# BLEACH

Copyright © 2008 by David S. Grant

All rights reserved.

No part of this book may be used or reproduced in any manner whatsoever without written permission, except in the case of brief quotations embodied in critical articles or reviews. For information, address Offense Mechanisms, an imprint of Silverthought Press.

*Bleach* first published by AuthorHouse 04/14/04
ISBN: 1-4184-2236-3

Printed in the United States of America

Published by Offense Mechanisms
www.offensemechanisms.com

ISBN-10: 0-9815191-0-5
ISBN-13: 978-0-9815191-0-4

Designed by Paul Hughes

# BLEACH

by DAVID S. GRANT

OFFENSE MECHANISMS
PHILADELPHIA | NEW YORK

This story probably isn't for you.

Do you read mysteries? Do you enjoy books where an author wastes your time describing what a table looks like? Throw this away, buy a Nancy Drew novel, and please, do us all a favor and learn to use your imagination.

I'm not going to hold your hand through this story. In fact, it's going to jump around.

FIFTY-NINE, FIFTY-EIGHT, FIFTY-SEVEN...

It's New Year's Eve 2004, one minute before the New Year. I'm at a party. Everyone is here, and they've begun to count down the final minute of 2003. "The End of the World" by R.E.M. is playing on the stereo. Chip is here. He's standing in the corner talking to an intern who works for ABC. Chip is wearing a modified Garfield & Marks sheath dress that's riding up in the back, dark sunglasses, and is smoking a Marlboro.

FORTY-SEVEN, FORTY-SIX, FORTY-FIVE...

Sharon is here. She's wearing a long tan Claiborne duster, a black beret, leather pants, black boots, and a T-shirt that reads: PLAYER HATER. Kyle is here. He's sitting on a couch talking with Gordon, talking about how difficult the music industry is. Kyle is wearing a sleeveless T-shirt that's cinched up too high and bright orange hot pants. Gordon is wearing a tight Halogen denim army skirt, a fake gold necklace, and is looking very bored.

THIRTY-FIVE, THIRTY-FOUR, THIRTY-THREE...

Do you like romantic comedies? You know, the books where there's a guy, a girl, witty conversational dialogue, and in the end the guy and girl both ride off into the sunset. Is that what you're looking for? If so, I've enjoyed our time together, and it's nothing personal, but now we must part ways.

TWENTY-THREE, TWENTY-TWO, TWENTY-ONE...

This is a story about a girl, but she's not doing well.

I'm on the bathroom floor holding this girl, who's wearing a bloodstained leather Calvin Klein trench coat. In fact—now is not the time to mince words—the girl, she might be fucking dead. My head is throbbing. The girl's jacket is open, exposing her left breast. A spot of blood is on the upper left area of her nipple. A shard of glass rests under her left eye.

FIFTEEN, FOURTEEN, THIRTEEN...

Dakota, the other girls from Showgirls, they're all here. Dakota was wearing a purple pinstriped Armani suit with matching top hat. Now she's in a pink bikini dancing around topless with a glass of champagne raised...

TWELVE, ELEVEN, TEN...

You still here? Go sign up for a class. Learn something. Do something productive with your life. Don't you have something better to do? Go watch a rerun of *Everybody Loves Raymond.* You make me sick!

NINE, EIGHT, SEVEN...

How did I get myself into this scenario? Do you really care? Well, you really have to start eight days ago. Somewhere pinched between corporate America, *Magnum, P.I.*, and my repulsion for every facet of society, I've gotten tangled into my present quandary. I'm going to take you back just as if you were there. This is where it gets a little strange.

SIX, FIVE, FOUR...

# 1

I hope this email finds you well. This is how Ski (pronounced "sky") ends all her inter-office emails. I can only surmise that this is how Ski ends all her personal emails as well. All Ski's funny little jokes, humorous observations, funny attachments, and links most will be unable to access. This is what I picture. Ski. If I didn't know her as the Vice President of Sales for Jameson Investments, I would assume Ski was in the porn industry based on her name alone. Ski only knows me by email. We have never met, nor have we ever talked on the phone. All we have is our limited correspondence via email. Every month Ski sends me an email that begins with: Hi Jeremy, how's life treating you? and then continues on, requesting the monthly cash budgets. Every month I reply, telling her she needs to contact my boss for the budgets. Ski then replies to my reply, apologizing for the confusion, and then asks me to forward the request to my boss. This has been going on for two years. Twenty-four emails. (Forty-eight if you count all her replies, seventy-two if you count my replies, ninety-six if you count the emails I forward to my boss as well.) This is my job. I work for Jameson Investments as a cost accountant. I'm thirty years old. I grew up during both the eighties and nineties, sandwiched between the Me Generation and Generation X. I want money—I just don't want to work for it.

As I forward Ski's message to my boss, a reminder window pops up on my computer screen. It's Friday afternoon, time for our weekly staff meeting. This is the worst two hours of my week.

"So let me reiterate what I said last week regarding the firm's debt ratio. Folks, I'll be frank, the ratio is low, meaning we need to finance more of our assets with liabilities, giving us more financial leverage." Maury. The Financial Controller. Despite there being eight of us in the room, he'll talk for most of the meeting. This is painful. All you need to know about Maury is he's old, somewhere between fifty-five and sixty, he spits when he talks, and he addresses everyone as *folks*, even when it's just a one-on-one conversation.

"Folks, we also need to discuss our payment obligations." Maury pulls a yellow-colored packet from somewhere under the table and grins as he distributes a document titled "Fixed Asset Payment Coverage Ratio" to everyone in the meeting. Maury drops my document a foot to the right of me. I wonder for a moment whether this was done intentionally. This is another one of Maury's political games.

"Folks, take a look at the earnings before interest and taxes for a moment. Now if we add the lease payments and subtract interest, principal payments, and preferred stock dividends, then take the total and..."

I zone out for a while. When I come back, Gerald, the Credit Manager, is discussing a problem he's found with the commissions program.

"We have brokers getting paid double commissions due to a glitch in the sales software program. I don't want to be held responsible for a computer problem." Gerald looks around the table. Everyone is nodding their heads in agreement.

What you need to know about Gerald is that he's in his early sixties (maybe seventies), is bald, has gray sideburns and a poorly-kept goatee, and refuses to take responsibility for anything where technology can be blamed. Everyone at the table knows it's not the system, it's the user. Gerald himself probably entered in the commission percentages twice. Gerald sighs and then continues, "It was different when I started. We didn't have these convoluted software programs, we calculated the commissions ourselves." Gerald glances my way. "Of course, some of you don't know any better."

I smile. I feel ill, unsure as to whether it's the fake office camaraderie or the boredom of this meeting that's making my head pound.

Next up is Howard, the V.P. of Finance. You only need to know one thing about him: he's the V.P. of Finance, a corporate man whose life dream was to be the V.P. of Finance.

Howard is not a fascinating man. Anything in the world not related to finance is a constant distraction in Howard's life. "We are working on establishing the amount investors are willing to pay for each dollar of earnings. We've implemented a new strategy called price earnings multiple approach. This technique uses the estimated firm's value, calculated by multiplying the firm's expected EPS by the average PE."

My head is killing me. I may have to get up and leave. I look around the table at the confused faces and wonder what will happen if I throw up right here on the glass conference table. Maury looks perplexed and slams his hand on the table. I should point out that this means Maury has something to say. My head is pounding. The constant distraction in my life.

"Isn't the..." Maury looks down at the table, where his precious brown Day-Timer lies. It is filled with notes he's been scribbling. A pink sticky note is on the cover of the Day-Timer. The sticky note simply reads: MAURY. An example of an approach to monogramming by a finance manager. "Isn't the multiple approach used mostly for valuing private firms?"

A speck of spit from Maury lands inches from me.

Maury looks around the room, where everyone is nodding in agreement with his genius idea. To Maury, the approving nod is the equivalent of smack to a junkie. Maury has a speck of tomato sauce on his tie.

Howard is getting defensive. "Well, yes, but it can be used to value public firms as well."

Maury slams his fist down again. "Is this the only indicator we're using from now on for calculating share value?"

Howard is holding on to his light blue tie. I've seen this before; he's nervous, his voice cracking. "No, Maury, we will also be using other calculations, but this is a new value we want to include in our valuation of the firm's stock."

I have no idea what they're talking about, but I'm pretty sure they had this exact same conversation during last week's meeting. Howard was wearing the same light blue tie at that meeting. I really need a hobby.

Maury continues, "Folks, we need to make sure we use everything available to us. Efficiency is the key. We need to be more than a necessary evil to Jameson. Gerald, you set up a meeting with I.T. to discuss the commissions problem, and Howard, don't put all your eggs in one basket when calculating share value." Maury slams his fist on the table. "Folks, we need to focus!"

Approving nods all around the table. Maury is such a star.

After the informative staff meeting, my boss, Jake, calls me into his office. All you need to know about Jake is that he's old, senile old, has a doctorate degree in Finance, and reeks of a rancid combination of Stetson cologne and cigar smoke.

Jake starts talking before I'm through the doorway.

"Is Rick up to speed on your projects, just in case any of the guys have questions while you're out?" Jake points up as he says the word "guys". I guess that means the executives one floor up, ironically consisting of four women and two men.

I sit in the chair opposite him, his pretentious mahogany desk separating us, and I tell him, "Yeah, Rick and I talked earlier today. I'm only out for a couple of weeks, and it's the holidays, so I don't anticipate any problems."

Jake's shaking his head. "Good, very good, but you can never have too much information, Jeremy. Remember that."

You can never have too much information. You can never have too much information. Got it.

"In case we need to get a hold of you, you'll have your cell phone with you?"

"Yes."

"Your pager?"

"Yes."

"Your laptop?"

"Yes."

"Your PDA?"

"Yes."

"And you'll be periodically checking voicemail?"

"Yes."

"Good, very good."

Thank God we're moving toward a paperless society.

Jake is now staring out his window. The sun is setting over the Manhattan skyline. The Empire State Building is casting a shadow over Midtown. Jake continues, "And you'll check in with me during the week?"

"Yes."

"And you're sure Rick is up to speed with your projects?"

"Yes."

I believe Jake is starting to lose his mind. I bet he smokes cheap cigars. It's hard to find a finance person who enjoys the finer things in life.

"Good, very good. You're sure Rick can handle this?"

If you looked up the word "old" in the dictionary, there would be a picture of Jake.

"Hmmm hmmm," Jake hums as he stares out the window.

After a minute, I finally break in. "Anything else?"

Jake spins around like he's surprised to see me there.

"No. Since I won't see you, Merry Christmas and Happy New Year." Jake continues to look at me like he has something else to say. He's studying me, squinting. "Jeremy, you're not Jewish, are you?"

I have bleached blond hair, pale skin, a few freckles, and a small nose.

"No, I'm not Jewish"

"Good, very good. Merry Christmas."

"Anything else?" I ask as I stand up.

"No, enjoy Minnesota."

"Wisconsin."

"Oh yeah, Wisconsin. Well then, have a Merry Christmas, Jeremy."

"You too, Jake. Happy New Year."

"*Wad* up JJ?" Rick is waiting at my desk. "What did Dr. J want?"

"Same old," I reply. "He wanted to make sure you wouldn't destroy everything I've worked on over the past four years while I'm out during the next two weeks."

"Word?"

Rick is the same as me, with even less ambition and the vocabulary of Puff Daddy, P Diddy, Diddy, and Sean Puffy Combs combined. It is also important to note that Rick is Irish. Rick is wearing a black shirt, black tie, black pants, and a pair of black Doc Martins. Rick has red hair.

Rick holds out his fist. "Don't worry, *dawg*, I got your back, most *def.*"

I make a fist and bump it with his. I'm down with it.

Rick cracks a smile.

I pull my fist back and scratch my face, despite not having an itch. Rick's ignorance makes me uncomfortable.

It's now my turn to continue this meaningless office conversation. "Thanks, man. What's up for the holidays?"

"Oh, you know, I'm heading upstate to kick it with my moms."

"Cool. You need anything from me, or are you all set?"

"Yo *dawg*, we've been through this, we cool, I'm *aight.*"

"All right then, I'm out of here."

"Yo, have fun in Michigan."

"Wisconsin."

"Whatever, yo."

I walk over to Karin's cubicle. She's staring at her computer screen. A Free Tibet bumper sticker is attached to the top of her monitor, a miniature Zen garden rests on her desk, the Knicks pre-game show is on her Panasonic portable. Latrell Sprewell is hurt and won't be playing tonight in New York. He's already left the team to be with his family for Christmas. "Enjoy the holidays, Karin. I'm taking off."

Karin is a middle-aged black woman with long braided hair who has entered accounts receivable transactions all day, every day, for the past ten years at Jameson Investments.

"You too, hon. Have fun in Iowa." She says this without taking her eyes off the screen.

"It's Wisconsin."

"Oh, right, hon. Have fun."

Karin holds up a peace sign as I walk away, her eyes still focused on the important work at hand.

Jenny pokes her head out of her office. All you need to know about Jenny is that in her early twenties she was a swimsuit model, she's now forty-two, still attractive (but showing her age nonetheless), and she hosts a Botox party every couple of months for the girls and gay men in the office.

On a scale of one to ten, Jenny is a seven. Today Jenny is wearing jeans and a tacky blue and red print shirt. It's Hawaiian Shirt Friday at Jameson Investments.

"Jeremy, I hear you're off for the next couple weeks. Now don't go getting any ideas about not coming back. We need you here."

Jenny begins yelling over Karin's cubicle, "Karin? Karin! Who was that guy who went back to Oklahoma for vacation and never came back?"

Karin replies without missing a keystroke, "Adam."

"Oh yeah, Adam, that's it. Jeremy, you better come back, unlike Adam."

His name was Aaron and he was from Washington. I keep this information to myself. I don't want to ruin their wonderful memories of Adam from Oklahoma. What would they talk about?

"Don't worry, I'll definitely be back," I lie.

"You better come back," adds Jenny.

I start walking away. This conversation is getting painful. "Okay, Jen, enjoy the holidays."

"You too, and make sure you come back. We need you, Jeremy."

I return to my desk to find six unread emails. The first email is from Human Resources, a reminder to everyone that next Friday is red, white, and blue day. The second is a response to the first email in which Doug from Marketing decided to reply to the entire company that he has just the shirt to wear next Friday. "It's fabulous," replies Doug.

Doug regularly attends Jenny's parties. Don't ask me how I know. I just do. Three emails are from people who decided to reply not only to Doug but the rest of the company pointing out the difference between replying to sender and replying to all. You can never have too much information. The final email is from Joe in I.T. He wishes me a happy holiday and hopes I have a good time in Indiana.

I push my chair back away from my desk and look across the aisle, where Chris is sitting at his desk eating a cold chicken leg. What you need to know about Chris is that every day while sitting at his desk he eats two chicken legs, two apples, a baked potato, and has five cups of tea. Not weak fruity-flavored tea, as he's quick to point out, but strong green shit called Gun Powder. Chris also lifts weights. Today is Friday, so it's bench night. Yesterday was Thursday, squat night. His license plate reads: W8SRUS. These are the things you find out when working ten hours a day next to the same person for four years.

"Ready for your vacation, Jeremy?" asks Chris, pointing at me with his chicken leg.

"As soon as I'm finished up here."

"Good." Chris is nodding his head while smacking his lips. I notice a piece of skin is hanging from the chicken leg as he points it at me. In my head I try to quickly calculate the odds of the skin sliding off the leg and hitting the floor. As much as I hate to admit it, I have a little Jake in me.

Chris's phone rings. He looks at the incoming caller ID and picks up the phone. "Hello, sport."

It's his wife.

I shut down my computer, change my voicemail message, turn on my email out of office assistant, and raise my hand to Chris as I walk out.

"Hold on, sport." Chris puts the phone on hold. "Hey Jeremy!"

I'm already starting down the hall, but still hear him. I yell back, "Yeah?"

"Enjoy your vacation in North Dakota."

Four years.

"Thanks, Chris. Have a good Christmas."

Walking down the hall, I announce that it's "Miller Time" to no one in particular and proceed to the elevator.

As soon as the fresh air hits me, I light a cigarette and grab my iPod from my bag, wrapping the headphones around my ears. "Everlong" by Foo Fighters is playing. Up next is "1979" by the Smashing Pumpkins, followed by tracks two through nine off Linkin Park's *Hybrid Theory*. I check my Nokia: two text messages, one from Chip that reads: DUDE I'LL PICK YOU UP AT THE FUCKING AIRPORT, the second from Angella that reads: WE NEED TO TALK - MEET ME AT THE W.

While listening to Dave Grohl belt out obnoxious lyrics, I walk north, stop, turn, look back at the building that's home to several investment firms including Jameson, and wonder if I'll be back.

My doctor is optimistic. He tells me there's an eighty percent chance I'll be back. The constant distraction in my life. My thoughts wander to Angella. Need to talk? The W? What the fuck is this about? I need a beer. Before meeting Angella, I stop off at O'Malley's Pub and have a pint of Guinness.

# 2

In a recent study on color preference conducted by the Pantone Color Institute, it was found that blue was the favorite color of Americans, men preferring spectrum blue and women preferring sky blue. In second place was green, followed by purple and red. Orange was second to last, followed by beige in dead last. Beige by definition is a light grayish brown, a combination of whites and browns. Brown has both organic and recycled meaning, white representing both innocence and secrecy. Recycled secrecy is the feeling I have as I walk off the elevator onto the seventh floor of the W Hotel. Four lifeless walls, all beige, surrounding leather sofas filled with beautiful thin pale people, too cool, and too thin for the room, all dressed in too much black.

To be fair, the room isn't entirely beige. There's a light illuminating behind the bar that seems to give the room an orange glow off the beige walls. No speakers in sight, but I hear light techno music coming from somewhere. At least it's light.

I spot Angella at the end of the bar and begin to walk over. I pass a guy with short brown hair, who may be German or may be from Oklahoma (maybe he knows Adam), at the bar who's staring at himself in the mirror while sipping a Red Bull and Absolut. I accidentally bump into him as I walk by, but he doesn't notice, remaining focused on the mirror.

The guy next to him with an expensive toupée and strong chin is asking a thin pale waitress named Dianne (pronounced De-Anne) whether she likes his new black shirt.

She says, "Is that the new Tommy? I love it, Paul. Fucking fabulous." Paul agrees. His shirt is fucking fabulous, so that means he's fucking fabulous. Two guys with light brown hair (with blond highlights) wearing black Kenneth Cole turtleneck sweaters, black DKNY pants, and black Prada shoes are commenting just loud enough so that I can hear how the bleached blond look for guys is "so nineties."

Sitting next to Angella is a woman, about thirty with short brown hair, reading page six of the *Post*, no doubt looking for some good gossip to talk about with her friends.

As her lips move, I notice a pleased look on her face. She must have read something involving Ben Affleck. She'll be a star tonight. I feel like an extra in a pro-abortion ad campaign.

"Hey, what's up?" I say as I approach Angella.

Angella is wearing a black dress, diamond earrings, and a silver necklace I've never seen before. She's drinking a vodka martini that I'm sure she didn't pay for.

"Hey, Jeremy. Thanks for coming."

All you need to know about Angella is that we met online (we both liked dogs, skinny dipping, and the color blue—so we were a 100% match), she works for Calvin Klein, and we have been seeing each other for six months. Oh, and she's been fucking some guy named Kevin for the last two months. All you need to know about Kevin is nothing.

Who really gives a fuck about Kevin! On a scale of one to ten, Angella is a six. She was an eight when I met her, dropping to a six when I found out about Kevin. Attraction is really mind over matter; when there's someone else, it just doesn't fucking matter. I order a Guinness. Dianne looks at me like this is the first time she's ever heard this order. "Is that some kind of vodka?" she asks. I order a Heineken. As I wait for my Heineken, I catch my reflection in the mirror. To be honest, the beige and orange lighting off my blond hair looks decent, despite what the tools on the sofa may think. I actually look more like a five tonight, rather than my typical four. Dianne brings me my beer. "Eight dollars."

I throw a ten on the bar and turn to Angella. "So what was so important?" I take a swig of my Heineken. "I have a plane to catch."

"I can't do this, Jeremy."

"Do what?" It's about time she admits that she's been banging Kevin.

"I can't deal with your problems."

"My problems?"

"Yeah, I mean, you know, your condition. It's like something I just can't deal with anymore."

It's only been a week since I mentioned it to her. I jump in, "Hey, listen, I told you because I thought you would want to know. Yeah, it's my fucking life we're talking about here, but still, I'm not looking for pity."

Angella takes a drink from her martini, checks her hair in a mirror behind the bar. "I know, but it's like I just have too much going on right now, with the spring collection and all, and can't be preoccupied worrying about you."

Angella glances across the bar. A small crowd of girls are gathering around Travis, the Crave Calvin Klein Model. Don't ask me how I know who it is, I just do.

"I'm not asking for that," I say. "I've never asked for that."

Angella continues, "The spring collection is very demanding, is all. I mean, you'll be so impressed when you see the new line. It's fabulous."

I'm sure. "Is this about something else?"

"Well, we've also started laying out the summer collection. It should be fabulous!"

"What about Kevin?" I ask.

"Who?" Her right hand involuntarily flips her brown hair. Her left eye twitches. She looks away.

I take a long drink from my Heineken. Paul is calling out to the new waitress, April, asking her what she thinks about his new shirt. She thinks it's fucking fabulous.

"Fuck it. Whatever. You want out, that's cool," I say.

"It's not that, it's just, I've got a lot going on right now. I don't have time."

I take another drink. "The spring collection. I got it."

"Jeremy, don't be like that."

Someone thin, pale, and dressed in black on one of the sofas makes a derogatory joke about Old Navy. Half the room erupts into laughter.

"Fine." I take another gulp of my Heineken and get up to leave.

Angella grabs my arm. "Merry Christmas, Jeremy."

Fuck you! You lifeless bitch! I hope you and Kevin both get stomach cancer and die painful deaths, dressed in black.

"You too, Angella," is all I say. I'm too nice.

I grab my Heineken, finishing every last drop, pushing my way past the consumers in black to the elevator. I wonder whether or not blue is really her favorite color.

Probably not. She seems more like a beige girl. It never would have worked. The techno music fades into the background as the elevator doors close. A bouncer is riding down the elevator with me. I pull out a pack of gum (Dentyne, spearmint) and offer the bouncer a piece, which he turns down. Who turns down gum? This place is fucked up.

Ass and piss. These are the identifiable odors permeating through the southbound S train as I try to steady myself against a pole. My head is still pounding despite the additional three pints I just consumed at Connolly's Pub, and the train has just stopped for no apparent reason. Standing to my left is a dark Latino man with biceps too large for his body wearing a black shirt that reads: I'M NOT GAY, BUT MY BOYFRIEND IS. To my right, two Italians are planning their attack on a white, maybe Irish kid sitting across from them wearing a Boston Red Sox hat and blue sweatshirt that reads: YANKEES SUCK—JETER SWALLOWS. Sitting across from me is a singing bearded homeless man wearing Wonder Bread bags as shoes, possibly an ex-rock star testing out some new lyrics: "She's my dirty girl, my dirty girl, she's my dirty girl..." over and over. My iPod is dead and needs to be charged.

The train resumes and minutes later comes to another stop. The conductor announces that there will be a delay. No reason, just a delay. The Latino shifts his weight from his left foot to his right, causing his right hand to flail out and brush up against my ass. I'm unsure as to whether I've just been hit on or had my wallet stolen. It's too packed in the train to drop my arm and check, and if I try, I may end up making contact with the Latino man's ass. I'll take my chances with my wallet being gone. The train resumes and the two Italian guys are moving in on the Irish kid, who, to my surprise, tells them to go fuck themselves.

The Irish kid then pulls a hunting knife from his black leather bag, causing the Italians to back off and move to the back of the train. The Irish kid puts the knife back into the bag and adjusts his Sox cap. A guy wearing a blue blazer with jeans eating a Big Mac turns around, looks at the Italian guys walking back, then looks over at the Irish kid, takes a bite out of his burger and with his mouth full tells the kid to "Fohgetaboutit." After taking another bite, blazer jeans guy smiles at the kid, says, "Nice fucking shirt, kid," and then turns around.

The Irish kid grabs his bag tighter and nods approvingly to everyone watching. Must charge iPod. The train stops at NYU, my stop. As I walk off the train I can still hear "She's my dirty girl, my dirty girl" fading in the background.

I'm walking down East Seventh Street heading toward the East Village. What you need to know about the East Village is it's New York, that's all. If you don't know, then you don't know. I stop off at Diangelo's Pizza House and grab two slices. A block away from my building, I come up on three homeless men. Homeless Guy #1 is smiling, humming, and pissing on the brick of a vacant auto parts store while Homeless Guy #2 is yelling to him about how the stock market dropped over a hundred points today on "The Street." Homeless Guy #3 is squatting near the end of the building with a sign that says INSULT ME FOR A QUARTER.

I finish my second slice, step over the stream of piss, dig into my olive green Dockers, pull out two quarters, and toss them into the weathered New York Mets hat sitting beside him.

I look down at him and tell him, "My life stinks." I pause. "And I hate my job."

As I walk away from the bums, I feel something fly by my ear and then something hits me in the back of the head. I look down and see it's a quarter. I look back at Homeless Guy #3, who tells me, "That wasn't an insult, fuckface." I pick up the quarter that hit me and continue walking toward my building, East River View Towers.

East River View Towers is a fifteen-story dilapidated building. As Billie Joe of Green Day said, some call it slums, some call it nice. I call it adequate. As my neighbor Rahul puts it, it was pure luck that I was able to get a one-bedroom in such an adequate neighborhood. The previous tenant killed himself the night before I came to New York looking for an apartment. It was spring of 1994, game seven between the Rockets and Knicks in the NBA finals. Sam, the previous tenant, was in to a bookie for ten grand and decided to let it all ride on game seven. As the neighbors would later tell me, it was sometime in between John Starks's tenth and eleventh consecutive missed three-point attempts when they heard the shot. I've heard the story a hundred times since I've lived here. Rahul always likes to point out that when the cops found Sam he was covered in blood and clutching a Starks jersey. So I guess in a way I owe my adequate apartment to John Starks. Thanks, John.

The elevator is out so I walk up to my apartment on the seventh floor. Out of breath, I enter my apartment and light a cigarette. My suitcase is sitting on my bed, empty.

While smoking, I pack the following: three pairs of jeans (two Levi's, one Polo), two Gap T-shirts (both blue), a black sweater, a blue sweatshirt, New Balance 1220 running shoes, black Skechers dress shoes, four pairs of socks, four pairs of boxers (including my lucky blues), black Dockers, a bathroom kit, faded Harvard sweatpants and sweatshirt (both from my freshman year), a black pointy strapless bra, black lace stockings, a black leather skirt, a wig, spiked black heels, and a tight leopard print half-shirt. I carry the suitcase to my kitchen, which is also my living and dining room.

I open the refrigerator and find two bottles of Miller Lite, half a gallon of milk, ketchup, mustard, and a half-can of Coke. Why do I live like this? I grab a Miller Lite, flop on the couch, and turn on the TV.

I flip on CNN. Today's terror alert code is Orange. Unsure as to whether that means we're at peace, war, or are supposed to remain vigilant, I decide to remain vigilant and annoyed, just to be safe. I flip on MTV, where the audience is laughing at a witty remark a young version of Carson Daly just read off a cue card. I turn to SportsCenter, where a reporter is live at an arena attempting to get an update on Shaquille O'neal's latest injury, a sprained ear. They come to the conclusion that he is questionable for tonight's game against the Celtics, then cut to commercial. I flip to MuchMusic, where the new Disturbed video is playing. My head is pounding. A constant distraction.

I grab three Advils, the only thing my doctors will allow me to take (recommended dosages, of course). The doctors told me that at this stage anything else would intensify my condition. I wash down the Advils with a swig from my Miller and light a cigarette. The next video is Eminem. An angry white guy is always funny.

The phone rings. On the other end is a heavy Arabic accent. My taxi is here. I grab my suitcase, walk down the stairs, and enter the cab.

"Where to, sir?"

"LaGuardia Airport. Go!"

# 3

"Do you know what the SoCal slow-ride is?"

This is the question presented to me by Jack as we sit on the runway at LaGuardia International Airport. All you need to know about Jack is that he introduced himself as "Jack, I work on The Street," has slicked back black hair, a square head, will be part of my life for the next two hours, and is a pompous ass.

I introduced myself as "Jeremy from Jameson." This is the first time I've ever introduced myself this way, but to be fair it was Jack who set the precedent regarding the introductions. The flight attendants are running all over the plane demanding that the busy New Yorkers turn off their cell phones or we will not be able to take off on time.

As the attendants approach the cell phone rebels, they all give the universally accepted mouthed "one more minute" with an index finger extended, and continue talking until the attendants rip the cell phones from their grips and shut them off.

I look at Jake, shaking my head. "No, what is it?"

"It's when you're standing behind the girl, you lift up her right leg, slide it in, and give it to her nice and slow, Southern California style."

We've known each other for less than five minutes.

"Oh."

"Yeah, let me tell you, Jeremy, that's the way this broad liked it last night, nice and slow." Jack smiles, nods, adjusts his wedding ring, and continues, "Oh yeah, I fucked her good. That's the way she liked it, nice and slow, SoCal-style."

"Is that so? SoCal-style, I'll have to remember that," I say.

The plane departs. At this point, I wish I could turn on my iPod and zone out to a Kid Rock marathon. Must charge iPod.

"Oh man, you want to talk about freaks?" asks Jack, I guess rhetorically, because I was unaware that I had wanted to talk about freaks. Good thing Jack is here. "Jeremy, you should have seen the girl I had last week, smoking body, like Britney—you know, Spears—and man, she was into some crazy shit, literally. Ever hear of a Cleveland Steamer?" Jack doesn't wait for my response. "It's when you squat over the girl and take a—"

I cut him off. "Yeah, I get it."

Jack smiles. "Yeah, I bet you get it."

What the fuck is that supposed to mean?

"What about a little yellow discipline? Have you ever done that, you know, a little yellow discipline?"

"No, I haven't." I make a disgusted face and stare out the window. Jack doesn't get it.

"Jeremy my man, you haven't lived until you've stood over a beautiful woman and just—"

I turn back. "Yeah, I get it." My relationship with Jack now dates back ten minutes. There's no such thing as too much information.

Two babies are crying. A man two rows up comments that all we need now is a couple of jackhammers.

Jack continues, “Do you want to know my favorite position?”

No, I don’t want to know anything about you. Actually, Jack, I hate you. I don’t say this because I’m nice.

“Sure.” I’m so bored.

“The rusty trombone.”

Jack has intrigued me. I take the bait. “Okay, what the fuck is the rusty trombone?”

Jack waves me off. “Forget it.”

“No, man. What’s a rusty trombone?”

“It’s when the girl is, you know, down behind you, then reaches around and strokes your—”

“Whoa, okay,” I cut him off. Two women are peeking over their seats, eavesdropping. I laugh uneasily. “Got it. The rusty fucking trombone.” This is all I can say. It would almost be worth the plane crashing, killing everyone aboard, just to remove Jack from civilization. Personally, I would make that sacrifice for society.

We are now well on our way west. I remove my watch and turn it back an hour. I once read that it’s bad luck to change your watch before you’re in the air. I’m not sure why. It’s not like the plane is going to crash while waiting on the runway. I put my watch back on, now set on Central Standard Time. The in-flight service has begun.

Our flight attendant, Becky, stops at our row and offers us each a quarter-can of Coke, ten salted peanuts, and asks if she can get us anything else. Becky is older, about forty, but looks good. On a scale of one to ten, she’s a seven and a half. I ask for a half-can of Coke. Becky tells me she’s unable to accommodate my request.

Across the aisle, a used up brunette in her thirties, probably from New Jersey, asks if they serve Starbucks coffee. Becky replies that she isn't sure what kind it is. "Well, I only drink Starbucks," says the woman.

"I'm sorry. Can I interest you in water, juice, or a soda?" asks Becky.

"No thanks, I only drink Starbucks."

Becky moves to the row behind us, where a man asks if he can have a full can of Coke. Becky informs him that she's unable to accommodate his request.

My Nokia phone is vibrating. I left it on. Sue me. It's a text message from Chip that reads: HURRY UP DUDE THE BARTENDER IS REFUSING TO FUCKING SERVE ME!

As Becky moves on to the back of the plane, Jack grins as he asks me if I'd like her to give me a rusty trombone. My head is once again pounding. A constant distraction. I ignore Jack, grab the *Sky Mall* magazine, and learn about a hundred different ways to store wine. I decide that the hundred-bottle cellar will suffice if I ever have the need to hoard wine. I rest my pounding head against my headrest. I fall asleep for ten minutes. I jump as I'm woken by the guy behind me, who's saying, "Oh, you gotta see it, you gotta see it!" He's apparently talking about the latest Wayans Brothers movie. I take a look back, and it's two fifty-year-old men discussing movies. The guy on the left is wearing a New York Giants jacket, the one on the right a black trench coat. Giants jacket continues, "There's a scene where he's trying to bang this little hottie and there's the Internet, and... You gotta see it, you gotta see it!"

Little hottie? I look back to confirm that this guy is actually fifty. Yeah, he's at least fifty.

"Okay, I'll see it," replies old trench coat guy.

I chuckle to myself. That, I believe.

Giants jacket continues, "You gotta see that, too, you gotta see it!"

"Okay!" replies trench coat guy.

My Nokia is vibrating again. Another message from Chip: HURRY UP MAN IM DYING HERE!

"Have you ever seen *Dude, Where's My Car?*" asks Giants jacket old guy.

"No."

"Oh, well, you gotta see it, you gotta. It's hilarious. Did you know they made a sequel?"

"No."

"Yeah, it's called, *No Really Dude, Where's My Car?* Oh my God, that's so funny. You'll have to see it," says Giants jacket.

"Sounds good. I'll have to see it," agrees trench coat guy.

After a minute he asks, "Did that really happen, a sequel for the *Where's My Car* movie?"

We arrive ten minutes early and have to wait for our gate to open. The captain chimes in, "Welcome to Milwaukee, where the local temperature is... Holy sh—" He catches himself. "Ladies and gentlemen, it's a brisk ten below zero!"

Jack looks over and says both jokingly and mockingly, "Vacation?"

"Actually, yes. I'm from SoHo."

Jack looks perplexed. "SoHo, New York?"

"No, SoHo, Milwaukee. It's Northside Milwaukee."

"Oh. Never heard of it," says Jack, meaning that my life is now irrelevant, and we will only talk about him. Jack continues, "I'm here to visit my sister, not to mention I've got a little girlie who moved to Wisconsin a year ago. I've been dying to see her again."

I want to ask whether she enjoys getting shit on or if she's more of a pissed on kind of girl.

"That's nice," is all I say.

"Oh yeah, she's nice. I'll find her and you know." Jack makes a fist and air jabs the seat in front of him. "Bada-bing!"

You can never have too much information.

"That's great. Good luck with that," I say. Must charge iPod.

Thirty minutes later, we pull into our gate and deplane. As I'm walking through the gate area, I see Chip standing there. Actually, he's swaying. All you need to know about Chip is that we've been friends since seventh grade, when we both got pinched by the principal for selling pot. To a teacher. The tragedy wasn't that we got caught, but that the teacher, Mr. Ross, was fired on the spot. Mr. Ross was our best customer.

Chip is wearing dark sunglasses despite it being pitch dark outside, has a cigarette sticking out above his ear, and appears to have bleached his hair blonder than mine, if that's possible.

Chip has a shitfaced grin as he spots me. As I get closer, I can see he's cut his hair short. In the eighties, Chip had long blond hair like David Coverdale. That changed in the early nineties when he got it cut shorter, refusing to wash his hair more than once a week, ala Kurt Cobain. In the mid-nineties he had a bit of an identity crisis, attempting a Layne Staley haircut that came out looking more Lance Bass.

Now starting to lose his hair, Chip has gone with the Art Alexakis look. "JJ, it's about time, man."

"What's happening, Chip?" We lock hands Dr. Dre style.

"Not much, dude. Welcome home. I'm smashed. Let's get out of here."

We maneuver through the crowd to the baggage claim, where we wait for my bag. It's an uncomfortable wait as I fear my bag is missing and I'll have to describe the contents to a baggage handler.

After fifteen minutes, my bag appears on the carousel.

Chip bumps into at least four guys as we walk though the terminal to the parking garage. As soon as we're in the garage, we both simultaneously light up cigarettes, Chip pulling a Marlboro from a pack, leaving the one in his ear. Chip looks over at me, dark glasses still on.

"So, who you fucking, dude?"

# 4

Eighty, eighty-five, ninety miles per hour. This is how fast Chip is driving his 1987 Camaro north, through downtown Milwaukee on Route 43. Under the city's illuminated beer signs, Uncle Kracker is playing in the CD player. I think it's the *Double Wide* CD, but I'm not sure. He's singing about Detroit, I know this for sure. Chip is talking with a Marlboro dangling from his lips, a can of Old Milwaukee in his right hand, left hand on the steering wheel tapping along with the music.

"Crabs? Oh dude, that sucks." Chip takes a long drag off his cigarette, then continues, "Yeah dude, I would have dropped her, too. Crabs. Fuck, dude."

"Yeah, what are you gonna do?" is all I can say. It was just easier to tell Chip that Angella gave me crabs. "You want a beer?" Chip asks.

All I drink is Starbucks.

"Sure," I say. Chip points to the back seat.

I reach into the back seat, where a cooler full of beer rests. While pulling out a beer, I notice a baseball bat behind Chip's seat.

"Playing ball?" I ask jokingly.

Chip smiles, takes a drag, continuing on the previous topic. "Yeah, dude, I got the little C's once myself. Itched like a motherfucker for weeks." Chip takes another drag, exhales, then continues, "Still, man." Chip checks his rearview mirror. A '78 Impala is following. "Consider yourself lucky. Remember Bonnie, the brunette college girl from Madison?"

"Yes." I don't.

Chip taps his brakes; the Impala backs off. "Dude, she gave me the big C."

"Cancer?" I ask.

"No, dude, the *big* C. You know, the clap. You talk about pain—that hurt like two motherfuckers."

"That sucks."

"Dude, you don't even want to know."

We both toss our cigarettes out the window. Chip removes Uncle Kracker and puts in POD's *Satellite*, skipping directly to the third track, "Boom." Under the CD player is an ashtray that Chip opens up. The contents of the ashtray are as follows: a bag of pot, I'd say about a quarter, a red Bic lighter with a green palm tree on it, and a freshly rolled joint.

"You still smoke herb?" asks Chip.

"Of course, man." The last time I smoked herb was with Chip last New Year's Eve.

"Oh, sorry, dude. I didn't know you still smoked. You do wear suits to work, right?"

"Fuck off. I still smoke."

Chip sparks up the fatty, taking two large drags, laughing as he exhales. Then in one motion Chip slams the rest of his beer, crushes the can in his hand, and tosses the can out the window. We're now going well over a hundred miles per hour. Chip is still wearing his sunglasses. He passes the joint to me. “Rock ’n’ roll, man.”

I’m baked after two hits.

“Boom! Here comes the boom!” Chip bangs the dashboard with his right fist as he sings along with the lyrics.

I take one more hit, tap out the joint, and put it back in the ashtray. I reach into the back seat and grab two more beers, putting my empty can back in the cooler. Chip is hammered. I’m not far behind.

“So dude, what are you wearing to Sharon’s party?” asks Chip.

Sharon Winkler’s party. *The* New Year’s Eve party, ten years running. This year, like last year, is a take on the Pimps and Ho’s party, with one twist: the guys dress up as whores and the girls dress up as pimps.

“Same thing as last year,” I tell Chip as I take a gulp of beer.

“Oh yeah, dude, I remember, that leopard thing. Cool.” Chip slams his beer. “Beer me, dude.”

“What are you wearing, same thing as last year?” I ask as I reach into the back and grab Chip another beer.

“No, dude. The mini-skirt doesn’t fit anymore, you know, since the operation.”

“Operation?”

“Yeah, dude, I told you.” Chip looks over at me while pulling out a cigarette.

“No, what operation?”

Chip laughs and lights his cigarette. “Dude, I didn’t tell you? Oh man, remember I got that Christmas bonus last year from Mansky Steel? Well, I took the cash and,” Chip takes another drink followed by another drag, “you know, got three inches added.”

“Fuck you.”

"Seriously, dude. I'm packing nine and a half, even ten some days."

I take a quick peek. Luckily I don't notice anything.

"Holy shit," is all I can say.

"Yeah, dude. The girls call me the blond white brother."

"Holy shit."

"Yeah, dude. Remember Janelle, that hot piece of ass from Kenosha who told you to go fuck yourself that one night you hit on her?"

"Of course." How can I forget?

"I'm fucking her, dude."

"Holy shit."

"Rock 'n' roll, dude."

As we exit the highway, a sign reads: "Welcome to the other SoHo, a true American city." Three minutes later, we pull into my parents' driveway. I grab my bag from the trunk as Chip calls me over to his window.

"See you at the Pour House?"

"Yeah, I'll be there."

"Cool."

"You don't mind if I stay at your place?"

"No way, dude, I don't mind. I'm off all week."

"All right, later."

"Later, dude."

Chip drives off and I look down the street where two black guys, one with dreadlocks, the other with a shaved head, are standing next to a Mercedes in front of the Super America convenience store. Two young boys around ten years of age approach the two men and exchange money for drugs. Several sirens sound in the background. A woman screams in the distance and everyone in a five-block radius is high. Welcome to a little place called SoHo. A true American city.

My parents are waiting in the doorway, both with tears in their eyes. They are the only two (other than that bitch Angella) who know that in eleven days I'm going in for surgery.

# 5

A brain tumor is an abnormal mass of tissue that results in multiplication of cells. This is the definition my doctor gave me. Since the tumor originated in my brain, I have what the medical practice refers to as a "primary tumor," an extremely rare diagnosis. If there's one thing I've learned it's that a brain tumor is a constant distraction in your life.

The medical term for my tumor is a "parietal lobe hamartoma." It is also referred to as an "orphan disease" because only a handful like this have ever been diagnosed.

For this rare type of tumor, radiation or chemotherapy are not options, only surgery. My doctor told me there's an eighty percent chance I'll walk away from the table. The last bit of information I've kept to myself. I despise pity.

My mother is serving dinner in the dining room: turkey, potatoes, gravy, and carrots. My father and I are discussing the Packers' playoff hopes (he believes they have a chance to win it all this year as long as Brett

Favre doesn't get hurt), work, and traffic. Next to the television is a stack of video tapes, mostly *Magnum, P.I.* and *Hunter* episodes.

*Hunter* is on TV. It's the episode where Hunter goes undercover to break up an organized crime ring. I'm having difficulty concentrating; the drugs and alcohol are starting to wear off and my headache is returning. Dinner is served.

"So Jeremy, we're flying in on the second. We'll drive you to the hospital that night. Do you want us to bring you anything?"

I stuff a large piece of turkey into my mouth. "No, Mom. I'll be fine."

My father speaks. "Do the doctors have anything new to say, you know, as far as the procedure goes?"

"Not really. It all sounds pretty straightforward. They go in, they remove the tumor."

"Did the doctor say when you'll be able to go back to work?" asks Mom.

"The following week. Like I said, it all sounds pretty standard. No need to worry."

"Jeremy," Mom looks disgusted, "you know that's not an option."

"Yeah, well, it all sounds pretty routine to me."

"Good," says Dad.

Mom is still disgusted. "Well, I just don't know. Did you hear about Uncle Rick?"

"No."

"He's not doing well."

"Oh?"

"Well, he's getting up there in years, and you know, he's got chronic pneumonia."

"Yeah, that's too bad." It is too bad, but there's also the fact that I haven't seen Uncle Rick for fifteen years.

"He's losing most of his hair. He looks like Fred Dryer," says Dad.

"So, Jeremy, other than your surgery, how are things going? Are you still seeing that nice Angella girl?" asks Mom.

"No, that didn't work out."

"Oh," is all she can say. Then she continues, "Are you happy? Jeremy, you know, you don't look very happy."

"I'm fine, Mom." I get this a lot.

Am I happy? I don't know.

***NEW YEAR'S EVE, 1995:***

*"There's nothing better than a dealer who's high." This is what I remember most about Sharon's first party, this line from the song "Junkhead" off the Alice in Chains* Dirt *CD. Chip, Johnny, and I started off the morning at 8 a.m. drinking Bloody Marys, only taking a break to drive to 10th and Capital to score herb. By noon we were smoking herb and working on our first case of Meister Brau, with another on ice. This was my first New Year's Eve as a Harvard graduate and I was planning on moving to New York the next spring. If the combination of fear, anticipation, and excitement counts as happiness, then yes I was tickle me fucking pink happy. Around 5-ish Sharon called, telling us she was throwing a party, no theme, just show up. At the time, we didn't know Sharon very well, other than the fact that she was known for throwing legendary parties. Initially I'm pretty sure she only wanted us there because she knew we would bring the chronic herb, but whatever, it was 5, we were trashed, and there would be girls at Sharon's. We show up and everything is pretty mellow until about 8, when a group of girls from Marquette showed up. More importantly, this is when Lauren showed up. As soon as I saw Lauren, I was immediately attracted to her. On a scale of one to ten, she*

*was an eight, and it was my mission to see what she was like. After drinking, talking, and more drinking, Lauren and I decided to go to George Webb's and eat cheeseburgers. I remember being so drunk I was unable to finish my fries, just sitting there poking at them. Lauren cleaned her plate, then ate my fries. Afterward, as we were driving, Lauren tells me she wants to do something crazy like shoot heroin. I'd never used heroin before, but what the hell, everyone else was. This was '96. You had Black Tar flowing out of Seattle and White China flowing from New York, take your pick. We pull over to a payphone and I call my guy, Jerry, on 10th and Capital to see if he can hook us up. "No problem, Jeremy. Stop by now." We stop by and I invite Jerry along, back to Sharon's party. Next thing I remember, we're in Sharon's basement, just the three of us and Layne Staley. Lauren is sitting on an upside down box, Jerry is sitting on the floor in the lotus position, and I'm sitting on a weight bench. Since it's our first time, Jerry tells us to shoot the heroin between our toes. I go first. The first time, I miss my vein but draw blood. The second time, despite blood all over my foot, I get it right and I immediately feel my heart go flush. I pass out, waking up thirty minutes later, Lauren and Jerry both gone, blood dripping from my foot, a pool forming on the floor at the foot of the weight bench. That was the last time I used heroin. I never did find out what Lauren was like. Three years later, she died from AIDS. A year after that, Jerry overdosed on crack cocaine.*

*I'm the only one alive from that night in Sharon's basement. This was the first New Year's Eve party at Sharon's.*

"More carrots?" asks Mom.

My mom is staring at my hair. "Why don't you get your hair cut? And why do you bleach your hair?"

"Because this is the way all the cost accountants wear their hair in New York, Mom."

"Oh," is all she can say.

My dad is shaking his head. "That's ridiculous, Jeremy. Don't lie to your mother."

My Nokia is vibrating. My mom looks at me. "Not at the table, Jeremy."

"Sorry." I pull the phone out and hold it under the table. There's a text message: DUDE HURRY THE FUCK UP!

*Hunter* has finished. My dad gets up, removes the tape, and puts in another. Within seconds, *Magnum, P.I.* is starting. It's the episode where Magnum meets a beautiful woman coming out of a pool, and offers her a towel. He's wearing his Tigers cap. TC is nowhere to be found.

After dinner, I change into my Harvard sweatpants, put on my New Balance sneakers and go running down the cracked SoHo sidewalks. A cop flies by with his lights on, putting his siren on right as he passes me, causing me to jump. An old man sitting on his porch drinking a forty of Hamms sees the whole thing and laughs. I make it about a mile before my sight goes blurry, causing me to fall to my knees to gain my composure. This has been happening more frequently lately. I walk back to my parents' house, past the old man, now sitting sleeping, the empty forty at his side. I change into my Polo jeans and blue Gap T-shirt and go into the living room, where my parents are watching another episode of *Hunter*.

"I'm going out."

My mom hits pause on the VCR. "Okay, have fun and be careful. You'll be here for Christmas, right?"

Life is very blasé at the Jenkins residence.

"Yeah, I'll be here."

"Are you sure you ate enough? You know, I can heat up the carrots if you want more carrots."

"No thanks, I'll be okay. I'll be staying at Chip's."

"How's Chip doing?" asks Dad.

"Good," I say.

My Polo jeans are vibrating, another message from Chip. I look down at my Nokia.

"That's good. I always liked Chip, such a sweet kid," says Mom.

IM SO FUCKED UP! DUDE ITS 80S NIGHT AT THE POUR HOUSE AND STONER IS HERE ROCK N FUCKING ROLL!

"Yeah, Chip is doing well," is all I say.

Mom hits play on the VCR remote.

# 6

I'm coughing as I hand the bowl back to Chip, who passes it back to Johnny in the back seat of the Camaro. We're sitting in the parking lot of the Pour House. Pearl Jam's *Ten* CD is playing. The song "Black" is on. Chip turns it up.

"Good herb? Ahahaaha," laughs Johnny, Stoner.

All you need to know about Johnny is that his nickname is Stoner, given to him because of his laugh (and other obvious reasons). Stoner has blond spiked hair, like Dexter Holland from The Offspring, a Born To Ride tattoo on his ass (trust me, I just know), and is the only one other than me from our group in high school to make it out of SoHo. Stoner lives a block off Venice Beach, L.A.

"How long you here for, Stoner?" I ask.

"Till Sunday. You going to the party?"

"Of course. You?"

"Fuck yeah, dude. That's the only reason I came back. I fucking hate Christmas, dude."

I look at Chip then back at Stoner. “Did you hear what Chip did?”

“Ahahaahaha, yeah, dude. Chip’s packing NINE AND A HALF.” Stoner announces this like he’s introducing a boxer into the ring. Stoner takes a hit off the bowl and passes it to me.

“How’s New York Fucking City, man?” asks Stoner as I grab the bowl.

“Cool, man, fucking cool. One giant fun cesspool.” I take another hit and start coughing again.

“Ahahaaahaha.” Stoner can’t stop laughing. I amuse him.

“How’s L.A. treating you?” I ask as I pass Chip the bowl.

Stoner looks at me seriously with his bloodshot eyes. “It’s good, man, real good.”

“You sure are tan, dude,” says Chip. “Damn, you look like a Mexican.” Chip passes back the bowl.

“Ahahaahaaaha.” Stoner laughs, composes himself, then takes another hit. We exit Chip’s Camaro and walk into the Pour House.

“JJ, Stoner, welcome back! The usual? It’s two dollar rails tonight, eighties night,” says Face. “Always good to see you guys.” Face points over at Chip. “And this guy, I don’t see you as often.”

All you need to know about Face is that he has been bartending at the Pour House for twenty years, will be bartending at the Pour House until he dies, looks like a tall Joe Pesci, and no one knows why he’s called Face.

“You know,” says Chip, holding up his arms.

“You guys here for Sharon’s party?”

“Yeah, dude. You going?” asks Stoner.

“Yeah, Stone, I’ll be there.”

“Cool.”

Face puts three drinks in front of us: a Beam and Coke for Chip, a Captain and Coke for me, and an Alabama Slammer for Stoner. "Just like old times, eh guys? This one's on me."

"Thanks, man. So how's SoHo treating you?" I ask. I take a drink of my Captain. It's strong, the only way Face knows how to make them. I light up a Marlboro.

"You know, everything is changing, yet nothing really changes. It's SoHo. There's a lot of crime, what the hell you gonna do? How about those Packers?"

"Yeah, they look good. Did you see the Chicago game?"

"Great game. How's the crime in New York?" asks Face.

I survey the bar, then look back at Face. "It's bad," is all I say.

The Pour House is dark and narrow, only about fifteen feet wide with a bar that runs down ninety feet with televisions hanging from the ceiling by chains. The DJ, who looks to be both new wave and retro, is at the far end of the bar. Poison's "Talk Dirty to Me" kicks off eighties night, followed by Whitesnake's "In the Still of the Night" and then Def Leppard's "Pour Some Sugar on Me." The bar is just starting to fill up. Stoner is wandering over by the pool table. I'm standing next to Chip. He's watching *Survivor*, smoking a Marlboro. Chip is still wearing his sunglasses.

Chip drinks half his Beam and Coke down and turns to me. "Dude, I've got an idea for a reality show."

I finish off my Captain and motion for Face. "What is it?"

"All right dude, ever see the show *The Bachelor*?"

"No, man, I'm proud to say I've never seen it."

"Well, it's this show where there's one guy and about twenty beautiful women, and they compete for the guy, the Bachelor dude, who marries one of the women in the end."

"Sounds awful. What are you watching that for?" I ask.

"Fuck, dude, I don't, I'm just saying, you know, that's what the show is about."

Face brings over my Captain. Chip motions for another Beam, throwing a ten on the bar.

"Okay, so what's your idea? Hookers?" I ask.

"Dude, you know me too fucking well, but it's not hookers, fucking better, dude."

Stoner, looking too tan for Wisconsin in December, walks over from the pool table and orders another Alabama Slammer. "JJ, next game, partners?"

"Sure." I nod to Chip. "Go on, man."

"So my idea is there's one bachelor and twenty-four women."

"I'm with you so far."

"The show runs for twelve weeks."

"Okay, man, go on. You're killing me. What's the catch?"

"The bachelor sleeps with one girl each episode, twelve girls in all."

"Okay, so the bachelor is going to fuck twelve out of the twenty-four girls and then marry the best fuck?"

"No, dude, fucking listen. The bachelor's not marrying anyone. He gets to fuck twelve girls, who will get paid for their time, of course, but that's for the networks to decide how much. Here's the catch."

Chip slams his Beam and Coke, I slam my Captain and Coke, and Face pours us two fresh drinks. Chip grabs his drink and continues, "One of the girls has AIDS."

"What?"

"Yeah, think about it. It's the odds game. Twenty-four beautiful girls. He fucks twelve. It's all about the odds."

It's always about the odds. Twenty percent. I hadn't thought about the distraction of my surgery for over two hours. Thanks, Chip. I drop my Marlboro on the floor, twisting it with my shoe while lighting another one.

Chip drinks down half his Beam and Coke, burps, and then continues, "The best part is at the end of each episode, the girl the bachelor fucks tells him one of two things, either Thank You For Picking Me, or You Have AIDS. Now that's reality fucking television."

I finish my Captain and Coke. "You're one twisted fuck." I motion to Face for another round. "What happens if the first girl has AIDS?"

"Well, that's for the networks to figure out. I just come up with the ideas."

Stoner motions for me; our quarters are up on the table. I grab my fresh Captain and Coke and walk over to the pool table, followed by Chip. "Youth Gone Wild" by Skid Row is playing.

"Their break," says Stoner as he looks my way.

Stoner pulls out a Marlboro Light.

"What the fuck, dude?" asks Chip, looking at Stoner's smoke.

"Sorry, dude. I can't handle the reds anymore," says Stoner.

"Bummer, dude," says Chip.

I'm so drunk we lose after five minutes to two hicks from Omro. The quarters are stacked so high Stoner says, "Fuck it, no more pool," so we walk back toward the front of the bar. "Dr. Feelgood" by Motley Crüe is playing. Troy, an acquaintance from high school, walks up to us. He's wearing a San Antonio Planet Hollywood shirt and a jean jacket with a Metallica *Ride the Lightning* patch on the back. "Jeremy, how's Boston?"

"I live in New York now."

Troy rolls his eyes. "Oh, really, New York?"

"Yeah, how you doin'?" I say in a fake accent while finishing my Captain and Coke.

"Well, you know, I've been married for five years. Got the house in Brookfield, and have my second child on the way. I work in the finance department for Johnson Electric."

"I thought you were going to be an architect." Chip is pointing at him for emphasis. I grab Chip's arm, looking over my shoulder for Face. Chip needs another Beam and Coke. At this point Chip can barely stand, not to mention he has never particularly cared for Troy.

Troy gets defensive. "I was going to be, but... no... It's not like—"

Stoner jumps in. "Ahaaahaaa, sorry, dude."

Warrant's "Cherry Pie" is playing.

Troy's had enough. "Good to see you again, Jeremy."

Troy extends his hand. I slap him five and light up a Marlboro. "Yeah, man. Take care." I'm still looking for Face when I hear her voice.

"JEREMY!"

I look over toward the entrance, where I see Sharon walking through, screaming my name.

"JEREMY! JEREMY FUCKING JENKINS! JEREMY FUCKING JENKINS!"

All you need to know about Sharon is she's cute in a party girl sort of way, talks a mile a minute, throws the best New Year's Eve parties, and we've all fucked her. She's a party girl. Enough said.

As she approaches us, she notices Chip. "CHIP, HOW THE FUCK ARE YOU!" She gives him a long open-mouth kiss, then grabs me and does the same. Poor Stoner doesn't know what hit him when she plants one on him. I can taste Jim Beam. Sharon is drinking a Miller. UGHH!

Sharon steps back and takes us in. She is wearing a shirt that says only SoHo. I got it for her a couple of years ago in New York because you can't find a SoHo shirt in Wisconsin. Sharon is also wearing a pin that says Where's The Fucking Party?

"You guys look really fucked up. Love the hair, Jeremy. What's up with the sunglasses, Chip? How's New York, Jeremy? How's L.A., Stone? Oh, fuck, it's been a year, how the fuck are you guys?" Guns N' Roses' "Welcome to the Jungle" is playing. All of this in under three seconds.

The three of us stand there drinking, smoking, swaying and smiling.

"You're coming to my party, right?"

"Fuck yeah, we'll be there," is all we can say.

Sharon looks over by the pool table and sees someone she knows, and starts screaming, "JOE! JOE! HOW THE FUCK ARE YOU, JOE?" Sharon heads over to the pool table. We're still drinking, smoking, swaying, and smiling.

"Last call," says Face. We get another round and sit at a small round table. We're hammered. The three of us are leaning into each other, almost knocking heads talking.

"Jeremy, you never fucking change, I mean, you change, but in a good way, you don't, oh, you know what I'm trying to say," says Chip as he lights a Marlboro. Stoner follows, lighting a Marlboro Light.

"No, man, what do you mean?" I take a drink from my Captain and Coke. We almost knock heads.

"You went to Harvard, man. You live in New York. Why don't you hang out with more, like, fuck, I don't know."

"Society types, eggheads, arrogant motherfuckers?" inquires Stoner as he takes a drag off his Light.

"Yeah," says Chip. "Why do you keep coming back to SoHo?"

"For starters, I hate those fucks! I guess deep down, man, I'll always be a blue collar guy from SoHo."

"Cool, dude. That's why I like you. You too, Stone. You guys are the greatest. I love it when you guys are here."

"Dude," says Stoner, looking at the suddenly affectionate Chip. "You've had enough. We gotta go."

"Yeah, you fucking nine and a half inch prick, you're fucked up, man," I slur.

"Ahaaahaaahaa," is all Stoner can say.

# 7

It's a beautiful Saturday morning. Light snow fell overnight, coating the trees that are now glistening in the sun. It's Christmas Eve. Children are rehearsing their lines for tonight's church services and parents are planning their Christmas mornings.

I'm still drunk, passed out on the floor. It's eleven in the morning when I open my eyes at Chip's house. I remember falling asleep on the couch. Stoner is sleeping on the living room table with his head hanging off the side. Chip is waking up on the other couch. Chip is still wearing sunglasses. My head is pounding from dehydration, my mouth is dry, and my lungs have just drawn up a petition requesting me to quit smoking. MTV's *Cribs* is on the television with the volume turned down. It's the episode with the rapper who's showing off his collection of Bentleys.

"How did we get home? Did you drive?" mumbles Chip.

"No... uh... I don't think... Well, I guess it's possible," I say.

I stand up. It takes me a minute to gather my balance, then I'm okay. On the way to the kitchen I pass the living room table, where Stoner is. He lifts his head, says, "Dude, keep it down," then passes back out, slinging his head back over the side of the table. I proceed to get water. I slam three tall glasses of water and immediately head for the bathroom, dropping to my knees when I reach a toilet that looks like it hasn't been cleaned in years. I'm throwing up for what seems hours (it's been about five minutes), Stoner is yelling, "Keep it down, dude!" and Chip is standing in the bathroom doorway staring down on me, sunglasses in his right hand.

"Dude, did I ever tell you about my idea for a restaurant?"

In between dry heaves, I look up. "What?"

"Yeah, I'm going to call it Café Bulimia. What do you think?"

I come up for air, say, "What?" then go right back down.

"Dude, picture it: somewhere out west, probably L.A., but that's for the owners to decide." Chip puts his hand up the front of his shirt, scratching his chest, then continues, "The restaurant is all good, you know, top of the line chef, real posh atmosphere, real Hollywood chic." Did Chip just say *chic*? Chip scratches his chest again. He should really have that looked at. He continues, "Tables, all around the outer edge of the restaurant, and right in the middle, a toilet. How about it, dude? You socialize, you eat, you drink, you fucking puke! Café Bulimia."

I'm still on my knees, but I think I'm finally finished. I look up at Chip. "That's not bad," is all I say.

I'm spinning as I sit down at the kitchen table. Chip is digging in the cabinet above the sink. Glasses are clanking together. Stoner walks in. "Dudes, I don't feel so hot." Chip walks over, grabs a bottle of Valium next to the sink, takes one out, swallows it, and offers the bottle to Stoner.

"No thanks, man, I'm good." Stoner reaches into his pants, pulls out a bottle of Xanax, and pops two pills. I pull out my bottle of Advil, dump five into my mouth and swallow.

I'm about to tell them when the phone rings. Stoner cringes. Chip picks up the phone. "Yeah. Yeah. He's here. Just a sec. J, it's for you. It's Jackie."

***NEW YEAR'S EVE, 1996:***

*After the first party, everyone was talking about how great the herb was, so naturally we were invited back. Hip hop was the theme of Sharon's second New Year's Eve party. I wore baggy pants, a baggy hooded sweatshirt, Nikes, and a hat with a big G on the front (okay, so it was a Packers hat, I know, I'm a fashion abortion). Chip, Stoner, and two other guys were on the porch doing beer bongs, two lesbians were making out on a beanbag chair across from me (I think one was flirting with me), and Young MC's "Bust a Move" was playing on the stereo. This was my first visit back to SoHo since I'd moved to New York six months earlier. I was sitting on a couch, smoking herb, drinking a bottle of Blatz when Jackie sat down next to me. All you need to know about Jackie is that she has strawberry blonde hair, claims she coined the phrase "let it slide," and likes to wear spandex shorts. Everywhere. On a scale of one to ten she was a seven, moved up to an eight with her "let it slide" personality, until she started dating a plumber with bad hair named Greg, then she dropped down to a six. Back on the couch, Jackie turned to me. "What's wrong? You don't look happy." I got this a lot back then. I still do. "I'm good," is all I said. We smoked pot, smoked cigarettes, drank beer, and made meaningless small talk. Her favorite color was blue. I'm not sure if it was the alcohol, pot, or the fact that she found out I'd gone to Harvard, but sometime around midnight she couldn't keep her hands off me. Tone Loc's "Wild Thing" was playing in the background. "Do you know someplace we can, you know, be alone?" I knew just the place. Five minutes later our clothes were littered all over the bloodstained basement floor. Jackie pushed me onto the weight bench. Cupping the back of my head with her right hand, she pulled me forward while shoving her tongue into my mouth, her breasts exposed. I kissed her left breast and caressed her right nipple while sliding one, two, then three fingers into her. She purred, grabbed my rock hard cock, then whispered into my ear that she wanted me inside her right that minute. She started on top, grinding slowly up and down, then I was on top, thrusting until our pubes touched. We had sex off and on for the next two hours. She was on top, then I was on top, we faced each other, then I was behind her. It was sweet, it was nasty, it was gentle, and it was rough. We only stopped for cigarettes, taking turns going down on each other, and herb... She came four, maybe five times, and we promised to see each other real soon. I was 21. She made plans to come to New York in two weeks. She canceled the night before. She couldn't come to New York. "I'm in love with Greg," is all she said.*

I pick up the phone. "Jackie?"

"Hey, Jeremy."

"What's happening?"

"Not much. You in town for Sharon's party?" she asks.

"Yeah, you going?"

"Probably. That's kind of what I'm calling about. Would you mind if I went?"

"Why would I mind?"

"Well, there was that one time, and I didn't know if..."

"Oh, that, yeah, wow, I had almost forgotten about that. Water under the, how does that go?"

"Bridge?"

"Right, water under the bridge."

"Cool. I'm so looking forward to it. I've been so bored since Greg and I broke up."

"Greg? Oh yeah, I remember him. That's too bad."

"Not really. He was driving me crazy."

"Well, I guess that's good then."

"Yeah, it is good. Hey Jeremy, what are you doing for lunch?"

"Lunch? Uh, nothing."

"Oh... Do you want to meet somewhere and catch up?"

"Sure, why not? Where?"

"I don't care, anywhere."

"Pick a place."

"Okay, how about that place on 14th and Beecher? What's the name of that place?"

Café Bulimia?

"I have no clue," is all I say.

We're silent for a minute. Finally, Jackie speaks up. "Claire's Diner, that's it."

"Okay, I'll meet you there."

"Great. I can't wait to see you, Jeremy."

I hang up the phone, take a shower, put on my clean Gap T-shirt, lucky blue boxers, and Polo jeans. I walk into the living room, where Chip and Stoner are watching Jerry Springer and drinking Bloody Marys. One is waiting for me on the table. Chip points to the Bloody Mary. "Rock 'n' Roll, dude!" As I choke down my first sip, Chip and Stoner are engaged in a philosophical debate.

"I fucking know her," says Stoner, pointing to the television.

"Fuck you," says Chip.

"Seriously, dude, I know her."

"Fuck you."

"No, dude, seriously. I think I met her in Chicago, at that fucking Crobar club, remember, where we saw Rodman?"

"Oh yeah, dude. No shit, you really fucking know her?"

Two minutes later it's revealed that she is actually a he.

"Ahahaahaaa, oh no, dude, I was wrong. I don't fucking know that dude."

"Fuck you, you know him," is all Chip says.

It's the end of the show and Jerry is giving his thought for the day. For some reason we're all silent, actually listening to this shit. When he's finished we all feel a little wiser. We light cigarettes. Stoner pops another Xanax and Chip goes to the kitchen to make another round of Bloody Marys.

"Hey Stone, you see Mickey yet?" I ask.

"No, dude. I'm thinking about going over there in a little while. Have you?"

"No."

"Dude, fucking come with me."

"Can't. I'm meeting Jackie."

"Oh, dude, that sucks. I hate going over there. He's so different now, and the kids... Fuck, dude, it's brutal."

"Yeah, man, I hear you. I'll probably stop over tomorrow, or the day after."

"Maybe I'll wait until then," says Stoner.

Chip walks in, handing us another drink. I still have half of my first one left.

"Chip, you want to go see Mickey with me?" asks Stoner.

"Can't. Janelle is coming over. Dude, wait, let's go tomorrow, or the day after," says Chip.

"Dude, I'm not hanging if Janelle is coming over."

"It's cool, hang out, she's on the rag anyway, and I'm not in the mood for crime scene sex. Dude, I just did laundry two weeks ago."

"Dude, that's awful. Ahaahaahaa."

"Of course, if you want to go to Mickey's so bad, take J with you."

"He's meeting Jackie."

Chip looks my way, smiling, nodding. "Good fucking move, dude."

"It's just lunch."

"Dude, she dumped that Gary—"

"Greg."

"Who fucking cares what the fuck his name is? She dumped him, got a boob job, and now you're meeting her."

"Boob job?"

"Yeah, dude, nice fucking work, too. She went from B's to D's. Fucking beautiful, dude."

"How do you know?"

"Dude, I just fucking know."

"I gotta go," I say.

"Nice fucking work, too," Chip repeats to Stoner as I leave.

# 8

I'm so bored and I hate the way my life is going, but I hate the alternatives even more. I don't even know why I'm here at Claire's. This place is such a shithole. I'm early so I grab a table near the counter under a framed certificate that says "Voted Favorite Milwaukee Diner by the Milwaukee Journal for 1980." Why did I agree to meet her? What's it been, almost a decade? This is a fucking disaster waiting to happen. As I dwell on my destined-to-be-doomed situation, I notice two cops who are sitting at the counter discussing the Packers' playoff hopes (they feel they have a good chance as long as Brett Favre stays healthy). Across from the cops are two construction workers who are busy trying to figure out which waitress they would "most like to nail." My head hurts and I'm about to call Jackie and cancel when she walks in. I motion to her, unsure if she will recognize me.

She's walking toward me with her arms wide open, her new accessories jumping out at me, and she says, "So what do you think?"

"They look great."

"They? I meant my new blue sweater. What do you think?"

Sweater? Blue sweater? Oh my god, I'm such a dumbass.

"Great, that's what I meant, the sweater."

"Yeah, I'm sure, Jeremy. So you like them, too, huh? They're not, oh, you know, too big?"

"Fantastic, I mean, you know, I'm sorry, you look great, is all I mean." I want to crawl into a hole.

"You too. You look good. You haven't changed at all, except for your hair. It's blonder than last time."

"Maybe a little."

Our waitress approaches us. She's in her forties and has a red bandana on.

"Can I get you two drinks?"

I let Jackie order first. "I'll have a Coke," she says.

"And you, sir?"

I only drink Starbucks.

"I'll have the same."

"How's work?" asks Jackie.

"It's fine." It's just easier to answer this way. This is America; everyone hates their crummy jobs.

"What are you doing these days?" I ask.

"Not much. Still working at Johnson's Sporting Goods as a buyer."

"Sounds interesting." Conversations kill.

"Not really. I hate my crummy job, but what the hell, let it slide, right?"

"Yeah, let it slide, I guess." My head is pounding.

When Jackie isn't looking, I pop three Advils. A constant distraction.

Jackie points to a girl and says she looks anorexic. I think she looks to be about average weight, but this is the Midwest so maybe Jackie is right. "Sorry to hear about you and Greg," I say because I don't want to talk about work.

"You already said that on the phone."

"Oh, sorry."

"It's okay. I'm glad it's over with Greg. It's just too bad, you know, I missed all those years when I could have been having fun. He was so boring."

"Yeah, I hate boring people," I say.

"Yeah, well, he also had bad hair," says Jackie.

"Oh, really? I never noticed," is all I say.

Our waitress comes back with our Cokes. Jackie orders soup and salad because she's dieting, she says. I order a cheeseburger with pickles, then light up a Marlboro. Jackie pulls out a pack of Newport 100s and lights one up. A waitress is smoking, the cops have reached the conclusion that the Packers will get to the Super Bowl and lose, and one of the construction workers is bitching because he just got paged, but none of that is important.

"Yeah, plus he was terrible in bed," says Jackie.

"What?" I say softly.

"What?" Jackie says mockingly. "Is this the new shy Jeremy? I said he was fucking terrible in bed!"

"Oh, well, it couldn't have been all that bad." I don't know why I say this.

"Jeremy, he knew he couldn't satisfy me. Why else would he always finish me off with my vibrator!"

You can never have too much information.

The waitress returns with our food just as Jackie is finishing her last sentence. The color of her face matches her bandana. She just places the food on the table, smiles, and leaves, heading for the kitchen, where there's no doubt an entertaining story is about to be told.

"You know, other than Greg, you're the only other guy I've had sex with."

"Really?" My Polo jeans are vibrating. "Speaking of vibrators, I've got a call. Sorry, I need to take this." I regret saying this as soon as it leaves my mouth. Jackie sits there, looking at me like I'm retarded.

"Hello?"

It's Chip. Chip asks, "How nice are they?" then tells me that Janelle is pissed off at him and that Stoner and him are going to Joe Mamma's later. "Are you in?" he asks. I tell him sure and that maybe I'll invite Jackie. Chip tells me that I should tell her his idea for a reality show. "Dude, you can say it's all your idea, it's cool."

We finish our lunch (Jackie doesn't touch her salad), only stopping to giggle when our waitress stops over. After we eat, we smoke and talk about meaningless shit. Her favorite color is still blue. She asks if I'm seeing anyone and I say I was, but it didn't work because of the spring collection, which Jackie doesn't really understand, but I let it pass because I don't feel like explaining. My Nokia is vibrating. I apologize for some reason and take the call.

It's Mickey. He wants to know when I'm stopping over to see the house, the wife, the kids, the new snow blower, the new station wagon, and little Dale's newly remodeled room. "It's beige!" announces Mickey. I tell him I'll be over on Monday, the day after Christmas, and I'm bringing Stoner.

"Wonderful," says Mickey. "It's been a long time since the kids have seen Uncle Johnny." I then ask him if he's going to the party and he says, "Yes I am, Jeremy." It's hard to believe this is the same guy who almost got his cock bit off by a hooker just a few years ago.

"That was Mickey," I say to Jackie for some reason.

"I remember him. How is he?"

"He's a married homeowner."

"Oh."

We share another laugh as the waitress walks over to grab our check and then I tell Jackie that we're going to Joe Mamma's later and that she should come. She says she'd like to, but she's meeting her friend Annie tonight. They are planning to see the new Ben Affleck movie. "Maybe after?" says Jackie, and then we agree that if we don't meet up tonight we should definitely meet up before the party on Saturday.

## 9

I'm back at Chip's and no one is home. I go to the kitchen, make a Bloody Mary, take another Advil, light a Marlboro, walk into the living room, and turn on Chip's computer. VH1 is playing an Aerosmith video in the living room. As Windows loads, a "Who's your daddy?" MP3 clip plays. I remove a February *Playboy* that's resting on the keyboard, dial into the net, access Hotmail, where I enter my email address, JeremyJenkins9997@hotmail.com. I've never met another person with my name, but if I ever do, the first question I'm going to ask is: What's your Hotmail address? My head is pounding and I don't feel well. Maybe I have a fever; maybe I'm still hung over. I'm not sure. I click on my inbox; I have three new messages. The first message is from Patrick. Patrick is the sort of friend you hang on to for the really boring times, you know, when you just can't watch another *Cheers* rerun, that's how boring. Patrick always has to bring a change of clothes when he goes out, changing before he goes home to his wife. Enough said. His message reads: Jeremy, where are you? You haven't returned my calls the last couple of days. I heard of a party on Thursday, do you want to go? Should be a lot of people. How's Angella? Talk to you! — Pat. I decide that I'll wait until I'm back in New York to reply to him. I may despise pity, but it's only human to like having others concerned about your well being. Then I change my mind and reply, explaining that I'm out of town and will call him when I'm back in the city. I do this because I'm nice. My drink is gone and my head is still pounding. I grab my bottle of Advil and realize I'm out. I walk back into the kitchen, pick up Chip's bottle of Valium, think about doctor's orders, out loud say, "Fuck it," pop one of the pills, make another Bloody Mary, and sit back down at the computer. The second message is from Angella. It reads: How's Wisconsin? How are your parents? Not too much is new here. The spring collection is looking fabulous! Merry Christmas Jeremy! Call me when you get back. Angella. I delete the message; she's such a phony. The third message is from Muriel. All you need to know about Muriel is that I met her my senior year at Harvard, she's a bit of a prude, and we've gone out off and on over the last five years with nothing sexual ever occurring (because she's a bit of a prude and I'm nice). On a scale of one to ten she's a seven and a half. Here's her message: Hey Jeremy, I called you last night, you weren't home. Did you go home for the holidays? Went to your favorite Boston bar last night, Big City Brew. It was boring without you so we went to East Cambridge to a seedy bar named Joe's, it wasn't much better than the Big Shitty, have you ever been? I have to go, when are you coming for a visit back to Boston? Muriel. I reply, telling her that I'll call her when I'm back in New York, have never been to Joe's, but it sounds like fun, I love seedy! However, instead of typing "seedy," I type "seemy." When I send the message, spell check catches this, pops up a list of options, and out of habit I select the first option. I send the message, closing with "I love semen!" I notice this just as the message is sent.

I make another drink and walk into the living room, where a Kylie Minogue video is on. I sit down on a couch, light a Marlboro, and take a drink from my Bloody Mary. The Valium has put me at ease and my headache is subsiding. Matchbox 20 follows Kylie, so I change the channel to Fox. I fall asleep with *The Simpsons* on and dream about brain tumor surgery. I wake up, read a little from the latest Ian McKeown novel until I hear the Camaro pull in. Despite the closed windows, I can hear "So What'cha Want" by the Beastie Boys bellowing from Chip's ride. Chip, Stoner, and Janelle walk in with two cases of Miller High Life. Apparently Chip and Janelle have patched things up, a bummer for me. I was hoping to avoid Janelle if possible. We're all sitting around the living room table, where Stoner had slept the night before. Stoner is drinking a Miller, smoking a Marlboro Light, and picking at a scab on his arm. Chip is taking a hit off a bong while Janelle talks about how much she hates her hair today, and I'm bored. Chip asks me what would happen if pot ever got legalized in America. "Would the States be loaded with tourists from Amsterdam?" While continuing to pick at his scab, Stoner asks me how it's going with Jackie and I say fine, then Chip asks me whether or not Jackie and I are going to start things up. I say, "I live in New York, remember?" and Chip goes, "Dude, don't get pissed, I'm just saying." Janelle looks at Chip and asks him what happened with Angella. I'm sitting right there at the same table as she asks him this. Chip makes a small C with his hand and Angella seems to understand. I wish everyone would leave me the fuck alone. My headache is back. Janelle comments on how while crossing the street today she had an encounter with a homeless lady who grabbed her arm and told her to "Be careful, this is a dangerous intersection." Great story, Janelle.

I go to the kitchen, grab another Valium and a Miller. I sit back down at the table. Chip and Stoner get up to move the television so that we can all watch the Bucks game while getting high and drunk. As they leave, Janelle puts her hand on my knee and says, "I'm sure you'll meet someone great real soon." She doesn't get it. I hate her.

Chip and Stoner come back to the table, pissed because the Bucks are already down by ten in the second quarter. Chip asks me if Jackie and I are going to hook up at the party, and I tell him maybe, just because it's easier to say that. He says, "Cool." A debate ensues regarding the size of the bong. Chip says it's a foot; Stoner says half a foot. Chip pulls out a tape measure and finds it to be nine and half inches. Everyone enjoys a good laugh. I feel this whole situation is getting redundant. I want to go back to New York. Stoner grabs the bong, which is now posing as the table centerpiece, takes a hit, and asks me about a girl from last year's party.

"Dude, who was that girl you were talking with last year?" asks Stoner.

"She was a trip," adds Chip.

"Ahaaahaaaha, she WAS a fucking trip, dude!"

"Yeah, dude, whatever happened there?" asks Stoner.

"Nothing. She left and I never got her number, last name, or anything," I say.

"Ahaaahaaaha, sucks, dude. I only talked to her for a minute, but she was cool, dude."

"Yeah, she was a trip," I say.

"What was her name?" asks Stoner.

"Mary."

"Do you think she'll be back this year?" asks Chip.

"I have no idea."

I've been back in Wisconsin for one day and I'm bored so I go to Joe Mamma's by myself. I call Mickey and see if he wants to stop by for a beer. He says he can't because it's too short a notice to find a baby sitter. I ask him why his wife Clarice can't watch the kids. After all, I'm only in town once a year. He tells me to hold on for a minute, then comes back and says he can't go out tonight. I tell him no problem and I'll stop by after Christmas. Mickey says that would be great.

I then call Mark, who says he won't be able to stop by because his wife just rented *Titanic*. I'm sitting at the bar drinking a Guinness. I put my phone in my jeans and then look around Joe Mamma's. I'm glum and depressed. Glum because my head hurts and I don't feel well, I'm convinced I have a fever, and depressed because I'm surrounded by married homeowners. I light a Marlboro as I sit on my barstool in my dejected state. As I nurse my Guinness, I think about where I am in my life and wonder whether I should get married and buy a house. Isn't this what society tells us to do? We're born, go to school, then college, then get married, buy a house, have two point five children, and then work the rest of our lives raising children, buying shit we don't need, and trying to pay off our debt. Maybe it's time I joined society. I take a closer look. To my right is Matt, a guy I went to school with who's about to order a beer when his wife Jenny tells him he's already had two and he's driving tonight. He gets angry and orders a Coke. At the end of the bar, a guy I only know as Jackson is checking out the pretty brunette dressed in a black halter top and white mini skirt walking to the bathroom (as only a pretty brunette can), until his wife notices this and starts giving him the third degree.

Sitting next to me is Ted and his wife. I can tell Ted is an ex-smoker who still secretly smokes behind his wife's back, dying for a cigarette because he's watching every drag I take. He tells his wife Shari he's going to shoot a game of pool and she says, "What am *I* supposed to do?"

Fuck society!

As my eyes continue to wander around the hazy bar, a blonde in a blue dress notices me smile and approaches me, asking me why I don't smile more and if would I like to buy her a drink. I'm about to say yes, when I notice it's a he and tell him, "Thanks, but I'm waiting for someone."

The bar is relatively small and there are too many people in here tonight, most of whom are married homeowners that I don't care for. The transsexual sits next to me and looks disgusted as he—or she—looks around the bar. "Sad looking crowd. Mostly married," he says. I look around and watch everyone talk, and that's all I see, people talking. No one's listening. Nobody cares about anything but their own little married homeowner worlds. "This place is awful," is all I say back to the blue dress.

This is all making my head really hurt, so I order a shot of Jack Daniels and I feel a little better and a little less distracted. Still annoyed by my surroundings, I light another Marlboro. The jukebox must be preprogrammed for the married homeowner crowd because all that's playing is Johnny Cash, Neil Diamond, and the occasional Jimmy Buffett song. I order another Guinness. I'm so bored I'm thinking about books and I remember a book I once read where a guy would recite a lullaby in his head, focus on an individual who deserves to die, and they would die right that second. I don't know any lullabies, but I would settle for a song, something like the "Da Da Da" theme from the Volkswagen commercials. I'm confident if given the power I would use it for good, removing the married homeowners who got married only because society told them to. I've never been more bored than I am right now.

The guy wearing a blue blazer standing next to his wife at the end of the bar, last night he fucked the stripper from his best friend's bachelor party. Da Da Da...

The woman standing by the jukebox while her husband buys her a Cosmopolitan, she's having an affair with her male secretary at the office. This affair has been going on for six months. She's pregnant with her secretary's baby. The husband thinks it's his. Da Da Da...

The guy shooting darts while his fiancée encourages him, the guy he's shooting darts with is more than just a dart partner. Da Da Da...

On my right side, the guy who's talking to his buddies about the Packers (he thinks they have a chance as long as Bret Favre doesn't get hurt), he's been secretly spending his children's college fund to support his cocaine habit. Now they will have to go to community college and find work in the computer field—or worse, they may end up being cost accountants. Da Da Da...

The short guy with... My Nokia is vibrating. It's Jackie. She just wanted to call, say hi, tell me that she and Annie are heading into Milwaukee because Annie is meeting some friends at Luke's Sports Bar on Water Street. "Sounds like fun," I say. She tells me to call her sometime during the week and I say I will.

I look over at the pool table, where a blonde girl wearing a tight white T-shirt and faded jeans is flirting with me. I walk over and say, "Hi, I'm Jeremy." She smiles and says her name is Kelly. I'm about to ask her if I can buy her a drink when some hick taps me on the shoulder and tells me to go back to my stool. I apologize, saying I didn't know she was with anyone. I offer to buy both of them a drink. The hick asks me if I'd like to take this outside. For some reason, maybe because of all the married homeowners annoying me, I'm out of character. I tell him to fuck off.

He tells me, "Let's go," pointing outside. Kelly the blonde says, "Fine, Greg. If you're going to be that way, I'm leaving," and she leaves the bar. I'm drunk and confused.

Greg? I look at the hick's face, then I see the bad hair. OH SHIT! The next thing I know, we're outside in a dark alley next to Joe Mamma's. Greg calls me a blond faggot and pushes me. I may or may not have mentioned something about finishing me off with a vibrator, but regardless, he's really pissed. Greg pushes me up against a dumpster, sending rats scurrying everywhere. I knee Greg in the balls, causing him to back off a moment, which buys me enough time, because my guardian angel appears. Well, not exactly an angel, but a Louisville Slugger crushing down on Greg's head, causing him to immediately drop to the ground, losing consciousness.

Chip is holding the bat, looking down at Greg. "Looks like we got here just in time."

Blood is gushing from Greg's left ear. Stoner, who's standing behind Chip, asks, "Dude, is he dead?"

"No, dude is still breathing," says Chip.

Stoner walks up to him, spits on him, lights a Marlboro Light and says, "Wow... Dude really does have bad hair."

Chip puts the bat back into the Camaro and we walk into Joe Mamma's. The transsexual in the blue dress nods to me as we walk in. I don't even look at Chip or Stoner, both, I'm sure, wondering what in the hell is going on.

"Holy fuck!" says Chip as he walks into the bar. "What the hell happened to everyone?"

"I know," I say.

"Dude, this sucks," says Stoner. We grab a table near the back. A waitress comes over, and I order a round of Dr. Kevorkians. The jukebox has changed from bad to worse.

Alabama is playing on the jukebox.

"I need to get out of here," says Chip.

"Dude, let's go to the Pour House," says Stoner.

"No, it's not that, it's—I mean, look around. I need to get out of this town."

I've never heard Chip talk like this. Chip continues, "Now I know why you guys only come back once a year. I can't believe I'm just noticing this now."

"Yeah, married homeowners. Welcome to SoHo," is all I say as I light a Marlboro and slam my drink. I cringe. Too much Jägermeister.

"I'm never getting married," adds Stoner, finishing his drink and motioning for another round. We sit for five minutes, saying nothing.

Travis Tritt is playing on the jukebox.

"For most, marriage is a crutch," I say for some reason. Both Chip and Stoner are intrigued and I'm drunk so I continue as our Kevorkians arrive. "I mean, don't get me wrong. For some, it's great, but should everyone get married?"

"No way, dude," says Stoner.

"Fuck no," says Chip.

Approving nods all around the table.

We're drinking down our fifth round of Kevorkians and I'm about to tell them about my tumor because I'm fucked up when Kyle walks in.

"Holy shit! Chip, Jeremy, and fucking Stoner, what's up guys?" Kyle looks around. "What the fuck happened here? Everyone's fat and boring."

"Yeah, dude. Married homeowners," says Stoner.

Kyle is disgusted as he looks around the bar. "No shit. I haven't been back for three years, and to walk into this shit... Fuck, man."

Brooks and Dunn is playing on the jukebox.

"So what's up, Kyle? You want a drink?" asks Chip.

"Yeah, man, what are you guys drinking?"

"Dr. Kevorkians," I say.

"Cool. Get me two," says Kyle.

"Fuck it, let's all get two," I slur as I light a Marlboro.

The waitress comes over, tells us it's last call, takes our order, and slides a napkin with her number on it across the table to Stoner.

"Rock 'n' Roll, dude," says Chip.

"Now that's some good ass service," says Kyle. "You guys should come see my band. We're playing at Hammer's Monday night."

The waitress comes back and Stoner asks her what she's doing for New Year's Eve. She replies, "Going to Sharon Winkler's party, and you?"

"The party. I'll be there," says Stoner.

"Great, I'll see you there. Thanks, guys." She smiles as she walks away.

"I'll stop by Hammer's. What's the name of your band?" I ask.

"Johnny Come Lately. Mostly folk, with a little rock. You know, like the Femmes."

"Dude, that's cool," says Stoner.

We drink down our Kevorkians, stumble out of our chairs, and walk toward the exit. Kyle asks, "All you guys going to Sharon's party?"

"Yeah, we'll be there. You?" I ask.

"Oh yeah, I can't wait," says Kyle.

Chip walks around the side of the building to the alley followed by Stoner, and nobody is there. "Dude, I told you he was breathing."

# 10

It's Christmas morning and I'm at my parents' house. An artificial tree sits in the living room and tinsel is everywhere throughout the house, except on the tree. There's a note that reads: *Went to the neighbors' house to pick up Magnum tapes.* I'm walking around the house in red boxers and white socks brushing my teeth while my Gap T-shirts are in the washer. I walk into the living room and to my surprise my Aunt Betty is sitting there.

"Hi, Jeremy," says Aunt Betty, sitting in an antique wooden rocking chair.

"Oh, I'm sorry. I thought I was home alone."

"Oh, you were. The door was unlocked, so I let myself in."

"Oh." There's an awkward pause as my aunt stares at my body.

"You look thin, Jeremy."

"Thanks."

"Too thin."

"Oh."

"And white."

You look old, Aunt Betty. Really fucking old.

"Oh," is all I say.

I shower, look at myself in the mirror, decide that maybe I do look a little pale, flex, and do some pushups. I only make it to twenty-five and I become exhausted. I go running. After a mile, my lungs are burning, and I feel ill. I stop and throw up on the side of the road, then turn around and jog back to my parents' house.

I put on a pair of Levi's and my blue sweatshirt and walk into the living room, where my Aunt Betty is taking a nap. It's 9:30 in the morning.

I find a bottle of Advil and take three and one of the five Valiums Chip gave me to "help me make it through the day," as he put it. I turn on CNN. Today's terror alert color code is Burgundy. The FBI is advising that non-specific threats have been made against middle age women who walk dogs.

I turn on *NFL Today*, where they're talking about the Packers' playoff hopes. They come to the conclusion that the Packers have a good chance if Bret Favre stays healthy. I flip to an infomercial for the Ab 500, a new device guaranteeing great abs that only requires five seconds a day, two days a week of your time, and you can eat anything. I turn on MTV2 and zone out to videos by the Red Hot Chili Peppers and Soundgarden. I close my eyes for a minute and wake to find my parents' house filled with relatives. My dad is elbowing me in the ribs. "Look, look! Doesn't Uncle Rick look like Fred Dryer?"

"Yeah, I guess," I say, even though I don't really remember him.

I step outside with my Uncle Tony for a Marlboro, and he asks me if I've got any pot. All you need to know about my Uncle Tony is that he has giant furry eyebrows. I tell him no, I don't have any pot, and realize that since I've been back I've been smoking all Chip's herb.

I go back inside to the kitchen, where Mom is watching a ham in the oven, and grab a beer from the refrigerator, which draws a concerned look from my mom. I go to the bathroom and pop another Valium.

I go back into the living room, where my dad and uncles are talking about the Packers and my aunts are talking about the new Harrison Ford movie. *There's Something about Mary* is on television, which is odd because I was just thinking about Mary, and I know my mom is dying to pop in a *Magnum, P.I.* tape. Dinner is served, but the Packers game is still on, so everyone agrees that it would be a good idea to move the television into the dining room.

My Aunt Janice is walking around with a bottle of wine and I hold up my glass, which draws another concerned look from my mom, but it doesn't really bother me because the combination of alcohol, Valium, and Advil really is pretty awesome. I made my parents promise not to tell anyone about my surgery because I despise pity, but somehow during timeouts and commercials I'm still the center of attention at the dinner table.

"So how's New York, Jeremy?" asks Aunt Betty.

"Great, I love it."

"Really? That place is a cesspool," says Uncle Tony.

"Yeah, a giant fun cesspool." This comment draws disgusted looks from all around. Not exactly the response I was looking for. Where's Stoner when you need him?

My Aunt Betty asks me why I bleach my hair blond and my mom jumps in and tells her that this is the way all cost accountants in New York wear their hair. My dad just shakes his head.

"So, Jeremy, any special girl in your life?" asks Aunt Janice.

"Yeah, Jeremy, when are you getting married?" asks Aunt Cheryl before I have a chance to respond to Aunt Janice.

"Jeremy, what the fuck gives? You getting married or not?" asks Uncle Tony, which draws the evil eye from my mom because he said the word "fuck" at the dinner table.

"I don't know. We'll have to see. Nothing in the near future, that's for sure," I say because I'm nice.

"That's for sure? What does that mean?" Aunt Janice asks Aunt Cheryl.

"Leave the kid alone. He's enjoying himself," says Uncle Rick. I've always loved Uncle Rick.

"I agree," says my Aunt Betty to Aunt Cheryl. "He's got his whole life ahead of him." This is another one of those conversations that is happening as if I'm not at the table. The last comment from Aunt Betty causes my mom to think about the operation and her eyes well up, so my dad jumps in and says, "Time for presents!"

I get two presents. The first is a pen and pencil set that reminds me of work. My head starts pounding. I suddenly feel ill so I go to the bathroom and take two more Valiums and three more Advils. My second present is a beige sweater that causes me to think of Angella and the spring collection. I search for other presents, thinking there must be a pack of razor blades somewhere, but there isn't. After opening presents, I step outside with Uncle Tony for a Marlboro. He tells me I'm too skinny to be straight, and now Uncle Tony is really starting to scare me. I go back inside and everyone is voting on whether they'd rather watch *Magnum* or *Hunter* reruns. I'm really bored so I take my last Valium, have another glass of wine, go upstairs to my old bedroom and fall asleep. I dream about brain tumor surgery. Christmas blows.

## 11

"Dude, good herb," says Stoner as he takes a hit off the bowl. We're sitting in Chip's Camaro a block from Mickey's. Sublime's *What I Got* is in the CD player.

"Yeah, man, what do I owe you for all this shit?" I ask.

"Dude, nothing. Rock 'n' roll. Nobody pays for my herb. Now coke and shrooms, like the shit I've got for the party, your donations are welcome."

"Cool," I say as I grab the bowl.

"Dude, when was the last time you saw Mick?" asks Stoner.

"A couple years ago, I guess. Clarice wouldn't let him go to the party last year," I say.

"Dude, it's gotten worse," says Stoner.

***NEW YEAR'S EVE, 1997:***

*Stoner and I were getting high at Chip's when Mickey came over pissed because some girl from Oshkosh had just dumped him, so we took it upon ourselves to cheer him up.*

*Mickey wasn't a big herb smoker, so it didn't take much to get him high. Two hits off the rolling steamer bowl and Mickey was baked. We all went to Sharon's around six, drinking vodka and water for most of the night. Around nine, Mickey was fucked up and decided that he wanted to get out for a while so I left with him and we drove around while smoking cigarettes. Pearl Jam's* Vitalogy *was playing in Mickey's CD player when we took a turn down what is known in SoHo as Hooker Alley. I remember asking him "What the fuck?" but it was too late because as soon as we turned the corner a black homely hooker jumped in the back seat, saying, "I give blow job for fitty." I'm pretty sure I wasn't going to partake in the act, but being the Harvard educated cost accountant, I remember asking whether the fifty dollars was for each, or just one. Before I even finished the question, she jumped in the front seat and was giving Mickey a hummer.*

*As this was going on I was just sitting feeling awkward and holding my breath because the hooker's seedy smelling ass was six inches from my face. This is when a hand came crashing through my window, grabbing the hooker by the hair and pulling her out through the window. I'm not sure whether he was a pimp, husband, or father, but he was pissed. I've never ordered anyone to "Get the fuck out of here!" like I did at that moment, but Mickey didn't budge, he just sat behind the wheel. I asked what was wrong, but he was in shock and pointing at his crotch. The hooker had bit him when she got pulled out of the car. Blood was everywhere. I froze for a second until the pimp/husband/father came back waving something that at the time I thought was a gun (we figured out later that it was probably Mickey's wallet that the prostitute had stolen and the pimp, being the honest businessman he was, wanted to return it). So I quickly jumped over Mickey, pushing him to the passenger seat, and proceeded to drive out of Hooker Alley to the hospital emergency entrance. As I helped Mickey into the entrance, all he could say was, "Damn, it was going so well until she bit down." Mickey spent the rest of the night in the hospital. I was there when he explained the situation to the doctor. The doctor asked if the hooker had rabies, then laughed. Two years later, Mickey was married. A year after that, he bought a house. A year after that, he had his first child.*

"Jeremy, Chip, Johnny, great to see you guys." This is how we're greeted by Mickey at the door. All you need to know about Mickey is that he once drank two cases of beer in one day while taking Vicodin, has a skull and crossbones tattoo on his right arm, a barbed wire tattoo on his left arm, and is now a registered Republican.

"Hey, guys," says Clarice. "You all look very blond today." She's so witty. She has laid out chips, hot dogs, and Pepsi for us to eat. Stoner makes the gag gesture when Clarice's back is turned, and Chip and I laugh because we're high.

The house itself is a standard Milwaukee bungalow with kid shit littered all over the place. There is a matching La-Z-Boy, sofa, and end tables, all beige. A quaint coffee table sits centered perfectly in front of the sofa with *Time*, *Newsweek*, and *U.S. News* magazines spread out in a Republican sort of way. A sign leading into the kitchen reads: "Welcome to our home." It should read: "Welcome to Hell." Mickey takes us around his house, showing us the den, the living room, dining room, kitchen, master bedroom, Mikey's bedroom, and

Dale's freshly painted room. The beige color makes me think of Angella, which makes me think of Jackie, which makes me think of Mary.

Mickey stops halfway through the tour to tell us that the mortgage is pretty tough to come up with right now, but they plan on refinancing soon and that will make things more manageable. You can never have too much information.

As Mickey continues the tour, Stoner turns around and points out that there's a picture of Mickey wearing a lime-colored Speedo on the wall. We all laugh because we're high and because it's a fucking lime-colored Speedo. Mickey doesn't laugh. He can't laugh. He's a married homeowner.

The kids are now in the house and running all over the place, calling out for Uncle Johnny and Uncle Jeremy. Dale comes up and hugs Stoner, who tells Dale he doesn't have to call him Uncle Johnny, that Stoner will suffice, but this brings a scowl from Clarice so Stoner lets it go and says Uncle Johnny is fine. Mikey is playing his Playstation, and I say, "Oh cool, Mikey. Do you have Grand Theft Auto?" and before he can say no, Clarice gives me a scowl and says, "Absolutely not. We won't have that filth in our house." I look up at Mickey, who's just standing there looking lost. I give him a look of hey man what can I do, but he gives me the look back that says I'm a married homeowner, this is the way it is.

Mickey offers us a beer and I say, "Sure," Chip says, "Great," and Stoner says, "Fuck yeah, dude," which brings another scowl from Clarice. That's the third scowl, so Mickey grabs four beers and we have to go to the garage.

While we're drinking our beers in the garage, Mickey is talking about money and how Clarice and him are going to have another child once they have saved a certain amount of money in the bank. We finish our beers and realize that Mickey has only taken one sip of his beer. Stoner offers to go in and get some more, but Mickey says, "No thanks, I'll get them" and then goes into the house that we're no longer allowed in. We contemplate pulling out the bowl, but then decide that may not be a good idea, because if we get kicked out of the garage we'll be outside, and it's fucking frigid outside.

Mickey comes back with the beers and continues to talk about money and the kids. Stoner could talk about living in L.A., I could talk about New York, or Chip could talk about his operation, but none of that is as important as the life of a married homeowner. Mickey goes in for another round of beers and Stoner jokingly says, "I hope he tells the mortgage payment story again." He doesn't realize Clarice is listening from inside.

Clarice is yelling at Mickey in the house and he comes back saying we have to go. We say it was great to see him and we'll see him at the party.

Mickey says, "Thanks for coming over, guys. I've had a great time. See you at the party." Clarice brings the kids out to the garage to say goodbye and then opens the garage door to let us out. We pile into the Camaro.

"Wow," is all I can say.

"No shit," says Chip.

"Brutal, dude. Fucking brutal," says Stoner.

We all light cigarettes and within five minutes we're at Mark's. "One down, one to go," says Stoner as we knock on Mark's door. All you need to know about Mark is that he likes to tan, married an ex-stripper, bought a house, and is trying to have a child, because that's what you do. "Hey, fellas," says Janet (a.k.a. Nikki from the Body Shop). "Let me get Mark. He's tanning in our new bed in the basement." Mark comes up from the basement looking too tan for Wisconsin in December, not to mention too tan for California in July.

He says, "What's up, dawgs?"

We all give him a weak, "Hey, man, what's up?"

"Nice tan, Stoner. You guys want a beer?"

Chip and I look over at Stoner, who says, "Yes, that would be lovely, Mark." This causes us to giggle because we're still high, and starting to get a little drunk as well.

"What do you think of the house?"

The house is beautiful, with cathedral ceilings and bright artwork lining the walls. We all look around and nod approvingly at the house, which is actually a mistake, because Mark was looking for a reason to give us a tour. Mark gives us the tour that includes a room upstairs dedicated to Janet's days as a dancer. There are pictures all around the room of her half-naked. There is a pole in the middle of the room. Mark gives me an elbow to the ribs. "This is where we spend a lot of our time." I chuckle, even though I'm not sure what he means, and look closely at the pictures, wondering why someone would want a room in their house like this. "Fuck dude, ahaaahaaha," is all Stoner can say as he looks around. Chip is laughing hysterically in the corner.

"What's so funny, Chip?" asks Mark.

"Dude, that's me." He points to a picture where Janet is giving a guy with blond hair and sunglasses a lap dance. Mark doesn't laugh. He may be married to an ex-stripper, but he's also a married homeowner. Mark decides it's time for us to go.

We finish our beers and agree to hook up at Sharon's party.

"Six months," says Stoner back in the Camaro.

"One year," I say.

"Two months," says Chip.

"The usual, fifty dollars a head?" I ask.

Everyone agrees on fifty dollars. It's sad when you're betting on a friend's divorce, but what the hell, it's going to happen regardless of the bet.

It's Monday night at Hammer's, which means it's quarter tap night. The rest of the week is ladies night (go figure). Johnny Come Lately has just taken the stage.

Kyle is the lead singer and isn't all that bad, but may have been a bit presumptuous comparing his band to the Violent Femmes.

During the break, I tell Kyle they sound great and buy him a beer because I'm nice and it's only costing me a quarter. My head is hurting and I could really use a Valium, but I'm out and Chip is busy at the bar talking to the friend of a brother who works for NBC about an idea for a reality show.

Then I decide I shouldn't be taking any more Valium with my condition and all so I decide I will quit. Stoner is ordering another beer and smoking a Marlboro Light, and I'm bored so I decide to call Jackie, who says she's staying in tonight because she doesn't feel well. I tell her I know how that goes, and we agree to meet up sometime before the party.

I wonder whether Jackie really is ill or just doesn't want to see me. Is it possible to have high self-confidence and low self-esteem? I think about this for a second and decide it's a stupid question. I order another beer, light another Marlboro, and continue to be bored.

During Johnny Come Lately's next break, I walk into the bathroom, where Chip and Kyle are doing lines of coke. Three lines are cut on a small mirror resting on the sink. "You want some?" asks Chip.

I'm drunk so I say, "Sure, one line."

Chip hands me a rolled up five and says, "Rock 'n' roll, dude." I snort the line, tell Chip it's good, remember the paranoid agitated feeling I used to get from cocaine, and promise myself I'll never do cocaine again. I'll quit tomorrow.

There's weak applause as Johnny Come Lately is introduced before they begin their third set, then everyone cheers loudly when they hear the lead singer is from SoHo.

Why is it we always love our own more than others? Are they more deserving? I light a Marlboro, order another beer, and continue to be bored. Sometime after midnight, Sharon shows up. She's wearing a T-shirt that reads: GOT POT? Sharon is still wearing her Where's The Fucking Party? pin. We say hey and then she asks me why I don't smile more, and I tell her I get that a lot. We talk about the party, other meaningless shit, drink more beer, and watch Johnny Come Lately. I ask her about Mary and Sharon says she doesn't know where she is or whether she'll be at the party this year.

"I don't even have her phone number," says Sharon. "Last I heard, she was skiing in Colorado. Before that, she was hiking in Vermont. Before that, she was in Amsterdam."

I cut in. "Amsterdam? That's cool."

"You never know where she is. She's been running with the bulls in Spain, drinking at Mardi Gras, kayaking in South America. You just don't know with that girl. I was surprised to see her at my party last year. I had no idea she was going to be there. But, you know, that's just the way she is. How does she put it? She's random!"

"There's something about Mary," I say, which sounds cheesy as soon as it leaves my mouth.

Sharon just stares at me looking confused because either she's never heard of the movie or because it's just a cheesy thing to say, or both. Chip and Stoner walk over. Chip is happy because he's found someone who may pitch his reality TV show to NBC. Stoner is checking out one of the waitresses, which Chip is giving him shit for. "Dude, I just like waitresses," says Stoner.

It's now last call so we each order two more beers, drink them down, and leave. Chip invites Sharon back to his place with us to smoke herb. I'm glad we're leaving because my head hurts and I know there's a bottle of Valium at Chip's. I'll quit tomorrow.

That night I don't sleep very well. I have nightmares involving married homeowners with brain tumors who sing bad Violent Femmes covers.

# 12

"Only two? Her number is two?" asks Janelle. It's Tuesday morning. Janelle, Sharon, Stoner, and myself are sitting around the kitchen table while Chip makes omelets.

We're discussing Jackie and the fact that she's only had sex with two guys. Don't ask, I have no idea how we got here. In the background we can hear "It's Getting Hot in Here" by Nelly playing on MTV2 in the living room.

Chip says, "Dude, you were her first."

I say, "I know."

Stoner digs into his jeans, pulls out his bottle of Xanax, and pops two pills.

"What's your number, J?" asks Chip.

"I think it's twenty-one, but I've kind of lost track," I say.

"That sounds about right. You've shagged about a half dozen girls at my parties alone, Jeremy," says Sharon.

"Ahaahaaahaa," laughs Stoner.

"What's your number?" Stoner asks Sharon.

"Oh, honey, that's on a need to know basis."

"I need to know!" yells Chip while he's dancing to Nelly.

"No, hon, you don't," replies Sharon.

Stoner shakes his head. "Mine is seventy-seven. Can you believe that shit?"

There's an uncomfortable pause that lasts about a minute as we all do the math in our heads. I'm a little worried because if Stoner has slept with seventy-seven girls, and I know Sharon was one of them, and I've slept with Sharon, then that means...

Chip speaks up as he flips an omelet. "Dudes, my number is ninety-eight! Rock 'n' roll!"

Janelle gets up from the table and walks out. After Janelle leaves the kitchen, Chip asks, "What do you think her number is?"

Stoner says softly, "Less than ninety-eight, dude, less than ninety-eight."

Chip serves omelets and Bloody Marys. We eat in silence.

After, Chip pulls me aside and says, "Dude, I was even counting threesomes as only one each. I mean, Janelle, you know, she knows I've been around the block." Around the block, or around the world? I pat Chip on the back, because it just seems like the right thing to do.

I leave the drama at Chip's and go to my parents' house, where no one is home. I figure now is as good of a time as any to check in with work. I plug in my laptop, which causes my head to hurt, then dial into our corporate email system. I have 175 emails waiting for me.

I've been out of the office for one working day. Here are some of the highlights: Jim from Account Services has puppies for sale. Jane Lansky is now known as Jane Machos (sometimes it's best to keep your own name when becoming a married homeowner). The next email is from Steve in Marketing, letting everyone know that Shawn's wife just gave birth to a baby boy named Todd. First of all, who's Shawn, and secondly, Todd? I don't think they really thought that one through. Other emails include: new hires, departing employees, three-week anniversaries, new dress code policies (you can wear open-toed sandals on Casual Friday, but you must also wear socks), two-week anniversaries, information on the building heating system that we have no control over, and finally an email from the cafeteria announcing that Friday's special will be New York strips. The final email has generated sixty-five reply-to-all emails asking if there will be a vegetarian alternative.

Next, I check my voicemail. I have five messages. The first message is from Ski, following up on the monthly budgets. The second is from Rick, who's pissed because he forgot where the monthly accounts receivable information is kept on the network. The next message is from Maury, informing me of a conference call scheduled for Wednesday morning. He would appreciate it if I'd be able to call in from Canada and participate in the call. Gerald has left a message requesting clarification on the new Purchase Requisition software program. "Jeremy, do I need to click once or twice on the icon? I was told to click twice to access the application, but yesterday I clicked once and it worked as well. Please let me know the proper procedure for accessing this application. Regards." What a fucking tool!

The final message is from Jake. He has a question regarding my expense account from my trip to California a month ago. "Jeremy, in regards to your expense account you submitted from your West Coast port trip, I'm a little concerned with your tipping habits. I see twice where dinners came to around fifty dollars and you felt it was proper to tip 22 percent and 24 percent. Not a major issue, but this is something we'll need to discuss when you're back in the office. I hope you're enjoying Alaska!" I hate my job.

Tuesday afternoons in SoHo are so boring. I'm at Radio Kaos, a CD store in West SoHo, reading the back of the new Jane's Addiction CD. A guy wearing a green turtleneck sweater is asking the bald owner (who's smoking a clove cigarette, making the store smell something awful) what he thinks of his new car.

"It's okay, I guess," says the store owner.

"I think it's a piece of shit. Looks like a space shuttle or something," says the car owner.

"Yeah, I guess," says the store owner. "But great parking spot!"

A teenage girl wearing a large gray sweatshirt asks the store owner about the new R.E.M. CD, and he says that it's really good. They really went back to their roots with this one, which, if I remember correctly, is what they said about their last CD. There should really be a limit on how many times you can go back to your roots.

I check my Nokia and I have two messages. The first is from Angella, saying she's sorry and wants to come to, no, she IS coming to Wisconsin for the weekend, and "Have you been checking your email?" She also says I shouldn't worry about the Kevin situation. "He wasn't that good in bed," is how she ends the message. I try to call her, but get voicemail and leave her a message telling her to not come to Wisconsin and we'll talk about everything when I'm back in the city in a few days.

The second message is from Chip, saying Stoner and him are really bored, being Tuesday afternoon and all, and that they are going to Showgirls to catch the matinee show.

I flip the Jane's Addiction CD over, take a look at the cover, and realize that I already have this one. I put it back on the shelf and head to the strip joint.

I'm stoned as we walk into Showgirls, pay the twenty-dollar cover, and grab seats at the bar. Tonight's special is thirteen-dollar bottles of Bud Light, so I buy three, leave a fifty on the bar, and wait for Stoner and Chip, who are standing at the stage to my left watching Jasmine dance.

My Nokia is vibrating so I answer it. It's Jackie, who called just to see what I'm doing.

"Uh, nothing," I say and then she asks if I'd like to go see the new Ben Affleck movie. I say I'd rather see the new Will Smith movie, and we end up agreeing to see the new Jackie Chan movie tonight at the Cineplex.

"Did you hear what happened to Greg?"

"No," I say and then tell her I have to go after agreeing to meet at the Cineplex around eight.

Jasmine reminds Stoner of the waitress from Joe Mamma's, so after she finishes dancing on the main stage, Stoner decides to buy a lap dance from her, and they go off into the corner. "More Human Than Human" by White Zombie is playing while the next dancer, Dakota, takes the stage.

After she's finished dancing, she comes over and starts talking to me about her boyfriend from Detroit who works for "The Big Three." I really don't know nor do I care what she's talking about, but it's okay because she smells okay and I haven't paid her a dime. The D.J. announces that Joy will be dancing next and that "she's yummy." He also announces that there's a red Corolla with its lights on in the parking lot, and for a limited time Bud Lights will be only twelve dollars each.

"Sweet Child O'Mine" is playing as Joy takes the stage dressed in a skimpy nurse's outfit.

Dakota exposes her crooked teeth as she smiles at me, asking me if I'd like a private dance. I tell her no because I have a headache and don't feel well, but I'll buy her a Bud Light if she wants, and she says she doesn't drink but will take the cash. I give her $20. She kisses me on the cheek. “Thanks, hon.” Then she leaves.

Stoner comes back from his lap dance and Chip asks him how she was. “Too much air,” says Stoner as Chip nods his head in a sympathetic way.

# 13

George Michael's definitive collection? I can't believe I just slept with a girl who owns this CD. It's actually partially hidden behind a Smashmouth CD, probably because she's embarrassed to own it. She should be. I'm embarrassed knowing I'm in the same room as this CD. It's Wednesday morning and I'm sitting at the edge of Jackie's bed in my blue boxers. She's still in bed, smoking a Newport with the sheets pulled up to her thighs. She's balancing an ashtray on her left fake breast. Ashes are landing around the outside. I'm not sure I've ever seen anything more fucking disturbing.

Last night we went to the Jackie Chan movie, which was okay, although I would have rather seen the Will Smith movie. Then we went out for margaritas because that's what she does after seeing a movie (it was a total bore) and then ended up back at her place.

During sex, while inside her, she asked me if I would move to Alabama with her, and I said no. Afterwards, I asked her why she asked that and she said she didn't remember asking the question. The sex wasn't anything spectacular, just okay. Now I find out she owns this CD.

I'm distracted and not feeling well, but it has nothing to do with the margaritas. This feels like one of those one night stand hangovers. George Michael? The definitive collection? Does he even have enough material for a collection? What was I thinking?

### *NEW YEAR'S EVE, 1998:*

*Latex beads. This is first thing I noticed, walking into Sharon's bedroom. The beads were sitting on top of her dresser. As I looked further I noticed a plethora of lubricants organized like most people arrange perfume or cologne. Astroglide and Liquid Silk among other lotions were on the dresser next to the beads. Sharon noticed me staring at the lubricants and laughed, saying, "That's nothing, hon." She opened the top drawer, exposing the following: a wand vibrator, a G-spotter, a coil vibrator, a crystal wand dildo, something called the Hitachi Maje, the Fukuoko 9000, and an anal toy just called Buddy. I looked at her, shocked. She shrugged her shoulders, saying, "Hey, you never know what you feel like, hon." I had been drinking and smoking herb all night, but I still think I knew what I was doing (for the most part, I mean, to be honest, thinking about the Fukuoko 9000 fucked me up more than the herb and alcohol). Sharon was pretty out of it, but she was the one who asked me if I wanted to fuck her just five minutes earlier. We were both bored... Earlier in the night, Chip and Stoner were chasing Old Thompson whiskey with root beer schnapps, challenging everyone at the party to do the same. I ended up doing a beer bong consisting of four beers, three shots of Old Thompson, and a fifth of root beer schnapps. I was fucked up. Barely able to walk, I met an old school hippie girl named Luann who used words like "groovy" and "far out" when describing her life, my life, and everyone else's life. She loved everyone and everything, and I instantly wanted to have sex with her. She referred to herb as "grass" and talked about moving to Montana to be with nature. "Pretty gnarly, eh?" she said when talking about Montana. We smoked herb (she smoked grass), and this was enough to cause me to pass out. I woke up three hours later on Sharon's couch, only a handful of people still at the party, Luann gone. This is when Sharon asked me if I wanted to fuck her. I looked around and realized I had nothing better to do. Afterward, while sharing a warm bottle of Becks, relieved that "Buddy" and I were never formally introduced, she told me I was the first guy she had been with since she stopped taking medication for Chlamydia.*

I'm in Jackie's kitchen on the phone trying to get a hold of Angella, but instead I get her voicemail, and tell her she needs to call me. Jackie walks in wearing only white panties with little red trolls on them and asks me if I'd like any amphetamines, which she refers to as "speed." "I've got both crosses and hearts," she says as she offers me a homemade wooden box filled with white and pink pills. I tell her that seeing her standing there is all I need to stay up. She lets out a fake laugh. I pop one of the crosses, then she pops three pills (two white crosses and one pink heart). Jackie asks me what I'm doing tonight and I tell her that Stoner, Chip, and I are planning on checking out a new bar called Tonic. Jackie says, "Sounds like fun." I say I'll call her, and I leave. As I'm walking out of Jackie's apartment building, I light a Marlboro. As I take a drag off my cigarette, I realize I still have the smell of Jackie on me, causing me to think of George Michael. I'm still embarrassed for her. I walk twenty blocks to my parents' house, where I shower, put on a clean Gap T-Shirt, and drink orange juice and vodka. My head starts to hurt when I remember I've got a conference call this morning with Maury. I take five Advils, washing them down with my screwdriver.

I'm thumbing through an Elmore Leonard novel while on the phone waiting for the meeting to start. On the other end, everyone is there: Maury, Gerald, Howard, a few other corporate yes men, and Jake. We're waiting for our UK office to call in. Gerald asks me if I've responded to his question on how to access the Online Purchase Requisition system. I tell him that it doesn't matter if he clicks on the link once or twice, which draws a response from Jake of, "Jeremy, you should really document that procedure." I say I'll take care of it when I'm back in the office. Gerald then asks Jake how I got two weeks off. Jake doesn't have a response. Gerald says, "Must be nice." I say, "Yeah, it is." Which causes Gerald (I presume) to put the phone on mute so that I'll be unable to hear what they're saying, probably discussing my future with the company, which at this point I really don't care that much about. Donald from Jameson's UK office finally calls in and Maury kicks off the meeting.

"Folks, I've called this meeting to discuss documentation as it pertains to our UK office." You've got to be kidding me. I put down the novel, turn on the television with the volume low, and flip to CNN. The terror alert color code for today is Violet, and the FBI is informing the public that they have received non-specific threats against anyone wearing a cowboy hat in Texas. I turn on VH1, where the Garbage *Behind the Music* is on. Maury is talking. "Folks, a company needs standards across the board. We can't be using one formula to calculate budgets in the States and have the UK using a different method. Folks, it just doesn't make sense." I'm watching an infomercial for the Juiceman II. I own the Juiceman I. Should I upgrade to the Juiceman II? The Juiceman's eyebrows mesmerize me as I contemplate buying the new model.

"Jeremy? Jeremy? You still there?" It's Maury.

"Uh... yeah, I'm here."

"Folks, we need Jeremy to take the lead on documenting all international procedures." I can actually hear the specks of spit hitting the phone as Maury says this.

Maury continues, "Jeremy, we're talking about international standards here, so be sure you take into account prices that our subsidiaries charge each other for the services traded between them."

"You mean transfer prices?"

"Yes."

Why didn't you say that?

"Okay."

"Folks, we need to focus on documentation. That's all. Jeremy, thanks for calling in from Utah."

"Wisconsin."

"Oh, right. Why can't I remember that?"

Because you're an old selfish bastard?

"No problem," is all I say.

Gerald asks if Jake and I can stay and continue our discussion regarding the financial workflow applications.

Jake says, "Okay" and "Very good." I don't have a choice in the matter.

"Jeremy, now when I fill out an Account Agreement form, it requires me to enter a total impact to the company field. What is that?"

"I believe it says in parentheses that you are to enter the dollar value."

"Dollar value of what?"

"The total impact to the company."

"Oh, so that's implied?" says Gerald.

"What? Well, it's right there. It's also in the help documentation."

"Help documentation? Where's that?" asks Gerald.

Jake says it's located near the top of the form and Gerald feels this is getting too technical. "Jake, can Jeremy document this procedure as well, since he's already documenting the clicking procedure for the Purchase Requisition system and all?"

"Very good. I think that's a super idea. Jeremy, put that near the top of your things to do," says Jake.

"What am I supposed to document? It says total impact to company right on the form, explains the dollar value right next to the entry field, and has extensive documentation throughout the help document," I say.

Gerald (I presume) puts the phone on mute.

They are back and Jake tells me I need to do a better job of documenting the procedures.

"Okay."

I'm a corporate whore.

# 14

I'm wearing my black sweater over my Gap T-shirt as Chip and I stand in line smoking, waiting to get into the Tonic bar. I've decided that tonight's the night I tell the guys about my condition. Just thinking about my stupid little annoying orphan disease makes me feel dizzy. Stoner is already inside because he knows one of the waitresses, well, he slept with one of the waitresses last year when she was then working at the Pour House. I remember Stoner had commented on how that during sex with the waitress she screamed, "Fuck me like you'd fuck your uncle!" We asked him what she meant and all Stoner said was, "Dude, I don't know, but I kind of liked it."

A homeless man is standing across the street, standing on a coffee can, reading from a dictionary. He sees us standing in line and quickly shuffles to the beginning of his book. "BLEACH, a verb, to make white or become colorless. Nothing," says the homeless man while staring at us. The word "nothing" stays with me.

Chip bumps me and nods forward at the lesbians standing in front of us and all I say is, "I know." They're whispering to each other (something sexy, I'm sure) with their hands in the back pockets of each other's jeans, and this makes me horny. What is it about lesbians?

We eventually get inside. To our dismay, we realize it's karaoke night. A pale guy wearing cargo pants is singing "Ring of Fire" really well.

"Fuck, dude, this guy has been burned. Listen to him. Only a guy who truly has been burned can sing this song like that," says Chip as he raises his hand to the guy singing in cargo pants. Cargo pants nods back to Chip. A bartender with a graying goatee and heavy Boston accent approaches us. He tells us it's two-dollar bottle beer night. I order a Miller, Chip a Budweiser. The bartender brings the beers over. "One *Millah*, one *Budweisah*." I ask him where he's from, and he says, "Southie." I tell him I went to Harvard. He doesn't seem impressed.

A brunette with fake breasts knocks over her drink and the bartender says, "That's a *pissah*, you want *anothah*, *sweethawt*?"

We pass an angry Golden Tee player who's kicking the machine while screaming, "I got fucking robbed!" We walk over to a table next to the darkened jukebox, where Stoner and Sharon are both drinking bottles of Rolling Rock.

"Hey, love your sweater, Jeremy. It's ghetto fabulous," says Sharon.

"Thanks," I say as I take a drink of my Miller and check out a girl wearing a blue tank top at the bar. Stoner is pointing over to a table right in front of the stage, where a homely lady with matted black hair is sitting, eating a bowl of popcorn.

"Dudes, look at her. She chews like a hooker."

"What?" asks Chip.

"She chews like a fucking hooker!"

"What does a hooker chew like?" asks Chip.

"Like her, dude. Just watch," says Stoner.

We all turn in our chairs, watching the homely girl chew like a hooker.

"She looks sick," says Sharon.

She says this because it's easier to say someone looks sick rather than say someone looks like they have AIDS.

An Indian gets on stage and rapes "Born in the USA."

Four girls who are too cute for their own good scream "Stop in the Name of Love."

A married homeowner sings "Margaritaville." The homely girl who chews like a hooker screams "Where's the fucking salt?" during the chorus.

The more butch of the two lesbians sings "Brown Eyed Girl."

Some guy in an orange Packers hat sings the worst version of "Johnny B. Goode" I've ever heard. Someone throws a bottle of Old Style at him. He leaves the stage. Everyone in the Tonic applauds.

My head is aching. I pop four Advils. Chip puts a full bottle of Valium in my hand. "Merry Christmas, dude."

I pop two Valiums.

I take a drink of Miller.

I light a Marlboro.

A Mexican wearing yellow sunglasses does a painful rendition of "American Girl."

"So what the fuck is going on with Angella?" asks Chip.

"I don't know. I think she might be coming here. I can't get a hold of her. She's not returning my calls."

"Coming to Wisconsin?"

"Yeah."

"Dude, that's fucked up."

Stoner and Sharon walk up to the bar to get another round. Chip lights a Marlboro, then slams the rest of his Budweiser.

"Dude, do you think she got the crabs taken care of?"

I ignore Chip's last question and finish my beer.

My Nokia is vibrating. I pray it's Angella. It's Jackie. She wants to know what I'm doing. I tell her I'm at the Tonic bar and she asks why I haven't called. I tell her it's lame and that I didn't think she'd have any fun and that maybe she should go see the new Ben Affleck movie.

"I'm going to see Greg tomorrow," says Jackie.

"Oh."

"Um, so I was wondering, if, you know, you wanted to go with me. Jeremy, I really don't want to go alone."

"Sorry, Jackie. I can't tomorrow. I've got too much going on."

"Oh. Well, what are you doing later tonight?"

"I'm not sure."

"Call me if you want to hook up."

"Okay."

"Angella?" asks Chip.

"No, it was Jackie."

"Dude, what the fuck are you going to do with Angella?"

"I don't know."

"Dude, I hear you. Fuck, Janelle is freaking out. She thinks I've got a sex problem."

"Man, I really don't want—"

"No, dude, whoa, no dude, not that. She thinks I'm like fucking addicted to sex."

"Oh yeah?" I say unconvincingly.

"Dude, what the fuck? You agree."

"No, man, you're fine. She's fucked up." Whatever.

"I know, but I kind of like her. Well, you know, I don't have to fucking tell you. Look at her. Fuck, dude, you were interested in her, but she shot you down."

"Yeah, I know." Whatever.

"So she wants me to go to counseling."

"Counseling? Like couples counseling, you and her?"

"No, dude, she wants me to go to this class, or seminar, or something. I don't know what it even is."

"That sucks."

Stoner comes back with more beers. He's smoking and bitching because some girl in a Polo shirt just called him a zero. Sharon is still at the bar. The bartender from Southie is showing her the tattoo that's on his ass. It's Minnie Mouse bent over getting railed by Mickey. Chip looks over at me and drops the bomb.

"Yeah, well, I was hoping you'd come along to this seminar, class thing, whatever the fuck it is. Please, dude."

"I don't think so."

"What the fuck? I'm asking you for a favor here, man. C'mon."

"When is it?"

"Tomorrow morning. We'll be there an hour max, I promise."

"I don't know. I've got a lot going on."

"Dude, one hour."

"Okay, one hour." Whatever.

"Cool. I've got next round."

Sharon comes back to the table, pinches my ass, and asks me what I'm doing later on.

***NEW YEAR'S EVE, 1999:***

*"You know, this may be our last night on Earth." This is how the worst New Year's Eve in my life began. Yes, this*

*was worse than being robbed in L.A., yes, this was worse than almost dying from shooting H, and yes, this was worse than listening to Wham. "You know, this may be our last night on Earth." Gerald repeated this numerous times throughout the night as we sat at Jameson waiting to test the financial system once the clocks switched to the year 2000. While millions celebrated the new millennium, I sat at Jameson listening to Gerald tell me how he had prepared for the end of the world. "I've got enough canned goods to last the family three months, all of my money has been pulled out of the bank and is in a safe, and I've got a bedroom full of batteries. Yes, my sixteen-year-old son isn't enjoying the fact that he has to share a room with his fourteen-year-old sister, but I'm not taking any chances. I knew this was going to happen. Technology isn't always a good thing, Jeremy. Now you'll see! Now you'll all see!" Jake was also there. Well, technically he was there. He spent the evening sleeping in his office. After all, it was four hours past his bedtime. Maury was there via conference call. Rumor has it that Maury spent the night in an underground shelter supplied by Jameson, I guess the thought being that if the entire civilization got wiped out, old senile Maury would be able to bring Jameson back to profitability all by himself. Maury is a star. "Folks, how are we doing?" Maury would ask every five minutes, sounding very tired as the night moved on. My only fun throughout the night was asking Gerald why the world would end on East Coast time. I asked this every five minutes. It was easy to remember; I would ask him right after Maury asked for an update. The entire Information Technology department was also there, a real fun group. A propeller hat guy named Wayne kept pressing me, wanting to show me the algorithm he used to complete the year two thousand conversion. I told him I didn't care what the stupid computer code looked like as long as it worked, but he kept pressing. I finally asked him to tell me in English how it worked and he said, "That's impossible." I said, "Well, isn't it really just increasing the year fields in all the files from two to four characters?" and he said, "Well, yeah, but it's much more complicated than that." I asked him how so, and he offered to show me the algorithm. This conversation went on for most of the night. When the clock struck twelve, nothing happened, just as nothing had happened in the Far East, and nothing had happened in Europe. The only thing that happened was Gerald made a complete ass out of himself again. We were allowed to leave around two o'clock. "Folks, you all did a great job tonight," said Maury from the phone. Fuck you, Maury. This was my worst New Year's Eve ever.*

It's late. Nobody is singing karaoke and the bar is starting to thin out. Stoner and Chip are sitting at the bar trying to talk the bartender into showing them his tattoo.

"Dude, I'm not gay, I just want to see it," says Chip.

The bartender calls them "*wicked retahded*" and goes on with his business. Sharon is telling me a story about how last Monday while getting dressed she accidentally dropped her shirt into the bathroom trash can. Thinking nothing of it, she put the shirt on and went about her day, shopping, seeing friends, and running errands. Later that night she looked in the mirror and realized she had something stuck to the back of her shirt. "A bloody fucking tampon!" is what she found hanging from the back of her shirt. "That's funny," I tell her and she agrees.

Stoner and Chip come back with another round and I go to the bathroom, passing a girl who's crying hysterically while a guy sitting next to her smokes a Winston. I walk into a stall, grab a seat, and pop two Valiums.

Sharp pains run through my head as I'm staring at the back door of the stall reading several phone numbers and stupid sayings written by morons with nothing better to do than scratch shit on stall doors. Under a phone number for Gayle (who LIKES A GOOD TIME) are the words GO HOME, scratched, alone, in the center of the door. For five minutes I stare at this, lost. More distractions in my life.

I walk back to the table, where Stoner and Sharon are giving Chip shit because he has to go to a sex seminar, and then they give me shit because I'm going with him. I drink down my Miller, smoke a Marlboro, and we leave. I climb into the back of the Camaro with Sharon. As Chip pulls onto the road and begins to accelerate, Sharon puts her hand on my leg, and that's the last thing I remember.

# 15

It's chilly on top of the mountain. A cool breeze blows through my hair, and I'm blinded by a bright light shining directly into my eyes. My head no longer hurts, but my body is in a restricted state. There are others up here. They are discussing the Packers' playoff hopes, but I can't see their faces because of the light.

"Jeremy, can you hear me?"

My feet are dangling eight thousand feet up as I rest on the summit's rock surface, and I'm not sure if I'm dead or alive. "Dude, wake up."

The others, who were discussing the Packers, have come to the conclusion that the Packers will make the playoffs if Brett Favre stays healthy. I come to the conclusion that I'm going to start doing things differently, even though I'm not sure what that means. The light is dimming. GO HOME.

I wake up on a hospital bed and see Chip, Stoner, and a doctor wearing black reading glasses on the tip of an abnormally large nose standing over me. A light is shining in my eyes.

"Dude, we thought you were in a coma," says Chip.

The doctor gives Chip an "Are you fucking stupid?" look and asks me, "How are you feeling, Jeremy?" My doctor looks a little like Mr. Kotter (with a much larger nose) and has a pack of Kools in his front shirt pocket.

"What happened?" I ask.

"Dude, you passed out then started going into convulsions, or something," says Chip.

"You were fucked up," says Stoner. The doctor looks over at Stoner, shakes his head, and motions for them to back away. Stoner says he's going to find something to eat. As Stoner walks out, he looks over at Chip, points at his nose then over to the doctor, and laughs. "Ahaahaahaa."

"Jeremy, I'm Dr. Robertson. You've been passed out for about an hour. You had a seizure."

I look over at Chip, who's leaning against the windowsill reading *Playboy*. As the doctor tells me this, he lowers the magazine and nods in agreement.

"Whoa," I say. I lift my head and see I've got a needle stuck in my right arm. I'm wearing a hospital gown, and my head is wrapped in a bandage. My black sweater and jeans are draped over a chair under the television. Conan O'Brien is on. What did they do with my Gap T-Shirt? Someone probably stole it.

Dr. Robertson asks me if I've ever had a seizure before, and I start to explain the situation. I tell him about the diagnosis, the surgery scheduled for next Tuesday, and that I've probably been drinking too much. As Chip hears me talking, he puts down the *Playboy* and walks over to the bed.

"Dude, what the fuck? Why didn't you say something before?"

"I don't know. I just didn't want to bother anyone."

"J, you're one dumb motherfucker, you know that? You could have died, and I would have thought it was my fault."

"What?" This is all a little too much for me right now.

"Yeah, dude. Fuck, man, I thought you were tripping from all the—" Chip looks over at the doctor, then nods his head at me. "You know what I mean."

I feel the bandage on my head and ask the doctor whether this is necessary. "You bumped your head," says Dr. Robertson, who looks over at Chip.

"Yeah, dude, you freaked out and your head was hunched forward in my car so I pulled over, and when pulling you out of the Camaro, I—I mean you—bumped your head on the door. Fucked up, dude. Blood everywhere. Sharon was freaked out, dude. I made her go home. Too much drama."

"There's a small cut on your forehead," adds Dr. Robertson, beginning to get impatient with Chip.

Dr. Robertson leaves to "look over some tests." As he walks out, he tells me that if everything looks okay, he'll let me go. GO HOME.

A nurse named Blanch with short blonde hair and a nose ring comes in and asks me if there's anything she can get me. I tell her no, and then she looks over at Chip, who's checking out the centerfold in his *Playboy*.

"Look at page 32. That's my cousin," Blanch says, looking over to Chip.

Chip thumbs through the magazine so fast he drops the magazine and looks a little embarrassed. Blanch giggles. Chip eventually finds the page, looks over at Blanch, then at me, and says, "Dude, she's fucking hot."

"She is hot. She used to be a lesbian. Now she dates a black guy from Chicago. Weird, eh?" says Blanch. You can never have too much information.

Chip reads the caption, then looks at me. "Her favorite color is blue," says Chip in a matter of fact sort of way. Blanch leaves and Chip comments on Blanch's "bunt" and says she should really start doing sit-ups on a regular basis.

There's a minute of silence and then Chip asks me about the whole "brain tumor thing" and I explain to him how I was having headaches, had blurry vision from time to time, and I tell him how I passed out one afternoon while playing football. After the football incident, I went to see a doctor, then another doctor, then another doctor, until I was finally diagnosed with my condition.

"Dude, are you scared?"

"Not really."

Stoner walks in. I get him up to speed on what's going on and he says, "Dude, that sucks." Stoner then walks over to the television, switches to MTV2, turns the volume down, and pops a Xanax. We sit in silence for a couple of minutes watching an Ice Cube video, then Chip speaks up.

"You guys remember Andy, from high school?"

"Oh yeah, the dude with the overbite?" asks Stoner.

I don't remember him. I remember a Tony with an overbite and bad skin, but no Andy.

"Yeah, him. He went in for a physical, and they found a spot on his ass," says Chip as Stoner leafs through the *Playboy*.

"Like a zit?" asks Stoner.

"No, dude, like a strange spot, so they do a test for cancer, and—"

"A biopsy," I say.

"What?"

"It's called a biopsy. A skin tissue sample," I say.

"Yeah," says Chip, who looks lost. "So, dude gets this test. It turns out he's got cancer, you know, the really big C."

"Dude had cancer?" asks Stoner.

"Yeah, so the test comes back positive. A week later, dude's in surgery."

Stoner puts down the *Playboy* and pulls out a Marlboro Light.

"What are you doing?" I ask Stoner.

"Dude, I need one. Don't sweat it, I'll put the fan on in the bathroom."

I shake my bandaged head and look over at Chip, who's also pulling out a Marlboro.

"Dude, so what happened to Andy?" asks Stoner as he stands up.

"Dude died on the table."

Chip and Stoner go into the bathroom to smoke.

# 16

Every now and then you come across something in life that you just know is going to be bad. Chip and I are standing outside the SoHo YMCA. My phone is in hand, and I'm still trying to get a hold of Angella while Chip tells me about a boring movie starring Charlie Sheen he watched last night while he was stoned and I was sleeping on the couch. "It started off good, a lot of violence, but then it turned into a romantic comedy. It was really a fucked ending." Jackie has left five messages since last night.

We walk inside and see a sign informing us that the sex support group (titled "Sexuality Wellness and Awareness Group") is going to be in the gymnasium on the second floor.

After mistakenly walking into a weight room where two gay guys in spandex are spotting each other, a locker room full of old wrinkled naked men, and the pool area full of elderly women doing aerobics (Chip points out that one woman, about sixty years old and wearing an orange bikini, still looks good for her age), we eventually find the gymnasium, where the support group has already started in the center of the gym.

At half court, twenty chairs are arranged in a circle, surrounding a table with a coffee maker, name tags, ashtrays, and an empty Krispy Kreme box.

We grab name tags, write our names (I write Johnny, Chip writes Stoner), sit down on two open chairs, and quickly realize that we shouldn't be here. This isn't a support group as much as it's a group of urban legends and bad clichés you thought never actually existed. They are all here.

Roy is talking. Roy has a habit of sticking things in his ass. About a month ago he was rushed to the hospital with a champagne flute stuck in his ass. A special team of proctologists from Johns Hopkins was flown in from Baltimore to remove the glass, well, not actually remove it as a whole object. The doctors had to take a special "ass hammer" (he says this like it's a medical term) and shatter the glass. For the next six hours, doctors carefully pulled shards of glass from Roy's ass while he swore he was never going to do that again. Roy was back at the hospital a week later, same style champagne flute. Roy is with his friends here. There's a girl here named Shannon who masturbates twenty times a day... before breakfast.

My jeans are vibrating, and this draws a lustful look from Shannon, who is disappointed when she realizes it's only my phone. I look at the display and see it's Angella.

I want to take this call, I need to take this call, but Jim is talking, so I send Angella to voicemail. Mindy, the woman running the group, gives me a stern look as I put my phone back into my pocket. Mindy nods over to Jim and asks him to continue now that this unbelievably rude interruption is over.

Since I'm sitting in the circle, everyone assumes I have a story, but I tell them I'm only here for support. This draws warm smiles from the perverts. I think Shannon is flirting with me.

Mindy nods at Chip, and Chip explains that he's had what his girlfriend thinks is a large amount of sex with a large amount of partners, and everyone looks at him, waiting for more. When Chip says that's it, everyone is disappointed. Roy says Chip shouldn't be here. He doesn't deserve this group. Everyone in the circle is nodding their heads except for Shannon, who is squirming in her chair, apparently amusing herself. Chip shrugs his shoulders, looks over at me, and we get up to leave. As we walk out of the YMCA, Chip comments on how he thought Shannon was cute, in a corkscrew in the ass sort of way.

## 17

Chip drops me off at my parents' house, where my dad is in the living room, busy organizing the *Magnum* and *Hunter* videotapes while Mom watches and offers advice on tape sequence. She suggests putting them in order by season, then changes her mind, saying that maybe the episodes with TC should be kept separate from all the other *Magnum* tapes. Then she asks whether or not they should start taping the reruns of the show *CHiPs*.

"That Ponch really makes me howl," she says. Then she gets up and leaves because the whole situation is getting too stressful for her.

I check my messages. There's only one. It's from Angella. The message says she's in town. She's staying at the Sheraton in Milwaukee (being paid for by Calvin Klein, I'm sure), and I should call her.

I grab a Miller from the fridge and my mom says, "Jeremy, it's not even noon yet!"

I tell her, "I know, but I've had a long morning."

She says, "Oh," in a way that says she understands what I've been through. She has no idea. I wonder what Roy is doing right now. My mom goes back into the living room and asks my dad if he'd like some coffee.

"Do you have Starbucks coffee?" he asks.

I don't wait to hear her response. Instead, I go to my old bedroom and stare at my Nokia, trying to figure out what to do with Angella.

I call Angella and she says the spring collection looks fabulous and that she really wants to see me. She says a lot of other things as well, but I'm preoccupied by a hole I notice in my blue Gap T-shirt, probably from a cigarette.

With my right index finger I pull at the hole and realize the shirt is ruined. This is my favorite T-shirt and I'm really bummed. We agree to meet at Rangolli's, a Thai restaurant that's near her hotel, the only Thai restaurant in Milwaukee.

Before I hang up, she starts to tell me about a new shirt that's part of the new Calvin Klein collection, but I'm not listening. I'm still focused on the hole in my T-shirt. I'm really bummed about this.

I put on my new ugly beige sweater, pop five Advils, finish my Miller, borrow my mom's car, and in about forty minutes I'm sitting in Rangolli's smoking a Marlboro, waiting for Angella. Two men, one wearing a white knit hat, the other wearing a green headband that says FIGHT ME, both with Irish accents and smoking Parliaments, are asking the waitress where they can get "a pint of the black stuff." The waitress just smiles and asks if they are ready to order.

After pointing to a half-dozen items on the menu and asking "What's in this?" they end up ordering something with chicken in it. As the waitress walks away, they mumble something about it being a bloody shame when you can't get a pint with dinner. Three guys, all wearing

Packers hats and jackets, walk in and sit at a table followed by Angella, who walks in wearing a long leather Calvin Klein trench coat, a white sweater, and black pants.

"It's too fucking cold here," says Angella as she sits down. "How are you, Jeremy?"

"Fine," I say. There's an uncomfortable pause while Angella surveys the restaurant, wearing an appalled look on her face.

"You should have seen the expressions when I said I was going to SoHo for the holidays," says Angella.

"Oh yeah."

"Yeah, un-fucking-believable. Everybody looked at me all crazy until I explained that it's in Wisconsin. Then I got even crazier expressions," says Angella.

"Oh," I say.

"Yeah, no one in New York has ever heard of it before."

Angella is watching as one of the super fans removes his Packers hat.

"So, are mullets still in here?" asks Angella.

I look over at the super fans, who are now leaving their table and exiting the restaurant because they just realized pizza isn't on the menu. The Irish guys are still pissed because they can't get a pint of Guinness. The one wearing the FIGHT ME headband is asking a cute married homeowner couple sitting next to him what they are looking at. I look back at Angella, who is staring at her nails.

"Why are you here?" I ask.

"Well, I wanted, I don't know, I guess I was concerned," she says, as if she had rehearsed this line before, but it didn't come out the way she had hoped.

"I'm fine. You didn't need to come here," I say.

"You say that, but I remember how you were when you broke your leg two months ago and were laid up, how you—"

"I didn't break my leg two months ago."

"Oh, right, that was K—well, whatever, I'm just concerned is all. New sweater?"

I look down at my beige sweater and cringe. "Yeah, Christmas present. Pretty cool, eh?"

Angella gives me the fake half-smile look. She never gets it.

"My blue Gap T-shirt has a hole in it," I say for some reason, maybe looking for sympathy.

Angella ignores me while she stares at a girl wearing a blue suede jacket. "Hideous," is all she says. She turns to me. "Jeremy, you're really going to like the new spring collection. It's fabulous."

"So you've said."

"It's fucking fabulous, Jeremy!"

A waiter walks over and introduces himself as Ned.

Angella orders tea and a salad, and I order a Coke and Spicy Basil Chicken. "Very good," says Ned, looking at me. Then he looks over at the chair next to Angella, where she has put her jacket. "Great jacket! Is that Calvin Klein?"

"It is," says Angella.

"It's fabulous," says Ned. "My grandfather, God rest his soul, always wore Calvin Klein. He was buried in a coat similar to that very one." You can never have too much information.

Ned looks over at me. "It will be about thirty minutes for the chicken, sir."

Angella shivers. "It's too cold here."

Ned agrees and walks away.

"How long are you here for?" I ask.

"Not long. It's too cold." Angella looks around. "And a little weird. But I was hoping to stay for New Year's. I want to see this party you've been talking about."

"It's really nothing."

"When are you going back to the city?" Angella asks.

"Sunday," I say.

"When is your operation?"

"Tuesday."

"Oh, that's the day of the Calvin Klein spring collection kick-off party. I really have to be there."

"That's fine. I don't want a lot of people there. Everything will be fine. My parents will be there."

"Oh, well, then I guess it all works out. So are you going to invite me to this big party?" says Angella.

"No invite required. Just show up dressed as a pimp." I shrug my shoulders.

Angella looks over at her jacket. "'I'll be looking fabulous."

"Okay," is all I say.

Angella shivers again and says she's going visit her parents in California next month.

## *NEW YEAR'S EVE, 2000:*

*Sharon decided that this year she wanted a Country Western-themed party. After hearing this, Chip and I decided to visit Stoner in L.A. The day before New Year's Eve, Chip received a call notifying him that Vin, his dealer, had been gunned down in a drive-by, payback for, well, who the hell knows? He was a drug dealer. These things happen. Chip cried for an hour and took the next plane to SoHo to attend Vin's funeral. "Vin was like a dad to me," confessed Chip while crying, "a cool fucking dad who sold me coke. Dude, I need to buy a suit." Chip has always had close relationships with his deal-*

*ers. It was the only time I've ever seen Chip sad. With Chip gone, Stoner and I decided that for New Year's Eve we would go to a club located at Fashion Island, a short drive from Newport Beach, where we had to drive to first because this is where Stoner's dealer lived. Stoner scored some herb and invited his dealer, known only as Jam, to come along with us. All you need to know about Jam is that he had a shaved head, was very tan, and shook my hand for longer than the universally accepted two seconds. We went to Finch's, a techno club that was neither hip nor a total dive. It was just okay, as far as bars go. A dance mix of "Come Out and Play" by The Offspring was playing as we walked up to the bar. Stoner immediately started to laugh when the bartender commented on how he "looks like a washed up surfer, no pun intended." Jam ordered bourbon on the rocks for all of us while lighting a Punch cigar and looking at me. "You look white," Jam told me. Stoner grabbed his drink, lit a Marlboro, and wandered off into the bar. Jam pointed out a guy sitting at the end of the bar wearing a Polo shirt and told me that Polo shirt guy used to fuck him for crack. "Yeah, it's too bad. He's cleaned up now. What a great fuck," said Jam. Stoner came back with three blondes who all claimed they were Laker girls (Stoner confessed a year later that they weren't Laker girls, but were actually Clipper girls), and they wanted to get high and take us all to a party in West Hollywood. On a scale of one to ten, they were all tens, as far as looks go. On an IQ scale of one to one hundred eighty, they were all in the seventies. "Cool," I said. "Fuck yeah, dude," said Stoner. "I guess," said Jam, still staring at Polo shirt guy. We went to the party in West Hollywood, a block off Sunset. It was neither fun nor dull; it was a typical L.A. gathering. Several pretentious actors and actresses, none of whom I knew by name, only by character, were there and they all looked very fit and tan. Eve, the "Laker" girl Stoner was with, was really into him and they disappeared. Jam hooked up with an actor from* 90210 *and then he disappeared. I was drinking Amstel Lights and talking with an actress from some sitcom that had recently gotten cancelled. She said I looked very white and needed to get a tan. She talked with her hands and liked to make quote signs with her fingers when referring to "the show," "Hollywood," or "the business." The struggling sitcom actress ended up leaving with some tan fit guy who was an extra in the latest Eddie Murphy movie. While drinking my Amstel and smoking a Marlboro, I realized it was already three in the morning. I was drunk and needed to find my way to Stoner's place in Venice Beach. I left the party and was walking up Sunset, where I approached a hooker wearing a blue skirt. I asked her where I could find a cab. She told me she would take care of me for forty dollars. I said I wasn't interested. Then she said, "Baby, forty isn't my price. I can get you a ride for forty bucks." I apologized for some reason and gave her forty dollars. The hooker waved toward the corner and within a minute a black Cadillac pulled up and a large black guy, who introduced himself as Tiger, motioned for me to get in. I got in and we headed down Sunset, pulled down a back alley, and Tiger put a gun to my head. He told me to empty my motherfucking pockets and get the fuck out of his motherfucking car. I obliged, handing over everything I had, and got the fuck out the car. Three hookers, all wearing red, approached me and said they saw the whole thing and added that that was the oldest scam in L.A., then left because I had no money. Ten minutes later as I was sitting on the side of the road smoking a cigarette that one of the prostitutes had given me, wishing I had just bought a cowboy hat and gone to Sharon's party, Jam pulled up in a purple Corvette. "Dude, need a ride?" I told Jam my story. He said that's the oldest scam in L.A., and gave me a ride back to Stoner's. I asked Jam how his night was and he said, "Dude, some guys just don't know how to suck dick. What do they teach these guys on the set of 90210?" As Jam pulled up to Stoner's apartment, he leaned over and said in a slow methodical voice, "You know, I'm not only into guys. I've paid for three abortions." Jam was lighting a Punch cigar when he said this. Then he continued, "Dude, you need to get a tan. Catch you on the flip side." Stoner was smoking herb on the couch when I walked in. "Dude, where did you go?" I told him what happened and all he said was, "Oh, dude, that's the oldest fucking scam in L.A. Ahaaahaaaha."*

Ned brings over our food and Angella asks about my parents and I tell her they are busy and she says, "Oh." And then she picks at her salad, pulling out the croutons and placing them on her napkin because she's dieting. I check my Nokia and see that I have four messages. The first is from Chip, asking if I want to go with him and Stoner to the Pour House, and the last three are from Jackie, asking "Where are you?", "Am I going to see you before the party?", and "Do you think my breasts are too large?"

I call Chip and we agree to hook up later in the evening. "Dude, I'm already toasted," he says as I hang up. Angella gets up to use the bathroom (probably to regurgitate the fifty calories she's just consumed), so I call Jackie, who sounds either a little high, a little pissed off, or in a state of melancholy. I can't decide. Despite hearing "You've Got to Have Faith" in the background as she's talking to me, I agree to meet her at her place after lunch. "Jeremy, I'm already toasted," she says as I disconnect my phone. Everyone is toasted except me. I'm distracted by my headache. I also have heartburn from the spicy chicken. I'm eating lunch with a girl I don't particularly care for and going to meet a girl who is in love with George Michael. Life is grand.

Angella sits back down and continues to pick at her salad while talking about a friend of hers she suspects has AIDS.

"She's lost at least six pounds in the last week, and she eats chocolate every day. She must have AIDS."

"Maybe she's working out," I say.

"Don't be naïve, Jeremy. I've seen this before. She's got AIDS."

Ned stops back over and asks Angella if there is anything else we need. She says, "No, we're all set." Ned walks away without looking my way. Angella tells me about the Sheraton and how the hairdryer isn't going to cut it and how she's glad she always travels with her own hairdryer.

I need to go.

I finish my lunch, Angella puts the pile of croutons back onto her half-eaten salad plate, I pay the bill, and we leave.

"What are you doing tonight?" asks Angella.

"I don't know. Probably going to a bar in SoHo. Do you want to go?"

"Fabulous."

As we stand outside the restaurant, Angella pulls out a notepad that has CALVIN KLEIN preprinted on the top of every page and takes down the directions to the Pour House.

My Nokia is vibrating. It's a text message from my mom that reads: PICK UP BLANK TAPES. When did Mom learn how to send text messages?

A guy bundled up in a North Face jacket with short hair on top, long in the back (all business up front, all party out the back) walks by, looks at Angella's jacket and says it looks fabulous.

"I know," she says, and then adds, "It's too fucking cold." The man agrees and walks away. As the man leaves, Angella points to her hair and mouths the word "mullet" while shaking her head.

# 18

I pick up blank video tapes from ShopKo and drive to my parents' house. As I walk into the living room, my dad announces that he's "almost finished sequencing the tapes."

I hand the tapes to my mom, who asks if I've ever seen the show *Picket Fences*. I say no and then she adds, "You have to see it," and I say okay. I go to the bathroom and pop a Valium, not because of my head, which doesn't feel so bad at the moment, but because I'm sick of being here. GO HOME.

I make a screwdriver, watch some MTV2, then flip to CNN, where they announce that today's terror alert color code is Autumn Rust. There's been non-specific threats made against any guy who has a seventies porn-style mustache. I finish my screwdriver, light a Marlboro, and begin walking to Jackie's.

As the Valium kicks in, a sharp dressed man approaches me and asks if I can spare any money because his car has broken down, he's stranded, and he needs to raise money to get home to Chicago. I give him twenty dollars because he doesn't seem homeless or smell like a crack addict. Then I think that maybe I've caught him on his first day of homelessness. I mean, if you think about it, at one point all homeless people were dressed neatly on their first day, before their fall. Whatever, as long as he has fun (or makes it home to Chicago). The Valium is really doing its job, and I feel okay.

Jackie greets me at the door wearing only blue panties. She grabs me by my beige sweater and kisses me. She pulls back immediately and asks, "What the fuck have you been eating?"

"I had a little Thai for lunch," I say. "You don't like?" I laugh.

"No, you taste like garlic and orange juice. Do you want any coke? You can snort it off my breasts if you want," says Jackie.

"Uh... no thanks. I'm giving up coke for the New Year."

"The New Year isn't until Sunday, remember?" Jackie reminds me of the obvious.

"Yeah, well, then I'm giving up coke for Christmas," I say.

"Whatever. Do you want some speed?"

"No thanks, I'm good."

"Suit yourself. I need a little something to keep going." Jackie grabs her wooden box, removes two crosses, pops them in her mouth, and washes them down with a Pepsi. "I went and saw Greg today. He mentioned that he saw you the other night."

"Oh?" I say, curious as to where this is leading. I light a Marlboro.

"Yeah, he said you guys shot pool at Joe Mamma's."

"That's all he said?" I ask.

"Yeah. He said you're a terrible pool player." Jackie laughs.

"Oh really?"

"Yeah, he said he beat you three games in a row. I didn't realize you knew each other. That's fucked up. He says he's getting out of the hospital tomorrow, but I think he'll be recovering for a while. He's got an eye patch."

"Which eye?" I ask.

"The right eye, I think. He's hurting pretty bad. Can you believe some people?"

"Yeah, that's fucked up. Maybe I do need a little something." I grab a white cross from the box and wash it down with Jackie's Pepsi. "What else did you do today?" I ask, hoping to change the subject.

"Not much. After seeing Greg, I came back here and started doing coke, you know, trying to forget."

"Yeah, I know how that goes."

"Are you sure you don't want any?"

"Yeah, I'm sure, I'm okay."

Jackie takes a vial of cocaine, puts some onto a spoon, adds two parts baking soda, water, and begins heating it over the stove.

"What are you doing?" I ask.

"Making crack, babe. You never?"

"No."

"You really should. It's twice as good as plain coke."

Jackie takes tweezers from a drawer next to the stove. Using the tweezers, she grabs a rock off the spoon, empties the end of a Newport, places the rock in the end of the cigarette, and lights it. Jackie moves over to the stereo, puts in a CD, and Wham begins to play. I ask her if we can listen to something else. Since she's high, she doesn't get pissed. She puts in Talking Heads.

Jackie moves over to the couch next to me, sits down, and asks me if I want to fuck her. I tell her sure. She removes her panties and bends over the back of the couch. Afterwards, she says that she could fall in love with me.

As I'm leaving, Jackie gets up and puts in her Wham CD. I can hear "Jitterbug" playing as I walk out of Jackie's building. What the fuck is wrong with me?

# 19

"Dude, it's over with Janelle," says Chip while lighting a Marlboro. We're in Chip's Camaro on North Avenue traveling east to meet G-Dawg, Chip's dealer. Since the crackdown on dealers in the Midwest, all dealers have decided to use a common alias to throw off the cops. Now most dealers in Milwaukee, Chicago, Detroit, and Cleveland go by G-dawg. Megadeth is playing on the CD player and my headache is back so I take another Valium because I've become immune to Advil.

We pull to the side of the street somewhere near 17th Street, an area I've never been, and Chip asks me whether or not I want to go in. I look around and can see what looks like transient zombies lurking around the corners, but I know this isn't the case. I've seen zombie movies and they're not usually living in the ghetto. There is no way in hell I'm waiting for Chip in the car. We walk to the second story of a duplex, where we're greeted by Snoop Dogg music, a lot of smoke, and a girl named Charlotte wearing a shirt that says HIGH,

HOW ARE YOU? Chip says we're looking for G-Dawg, and she points to the back room while adjusting her bra under her shirt. G-Dawg is sitting at a desk with stacks of cash sitting in front of him as we enter the "back" room.

"Yo, Chip, my man, how you been?" asks G.

"Dude, you know, same old. This is JJ. He's back for the holidays. We go way back. He lives in New York now."

"I bet you can't wait to get back," says G.

"Yeah." I grab a seat in the corner of the dimly lit room, light a Marlboro, and remove my jacket.

G looks at my sweater and says, "Damn, that's one ugly motherfucking sweater." He looks over at Chip, who's lighting a Marlboro. "Am I right?"

"Dude, it's an ugly fucking sweater," says Chip.

G speaks up. "What you need, my man?"

"Two ounces of herb, two grams of krell, and a gram of magic veggies." Chip takes a drag off his cigarette. G writes down everything like it's a shopping list. G stares at the list, then looks up at Chip.

"Whoa, what the fuck? I have to ask, Chip, with an order like this, not your typical order, man, what's up?" G rolls a cigarette on his desk.

"Dude, one fucking killer New Year's Eve party." Chip searches for an ashtray.

"Sharon Winkler's?" inquires G as he hands Chip a silver ashtray.

"That's the one," says Chip.

"Cool, man. My whole crew is going. I'll see you there." G lights his hand rolled cigarette and calls out, "Charlotte!" He looks over at me and says, "JJ, never fuck a girl named after a city. A little word of advice from your Uncle G."

Charlotte appears at the doorway. "What is it, G?" G waves the list in the air and Charlotte walks over, grabs the list, and walks out.

"Ten minutes," says G to Chip. He takes a drag off his cigarette. "Seven hundred."

"I've got some of it," I say to Chip as I pull out my wallet.

"Dude, put that away. Damn, dude, what the fuck?" Chip looks very disappointed. "Easy on the money talk, dude," Chip says softly as he motions for me to put away my wallet.

"Oh, sorry."

"Got to be smart, kid." G points to his head. "How's the nine and a half treating you?" he asks Chip.

"Dude, it's all good, you know," says Chip.

"Yeah, I do know. Last night I was pounding a sister in the booty and she was screaming like she was being raped," says G.

"Dude, that's fucked up," says Chip.

G looks over at me. "You know what I'm talking about, right?"

"I'm not sure." What's taking Charlotte so long?

Chip tells G, "JJ just got the little C's, so you know."

"Sorry, man, that's not cool." G gives me a sympathetic nod.

Charlotte comes back and whispers something into G's ear regarding the "veggies." G writes down an address on a piece of paper, gives it to Charlotte, and she's out the door. "Five minutes," says G.

"How's business?" Chip lights another Marlboro.

"Good, always good around the holidays, you know," says G. "What do you do?"

"I'm a corporate whore," I say, smiling.

"A corporate what? What the fuck is wrong with this kid?" G looks over at Chip, who shrugs his shoulders.

"I'm a cost accountant for an investment firm," I say.

I don't think Uncle G likes me anymore.

"Cool, man, that's cool. Your parents must be proud," says G, maybe sarcastically, maybe sincerely. He pulls out a cigar, pulls back the outer leafs, empties the tobacco, and wraps about a quarter ounce of herb using what's left of the cigar.

"Dude, now that's a fucking blunt," says Chip.

"Yeah, it's the only way I know how to make them." G lights it up, takes a drag and passes it over to Chip. Chip takes two deep drags, gets up and walks over to me, handing me the blunt. I take a drag and hand it back to Chip, who takes it back over to G, who's staring at me.

G gets up, walks over to a window and opens it. "It's getting a little cloudy in here." He sits back down and takes a long slow drag off the blunt. "JJ, you seem like an all right kid, but man, I'm going to have to ask you to put your jacket back on. That sweater is depressing me. What color is that?"

"I think it's beige." I put my jacket on.

"Thanks, man. I'd apologize for being rude, but come on, that's one ugly motherfucking sweater. Damn." G takes another hit.

Charlotte returns, whispers something into G's ear, and then leaves.

Chip and G stand up and slap hands. G tells me to "keep it real" and we walk out of the back room. As we walk through the living room, Charlotte gives me a strange look, maybe sexual (I really can't even tell anymore), and I can hear G in the background: "Remember, never fuck a girl named after a city."

Chip and I walk down a back alley where Chip pays a guy wearing a Chicago Bulls cap, then we walk another block, where a ten-year-old boy wearing new Air Jordans is holding two brown paper bags.

"You Chip?" asks the boy.

"Yeah, little man, I'm Chip."

The kid looks at me, "Who the fuck is this?"

"I'm JJ," I say.

"Hey, little dude, it's cool. G knows us," says Chip.

"Who the fuck is G?" asks the boy.

"What the fuck?" asks Chip, looking at me then back at the kid.

"Oh man, I'm just fucking with you. Here's your shit, fuckheads." The boy hands us the two bags and starts running toward a dark back alley. We walk back to the Camaro, where two black guys with large afros tell Chip he's got a nice car, comment on his blond hair, and then laugh.

As we drive away, Chip inspects the goods. He pulls out a bag of pot and puts it up to his nose. "Dude, this is the fucking shit." Chip puts his hand into the bag. "Oh dude, it's so sticky. I can't fucking wait for this shit."

Once we're out of the ghetto, well, the deep ghetto, anyway, Chip pulls over and packs a bowl with the new pot. He takes a hit and coughs as he passes me the bowl. "Dude, try it," says Chip between coughing spells. I take a hit and POW! I cough, the herb hits me, and I'm stoned. We stay parked on the side of the road for the next ten minutes, both staring straight out of the windshield into traffic. Nothing is playing on the CD player.

My Nokia rings. It's a number I don't recognize, but since I'm so high, I answer it anyway.

"Yeah, what the fuck is up?" I say.

"Is Jeremy there?"

"You got him, who is this?"

"This is Jake."

"Jake? Jake who?" I ask in an I don't give a rat's ass tone.

"Jake, your boss," says Jake, my boss.

"Oh, hi Jake. How are you?" I try to suppress the laughter that's building inside of me.

"Jeremy, I know it's late, well, it's six o'clock there, seven o'clock here, but we're here working. We're preparing for the year-end processing, and we're running into some problems with the budgeted dollars for capital assets spreadsheet."

"Dude, you want any more?" Chip holds the bowl in front of my face. I wave him off, cover my phone, tell him it's my boss, and please shut the fuck up.

Chip laughs because he's so stoned. "Dude, you are such a corporate boy." Chip yells.

"Jeremy, did I catch you at a bad time?" asks Jake.

"Uh, no. What specifically is the problem?" I bite my lip because I really want to laugh at something.

"Well, the spreadsheet doesn't contain anything for the new forecasting project. I thought that was your responsibility."

"Yeah, it's on the last version. I showed Rick where it was."

"Well, Rick is right here. Why don't you talk with him?" I hear the phone being handed off.

"Yo, wad up, J? Sorry about this, man, but the updated spreadsheet isn't where you said it was," says Rick, then softly speaks into the receiver. "Dr. J. is really pissed about this one, man. I don't know what to do, yo."

"Don't worry, Rick. Are you at your computer?"

"Yeah."

"Okay, look in the shared network drive under budgets."

"I've already done that, yo," says Rick, who's actually sweating this. He's never going to make it.

"Rick, look again."

"Yo, man, I'm there."

"Okay, now look under the capital assets folder."

"There, man. Hey J, are you high? You sound funny."

I cover the phone and explode into laughter. This causes Chip to start laughing. This lasts for about thirty seconds.

"You still there?" I ask Rick.

"Yeah, what the fuck is going on?" says Rick softly.

"Just out with some friends. Look in the 2003 folder," I tell Rick while I try to compose myself.

"I'm there, man. Do all you guys in Minnesota party like this?"

I ignore the last question.

"Now go to the file titled CAR underscore forecasting." Chip takes another hit and starts coughing loudly, causing me to start laughing again.

"Got it, but man, there's nothing here for the new project. I've already looked here."

"Click on sheet number two."

"What?"

"It's located on the bottom of the spreadsheet." This guy has a degree?

"Oh man, there it is! You da man, J!"

"All right, so are you all set?"

"Most def. You da man, J!" I hear Rick yell over to Jake, "Got it, boss!" A few seconds later I hear the phone being handed off again.

"Very good, Jeremy," says Jake. "Very good."

"No problem. Anything else?" I ask.

"I think we need to get you a new phone. Your voice sounds a little scratchy," says Jake.

"Oh." I bite down on my lip, drawing blood trying to suppress the laughter. "Okay, anything else?"

"No, sorry to bother you, but you know how it is. The finance world never sleeps, especially at year-end."

Chip puts the bowl two inches from my face.

"Okay, Jake. Happy New Year," I say.

"Happy fucking New Year, Jake!" screams Chip.

I quickly disconnect the phone, but not in time. We both laugh non-stop for ten minutes for really no reason at all.

***NEW YEAR'S EVE, 2001:***

*This was a weird year for me. I didn't make it back to SoHo for Sharon's party. Instead, I stayed in New York and had a quiet dinner with Lisa, a girl I was seeing at the time. Lisa and I were very big into Zen meditation, not necessarily the whole Buddhism part as a religion, but the meditation practice. It was during this time that I would say things like "If you are trying to attain enlightenment, you are creating and being driven by karma, and you are wasting your time on the black cushion" and "Moment after moment, everyone comes out from nothingness. This is the true joy of life." My friends didn't call very often. Like I said, it was a weird year for me. Lisa and I ordered in Chinese (I had the King Cheng Chicken, she had steamed Chicken and Broccoli because she was dieting), meditated, and then listened to "Careless Whisper" by Wham... because we were never going to dance again.*

"I love Ratt," says Sharon as Face brings over a round of drinks. "Round and Round" is playing at the Pour House as Chip, Stoner, Sharon, and I sit at the bar.

Sharon is wearing a black leather Harley Davidson jacket over a shirt that reads: LOSER. She's also wearing a pin that reads: LET'S GET FUCKED.

"Ratt is definitely my favorite band from the eighties," says Sharon.

Stoner lights a Marlboro Light while looking over at Sharon. "Dude, you're fucking insane. Winger was a band whose music still sounds good today."

"Better than Cinderella?" asks Chip. "Dude, I don't fucking think so." Chip slams his Beam and Coke and shakes his glass at Face.

"L.A. Guns, now there was a band," I say. No one comments on this. Face is on the other side of the bar giving me a very strange look as he makes Chip's drink. I go put quarters on the pool table.

Angella walks in, sees me at the bar, and walks over.

"Oh my God! Is this fucking Ratt?" she asks.

"Yeah, I think so," I say.

"This music should be kept in storage. It's bloody fucking awful!" says Angella. Sharon gets up and walks toward the pool table.

I introduce Angella to Chip, Stoner, and Face. While Angella orders a vodka tonic, Chip looks at Stoner and makes a C sign with his right hand while pointing at Angella with his left.

"Big or small?" asks Stoner.

"Small," Chip says softly.

"Duuude." Stoner nods his head.

"So this is your hangout?" asks Angella.

"I don't know. We come here, so yeah, I guess," I say.

"Music sucks," says Angella.

We sit drinking for five minutes. Sharon comes back over, everybody begins to smoke, and Stoner tells us about a girl he met at Claire's Diner earlier today. "Dude, by the way, where were you guys this morning?"

"Sleeping," is all Chip says as he looks over at me.

"Yeah, sleeping," is all I say.

"Well, anyway, she's an ex porn star. She's originally from SoHo and is back for the holidays, but lives in L.A. Fucked up, dude. She lives about two blocks from me," says Stoner.

"*Ex* porn star?" I ask.

"Yeah, well, she's thinking about shooting one more movie, but that will be the last one," says Stoner. Face brings over another round of drinks. My Captain and Coke is all Captain Morgan's.

"Dude, porn stars always think they have one more in them." says Chip. "It's a drug to them."

"Come again?" says Sharon. Angella stands there with a blank, maybe shocked, look on her face. She tugs at my arm.

"Are you high?" Angella asks me.

"No." Then I laugh and turn back to Chip.

"Dude, porn stars are just like the rock stars who think they have one more tour left, or the boxer who always thinks he has one more fight left. They can't admit when it's over." Chip drinks down half his Beam and Coke. "They should all just quit when their time is up. Why tarnish your image? How many times have you said so and so should have stopped making porn a long time ago?"

"Dude, all the time." Stoner takes a sip of his Alabama Slammer.

"Dude, I know." Chip raises his glass to Stoner then slams the rest of his drink.

"Dude, she's also thinking about becoming an escort," says Stoner.

"A hooker?" asks Sharon. Angella makes a disgusted sound then slams the rest of her drink and orders another vodka and tonic.

"No, a high class escort service." Stoner looks over at the pool table. "Dude, she's not a prostitute. Whatever, dude."

My Nokia is vibrating. I look at the incoming name. It's Jackie. I send her to voicemail. I look over at Angella and smile. She doesn't smile back. She continues to drink.

My quarters are up on the pool table, so I tell Chip and Stoner to go play. Sharon follows them. Angella asks me whether they all know about my condition. I tell her some of them do. She says she doesn't care for my friends. I say, "I know."

I see Troy walk by, trying to ignore me. I'm starting to get a little drunk and I'm still a little high, so I say, "Troy, what fuck is going on?"

"Oh, hey, Jeremy, how's it going?" Troy is wearing a Dallas, Texas Hard Rock Café T-shirt.

I introduce Troy to Angella. "I'm good, man, are you ready for the party?"

"Oh yeah, can't wait. When are you going back to Boston?"

"Sunday." Angella gives me a strange look and I whisper in her ear, "It's just easier this way."

"Oh," says Angella, not understanding a word I'm saying.

Troy leaves. Sharon stops over and says she's leaving and she can't wait to see me at her party. I tell her, "I'll fucking be there." I light a Marlboro and then say, "Oh, and Angella will be there as well."

"Ghetto fabulous," says Sharon, not looking at Angella, still pissed because she dissed Ratt. Sharon waves goodbye to Face and then leaves.

Chip and Stoner come back from playing pool.

"Dude, we got fucked up the ass," proclaims Chip, looking at Angella. We sit at the bar drinking. Angella tells me about the summer collection. Stoner and Chip have decided it's time to break out of their slump.

"Dude, we're breaking out tonight. You want in?" asks Chip.

I look at Angella, then back at him. "What do you think?"

"Oh yeah, well, Stone and I need to do this. You understand. You know, the whole Janelle thing, and Stone with his waitress rut and all," says Chip.

"No problem," I say. This is a trick that has been used for years by baseball players to break out of hitting slumps.

Go out, find a girl you're not attracted to, take her home, and more times than not, you'll be hitting in no time. Some might say it's coincidence, but it's really just taking your mind off your problems for a minute, allowing you to stop obsessing over a slump, so to speak. I've participated from time to time in the past. However, I will not be partaking in this righteous event tonight. There's only one rule. It's to ensure you don't pick a girl you're attracted to: someone else always picks the girl for you.

"Dude, look at her," says Chip, nudging Stoner and pointing across the bar at a girl wearing a large Ralph Lauren sweater.

"Okay, dude," says Stoner.

"No wait, you need something else," says Chip.

Angella catches on to what's going on, finishes her drink, and tells me she doesn't want to be a part of this and that she's going back to the Sheraton and that I should stop by later. I tell her I'm probably staying over at Chip's. She says, "Whatever, I'll call you tomorrow." Then she leaves.

Face is standing next to us. He looks at Chip and says, "What about her?" He points to a girl who looks a little bit like Nell Carter, only rougher.

"That's your girl, dude." Chip points at Nell.

"Whoa, dude. That will definitely make me forget." Stoner looks a little scared.

Face goes back around the bar, gets us another round, and we all light up cigarettes as Stoner scopes out the bar, looking for Chip's girl.

"No fucking way, dude, she's fucking here!" says Stoner.

"Who?" says Chip.

"That's your girl, dude, right over there. Ahaaa-haaha!" Stoner points straight ahead at a girl sitting by herself at a table.

"Oh, dude, no way. Is that who I think it is?" asks Chip.

"Yeah, dude, that's your girl. The homely girl who chews like a hooker."

"Fuck, dude, all right." Chip walks over to the homely girl and Stoner heads over to Nell, both looking a little uneasy. I turn around to the bar and light another Marlboro.

A guy next to me wearing Buddy Holly type glasses asks me if I saw the race today and I say, "No, I don't watch racing."

Buddy says, "Oh, I didn't know you were gay."

I say, "I'm not. I just don't like racing. I think it's gay."

Buddy is drunk. He gets close to my face. "So what the fuck do you like, blondie? Are you a Packers fan?"

I say, "Sure. They have a good chance this year."

Buddy backs off and agrees, saying that they have a chance to win it all as long as Brett Favre stays healthy. Buddy turns around to look out at the bar and dumps his bottle of Old Style all over the bar, some of it catching my arm. Buddy apologizes and I tell him it's okay, because I'm nice, even though it isn't okay. I go to the bathroom to wash off the beer.

I walk into the bathroom and over to the sink. I turn on the water and hear two very distinct voices coming from the stall. One voice is a low woman's voice, a little Motown sound to it, saying, "Oh baby." The other voice has a slight L.A. drawl to it and is saying, "Oh dude." I quickly wash my hands as they go at it. I exit the bathroom to the chorus of "Oh baby. Oh dude. Oh baby. Oh dude..."

I walk back to the bar and tell Chip that I think Stoner has broken his slump and then ask him what happened. "Dude, she wasn't interested. She said I drink like a slut."

Face stops over and asks us if we want another round. I tell him I'm done and ask if he could call me a cab.

"No problem," says Face as he dials the number. "Where to?"

"The Sheraton."

## 20

It's Friday morning and a commercial is on the television promoting the Chippendale Dancers, who will be appearing New Year's Eve at a club called the Yellow Banana. Angella asks me if I've ever had sex (she says "made love") to a stripper or hooker and I tell her no, which isn't totally untrue.

I'm sitting on a chair next to a desk wearing a robe that says SHERATON while Angella lies on a sofa in green striped pajamas with her left leg lifted, resting on the back of the sofa.

"Order room service," says Angella.

I call and an older woman answers. "Sheraton room service. Would you like to try our German style sampler plate for breakfast?" I say no, then order French toast, an eggs combo platter and a side order of bacon.

"The combo already comes with bacon," says the woman.

"I know," I say.

She says, "So you want two orders of bacon?"

"Yes, and a pot of coffee."

There's a pause until she says, "Okay, that's two orders of bacon, an egg combo that comes with one of those orders of bacon, and French toast."

"And a pot of coffee," I add.

Then there's another pause while the woman explains to who I presume is the cook the bacon situation, and then she says to me, "That will take fifteen minutes."

"Okay." I hang up the phone and stare at the television.

"I made love to a stripper once," says Angella.

I ask her why she uses the phrase "made love."

She ignores me. "It was my twenty-first birthday. There was a party. He showed up wearing either a cop outfit or doctor's outfit, I forget, anyway, it was a crazy night and we ended up waking up the next morning in the back of a limo." Angella brings her leg down from the back of the sofa and brushes her hair back.

"Great story," I say insincerely.

"Yeah, and the craziest part was that we didn't know whose limo it was!" Angella laughs. "God, I wish I could remember his name." We sit in silence for ten minutes with the television on mute. I'm not sure what the show is about, but it has something to do with religion and sending money to a man I've never heard of or seen before.

"I hate living alone," announces Angella, perfect timing as always. "I really need to get a roommate or something."

"Ever thought about buying a dog?" I ask, which draws a look that I've been seeing a lot of lately. Angella asks if the coffee I ordered is Starbucks and I say I don't think so.

My bacon is delivered by a guy wearing a bow tie and a name plate that reads: GUY. He comments on the large amount of bacon, says, "Yummy," and then leaves.

"What are you doing today?" asks Angella as she picks at her French toast.

I stick a piece of bacon in my mouth and mumble, "Stuff," and then say, "with Chip and Stoner."

"Oh. I'm thinking about going to the Grand Avenue Mall." Angella cuts the crust off her French toast. I offer her syrup and she shakes her head. "Are there any good stores in the mall?" I just shrug my shoulders as I eat another piece of bacon. A commercial advertising a tool show at some venue downtown is on the TV. I wonder how they will fit all those people into one room, then I realize they're talking about hardware tools. I turn the channel. The Chippendales advertisement runs again.

***NEW YEAR'S EVE, 2002:***

*This year was Sharon's "I Hate Myself And Want To Die" New Year's Eve party. Sharon was heavy into drugs, broke, and living near the bottom. Everything about the party was depressing, including the invitations Sharon had sent out two weeks ahead of time (the only time she'd ever sent out invitations). The invites said: "Come celebrate another shitty fucking year at my shitty fucking party." On the bottom of the invite were the letters BYOH. Some speculated that this was a typo, while others just assumed it stood for BRING YOUR OWN HEROIN. As soon as we showed up, I wanted to leave. Everyone was shooting H, snorting coke, or doing ecstasy. I sat on the couch smoking a joint, milking a Busch Light while listening to Marilyn Manson on the stereo, which was okay, but gets old fast when this is the only music being played. I was too high to get up and change the stereo. Sometime after midnight, someone dressed in black wearing a yellow wristband put in the Sex Pistols and then Nikki (a.k.a. Janet, my friend Mark's fiancée), who was really high on coke, sat down next to me. Chip and Stoner were standing across the room, discussing whether or not they would have sex with a homeless girl. Chip came to the conclusion that he wouldn't do that, then said, "Well, maybe if she had a nice smile." Janet was telling me about how she had recently given up stripping due to her engagement and how she was going to miss it because it really was a turn on for her. "Have you ever had a REALLY good private dance?" Janet asked me, and I said, "I don't know," and then Janet said, "Well then you definitely never got one from me, because you'd know, you know what I mean?" I said, "I guess," and then she got on top of me and proceeded to start grinding on me right in front of everyone at the party. I was going to tell her to stop, but I was really bored and she was REALLY good. As Nikki or Janet or whoever was gyrating over the top of me with her knee pressing against my crotch, Mark (who was both very high on coke and a little drunk on champagne) came over, grabbed Janet off me and told me he was going to kick my ass. Mark took a half-assed swing at me and missed, instead sending his fist through the window behind the couch. This sobered up Mark, who was also coming down from the coke. As Mark sat there bleeding all over Sharon's crème colored couch, he looked up at me and said, "You know, she really is good, isn't she?" I agreed, told him she was going to make a wonderful wife, and helped him bandage up his hand. Someone put Marilyn Manson back on the stereo, and then we left.*

I leave the Sheraton and I'm waiting for the 76 bus to take me to SoHo. My headache is back, I'm out of Advil, and I'm out of cigarettes. A guy with brown teeth and green sweatpants lights a Camel Light. I ask him for one. He says, "Sure, man. I was in the same situation yesterday and a guy wearing a T-shirt that said NO

BULL bummed me a Camel Wide. Wow, man, a Camel Wide. That was pretty harsh, you know." You can never have too much information. I tell him thanks and then he lights my cigarette for me, and this makes me a little uneasy for some reason.

"Circle of life, man," he says.

"What?"

"You know, circle of life. Yesterday I needed a cigarette and there was a guy with one, and now today you need one and I'm giving you one. Circle of life."

"Yeah," I say, and then introduce myself for some reason. He introduces himself as Fred.

We stand, smoking, waiting for the bus, and Fred is talking about how he never used to take the bus. Instead, he would hitchhike everywhere.

"Man, you can't do that anymore, you know, too many psychos." Fred flails his hands in a psycho sort of way.

"No kidding," I say, even though I've never considered hitchhiking.

"One time, I had tickets to go see the Head Wounds, a rock band from Queens that was playing in the Bronx. This was when I was living in Pennsylvania and didn't have a way to get to the concert." Fred tosses his cigarette and then offers me another. I take another. Fred lights it for me (I still feel uneasy about this) and continues after taking a long drag.

"So I'm right there on the Interstate and this eighteen-wheeler pulls up, you know, one of those big motherfuckers, man, and get this, he just happens to be going to the Bronx. Un-fucking-believable."

Fred takes another drag. I continue to smoke, every now and then saying, "Yeah."

"So we get to the Bronx and it's three hours before the show starts, so the guy says he can't just drop me off in the Bronx because I'll get fucking shot, so fucking get this, he takes me into Manhattan. Now remember, he's got this eighteen-wheeler in Manhattan. He gives me ten dollars and tells me to take a cab to get to the show."

"Wow, that's fucked up," I say, then add, "Cool."

"Yeah, man, very cool. That was a good deed he did. That's why I love telling the story; it makes me feel good to give this guy credit for his good deed."

"Right on," I say, even though I've never used this phrase before in my life.

I ask Fred what he's doing for New Year's Eve and he says he'll be watching the Peach Bowl during the day and that he's pretty excited about it, and this makes me a little sad, and then Fred says, "Then I'm going to Sharon Winkler's party."

The bus pulls up. Fred slides into a seat near the back and immediately falls asleep. I sit in the seat behind him and a girl wearing a teal colored jacket and a smile sits next to me.

"How are you?" I say.

"Great." She grabs a new CD from her purse and tries to unwrap it. "Why do they package these like this?"

"I know," I say. "It's a bitch."

She laughs and says her name is Gretchen and I tell her my name is Jeremy. I help her open her new CD.

"Do you like the Goo Goo Dolls?" she asks.

"Yeah, they're okay," I say. "I like their older stuff better."

"Oh my god, me too," she says.

"That's cool," I say.

She says, "Yeah."

We ride in silence and then she asks, "What are you doing for New Year's Eve?"

"I'm going to Sharon Winkler's party," I say.

She says, "Oh, I've heard of that party."

Obviously not thinking, I ask, "Would you like to go?"

"Oh yeah, that would be fab!"

"Cool."

"So guess who I saw while I was buying my new CD?"

"Who?" I ask.

"John Cusack."

"Oh, yeah, I think he's from Chicago."

"Yeah, it was so fab. You never see famous people here," says Gretchen.

"No kidding. That's fascinating," I say.

"What do you mean?" asks Gretchen.

"You know, you're right, you don't see many famous people here. Seeing John Cusack, that's cool."

"No, what does 'fascinating' mean?"

The bus stops, my stop, and Gretchen says, "You live in SoHo?"

"Yeah."

She asks me where the party is and tell I her I'm probably not going. I exit the bus.

***NEW YEAR'S EVE, 2003:***

*Yale. "She's a Yale graduate," said Sharon as she introduced me to Mary. All you need to know about Mary is that she went to Yale. On a scale of one to ten she was a nine, actually closer to a ten, but we don't need to go into the impossibilities of a four picking up a ten. Short blonde hair with bangs that fell over her forehead, green eyes, high cheekbones, full lips, and a body, well, you get the picture. Did I mention she went to Yale? She was drinking Olympia beer and complaining about the mixture of cigarette and marijuana smoke that filled the room, so we went outside. As soon as we walked out onto the porch, she pulled out a joint and lit it, took a long drag, and handed it to me. It was really good herb. I was stoned on one hit. She had just gotten back from Amsterdam, so we talked about the coffee bars, museums, and the Red Light District, which prompted her to reveal, "I could watch live porn all day long." I told her I knew a couple of porn stars, which didn't draw the response I was looking for, which I guess was okay, because I was lying to her anyway. As we were talking about the similarities and differences between Harvard and Yale, a convertible Mercedes with two guys in it drove by and Mary said, "God, those guys have no fucking idea what I'd do to them just for a ride in their car." Then my phone rang. It was Chip, asking me, "Dude, where the fuck are you?" and then, "Dude, get the fuck inside, NOW!" I told Mary to wait a second and then she said something that I didn't hear as I went inside and found Chip and Sharon standing outside the bathroom, where a young girl (maybe sixteen, maybe fourteen) was lying on the floor (maybe dead). "Dude, I didn't give her anything," Chip kept saying over and over. "Fuck, I don't care, just get her the fuck out of here. I don't need this shit tonight," said Sharon. We carried the girl out to a car, where we paid two guys in herb to drop her off at the hospital. I looked for Mary, but she was gone. Turns out the girl wasn't dead, she had just overdosed on heroin and would be fine after a month of therapy. Just my fucking luck.*

# 21

"Dude, what do you think about this? Does it make my ass look big?" Chip is wearing a leather miniskirt. He's sticking his ass out toward Stoner.

"What, dude?" asks Stoner.

"Dude, stop staring at my ass. It was a fucking joke."

Chip looks at the noticeable bulge in the front of his skirt. "Dudes, it's not always a blessing to be packing nine and a half... ten, some days."

It's three in the afternoon and we're at SoHo Thrift, where Chip and Stoner are buying their costumes for tomorrow night's party. A girl wearing a green shirt and red tie is trying to figure out what our story is while a man behind the counter wearing brown slacks, white ankle socks, and hiking boots watches to make sure we don't steal any of his priceless items.

My Nokia rings. It's Jackie. She asks me what I did last night.

I say, "Nothing."

Then she says she thinks she may be sick or hung over and that she really can't tell the difference anymore. "I'm taking NyQuil just to be safe," she says.

"Good," I reply, and then she asks me if I want to stop over later.

For some reason, I freeze. I don't have a reason not to stop over. "Okay, I'll see you later."

"I'm looking forward to seeing you, Jeremy."

I shut off my phone.

Stoner is thumbing through a rack of discarded clothing. He pulls out some South American tanga-styled knickers.

"Dude, what do you think?" Stoner looks over at me and then at Chip. I shrug my shoulders, take a drink from my Diet Coke, and then look at the girl in the green shirt and red tie. I wonder what she's doing for New Year's Eve.

She may be a lesbian. I'm not sure, but that's okay. I'm a lesbian trapped inside a man's body.

"Rock 'n' roll, dude." Chip nods over at Stoner.

"Ahaahaaha, cool," says Stoner as he pulls out a purple bustier from a box next to the rack. "How about this?"

"Dude, you're supposed to dress like a whore, not a fucking fag." Chip looks embarrassed for Stoner.

Stoner looks over at me, rolls his eyes, and throws the bustier back in the box.

The girl in green and red approaches us. "Can I help you guys find anything?"

"Yeah, we want to dress like sluts!" says Chip.

"It's for a party," I add.

"Do you have any more red ties?" asks Stoner, pointing at the girl's tie.

"Uh, I don't think so," she says.

"Dude, what the fuck?" Chip looks over at Stoner.

"Not for the party, dude. I just like it. You know, it's very unique," says Stoner uncharacteristically, smiling at the girl in green.

A man approaches the girl and asks her if she knows whether or not they have any corduroy pants. She says, "I think there may be a pair of beige pants in the back." The man's eyes light up as hurries past us to the back.

Chip finds a skimpy dress that "will work." Stoner buys a white cotton mini-skirt and tight yellow half-shirt. "Dude, this will have to do. I need a cigarette." They buy the garments. We walk out, all light up Marlboros (Stoner lights a Marlboro Light). "Dude, I feel like Chinese," says either Chip or Stoner. I'm not sure. My back is turned to both of them.

We're standing at Happy Go Lucky Asian Garden Restaurant. No one else is here other than a table of young boys. Chip says, "Dude, I think I'm going to quit."

"Quit what?" I ask.

"All of it, dude."

"Herb?" I ask.

"Herb, alcohol, smoking, and everything else, all of it, dude." Chip looks very melancholy.

We order the following: two vegetable spring rolls, beef teriyaki, scallion pie, wontons, pepper steak, and pork fried rice. The woman behind the counter yells three one-syllable words and magically our food arrives in five minutes.

"Dude, you mean, like now? You're quitting?" Stoner is talking to Chip but looking outside at a man in a blue hat and a T-shirt that reads: SMILE, IT'S FRIDAY, staring inside at us.

"No, I mean after the party. You know, the New Year and all that jazz."

"Yeah," I say. "A resolution," I mumble. "I fucking hate those," I add.

"Dude, fuck it, we'll see, I just don't know," says Chip.

Three black kids, all about twelve years of age, are talking about girls. One is telling a story about how he pulled down a girl's pants and was "ready to go to town," all his friends lean in closer, "and then she gassed me."

"Gassed?" asks one boy who's wearing a Michael Jordan jersey. The boy who was talking pulls the kid in the jersey closer, explains to him what he meant by "gassed." The boy in the jersey goes, "Gross," and then finishes his pepper steak.

"Dude, I'm never quitting herb," says Stoner.

After the restaurant, we agree to meet tomorrow morning to start partying. I'm really bored so I go over to Jackie's, where she doesn't look or sound sick, but she's taking a lot of cold medication because it makes her feel numb.

"You want a beer?" asks Jackie. "I've got Miller."

"Sure, I can get it." I walk to the kitchen and suddenly I feel like someone just hit me in the head with a sledgehammer. I grab my head and fall to my knees. Jackie is so out of it that it takes her a few minutes to notice what's happening. When she sees me on my knees, she makes a derogatory remark that I'm glad I can't hear, and then she helps me to the couch.

"I know how you feel. I get like this sometimes." Jackie hands me a beer. "Drink this. It will make all your problems go away."

"Do you have any Advil?" I ask.

"Oh, I don't know, I'll have to check." Jackie gets up and I can hear cupboards opening and closing in the kitchen.

"How about Xanax?" she asks. "Or speed? Do you want any speed? Will that help?"

I tell her no, and then she finds Tylenol. That will have to do, so I take five and wash them down with my Miller.

"Are you okay?" asks Jackie in a don't-be-a-fucking-baby sort of way.

"No, I have a brain tumor."

"Sure, hon, we all do." She unzips my jeans and puts my dick in her mouth, which takes my mind off my splitting headache for a minute, but it's very hard to concentrate with the pain so I tell her to stop.

"Whoa, this is heavy." Jackie pulls out a mirror and a small container meant for camera film, dumps a little coke from the container onto the mirror, cuts the coke with a razor blade into two lines, and then snorts them both. After wiping off her nose, she walks over to her stereo, puts in Bobby Brown, and then sits down next to me. I still have my head in my hands, thinking this will somehow deteriorate the pain in my head.

"What do you want to do?" asks Jackie.

I look up. "I need a minute."

"Whatever." Jackie looks around the room. "Want to see what I'm wearing to the party tomorrow?"

"Sure." My vision is starting to come back.

"Well, I'm wearing this purple suit." She picks up the suit that's on a hanger, pressing it against her body. "It's DKNY," says Jackie in a matter of fact sort of way. "And this jacket." She grabs the jacket that's draped over a black chair. "Isn't this jacket just marvelous?"

"Yeah, I told you I liked it before." I'm still holding my head.

"I just bought it today. What are you saying?" Jackie is waiting for my response as she holds onto her black leather Calvin Klein trench coat.

"Oh, yeah, I mean, I've seen the jacket before. It looks great."

"Thanks, I guess." Jackie turns the volume up on the stereo. "Can I get you anything else? Another beer?"

"Actually, I'm not feeling very well. I think I'm going to go back to my parents' house. Okay?" I ask her permission for some reason, I guess because I'm so nice.

"Oh, well, okay, I guess."

"I really don't feel well. I think I need sleep," I add.

"Yeah, I can see that. Okay, Jeremy, I hope you feel better. I'll see you tomorrow at the party?"

"Yeah, I'll see you tomorrow," I say as I walk out the door.

"Hey, Jeremy?"

I turn around. "Yeah?"

"Cheer up, tomorrow is New Year's Eve!"

I'm back at my parents' and I want a cigarette so I go outside. While I'm smoking, I look up at the stars and I swear the stars have spelled out the phrase GO HOME, but then I look closer and I'm not sure so I finish smoking and go back inside.

I'm in the kitchen and my mom is making a cup of tea. She asks me if I want something to eat and I tell her no and then she asks if I've been eating and I tell her I've put on five pounds since I've been back and this makes her feel good so she smiles.

"How are you feeling?" she asks before leaving the kitchen.

"Fine."

"You look white, a little pale," she says.

"Oh," I say.

My mom goes back to the living room to watch *Magnum* and I go upstairs to my old bedroom, where I try to get to sleep, but I can't because I keep thinking about my brain tumor, Sharon's party, and how all I really want to do is go home. After an hour or so I finally fall asleep. It will be morning soon, a new day. New Year's Eve, 2004.

# 22

NEW YEAR'S EVE, 2004: I wake up, put on my Harvard sweatpants and sweatshirt, New Balance 1220 sneakers, run five miles, do 100 sit ups, do 50 push ups, masturbate (but I'm really not into it), shower, look at myself in the mirror and realize I still look pale (and a little thin), shave, brush my teeth, put on my blue Gap T-shirt (the one without the hole), Polo jeans, black Skechers shoes, and comb my hair (realizing I will need to bleach it again someday soon). I take three Advils, two Valiums, and walk into the kitchen, where I fix myself a screwdriver. I walk into the living room and turn on the television and there's an infomercial with an attractive blonde, but then I realize it's for a kitchen appliance and since I don't cook I turn to CNN. Today's terror alert color is Beige. The FBI has also issued a warning that they have received non-specific threats against anyone who says they are going to quit smoking for the New Year.

I have a dull headache, which is distracting, but it's actually okay with me. I finish my screwdriver, read a short story by F. Scott Fitzgerald, and check my messages on my Nokia. I have one message from Chip that simply says, "I'm ready." One from Stoner that says, "Dude, I'm at Chip's, we're ready!" Two messages from Jackie, a message from Angella, and a message, obviously a wrong number, from someone named Bill that says, "Hey Johnny, I'll see you at Sharon's party tonight." This last message bothers me because I have a New York area code, and I'm pretty sure the number on my caller ID was an L.A. area code. This is going to be some party.

I switch back to the infomercial with the attractive blonde, think about masturbating again, then think of Shannon, and instead decide to make another screwdriver and have a bowl of Grape Nuts. I call Jackie back and all I hear is "Faith" blasting in the background. "Just a sec," she says. She turns down the stereo and says, "Jeremy, it's New Year's Eve! Get your ass over here." I tell her I'll stop by before I go over to Chip's and then she asks when that will be and I say not too long, and then she wants me to associate a time with not too long and now I don't even want to go over there, but instead I tell her about an hour and she says, "Okay, an hour. Don't be late!"

I call Angella and she doesn't say much. She just wants to know what I've been doing and I tell her, "Stuff," then add, "with Chip and Stoner." She says, "Okay" and wants to know what I'm doing today. I invite her over to Chip's house, but I get the feeling she doesn't care for my friends and we agree to meet at the party tonight.

I go back into the kitchen to make another screwdriver, but instead just have more orange juice because my mom is there (she's wearing a 1993 Badger Rose Bowl sweatshirt) and then she smells alcohol and asks me why I'm drinking and I tell her because it's New

Year's Eve. This isn't an acceptable response to her. I tell her I'm quitting drinking for the New Year and then my dad walks in while my mom is asking if I'm also going to quit smoking for the New Year and I tell her she needs to watch CNN and that it may not be a good idea to quit smoking. My dad is staring at my mom. "Dear, let the kid smoke. He's got enough on his mind." I smirk at my mom and my dad adds, "Don't be a wise ass, Jeremy." Then they both go into the living room, so I reach under the sink, grab the vodka, and make the strongest screwdriver I've ever had in my life.

I'm pretty drunk when I get to Jackie's. All she's wearing is a blue thong and a smile. "You're five minutes late," she says. "I want you to fuck me." I ask if she's got any orange juice. She points to the kitchen and I make another strong screwdriver. I ask her if she wants one, but she says no, because she's still on her NyQuil high. I walk into the living room, where Jackie has moved to the couch. I grab a seat next to where her purple suit and jacket rest.

"You look white," says Jackie.

"Yeah, I know." I light a Marlboro. "Did you hear about the FBI warning?"

"No, I don't watch TV."

"Oh." I take a drink. "So are you excited about the party?" I ask because we really have nothing to talk about.

"Yeah, I mean, I guess. I don't know. Right now I'm pretty out of it. I'm sure I'll be ready to go later on. So do you want to fuck, or are you still not feeling well?"

I move over to the couch, where we have sex, then again on the floor (at one point I was so twisted around I strained my neck), then Jackie tells me that she's thinking about seeing Greg later today, and I say, "Okay," and this upsets Jackie because she wanted me to be jealous, but I'm not, and I tell her to have fun. She tells me she bought Advil just for me, so I take two more, even though I have my own bottle. I make another screwdriver, pop two white crosses, slam my drink, and then leave.

# 23

"Hit the fucking bong, dude! Hit it like a fucking man!" says Chip to Stoner as he takes a hit.

Chip is wearing a dirty gray sweatshirt and sunglasses, AC/DC is playing on the stereo, and Stoner passes the bong to me.

Chip is leafing through a *Hustler* while he tells us about this girl from Memphis he hooked up with last night.

"Dude, so she tells me to talk dirty to her." Chip lights a Marlboro.

Stoner pops a Xanax. "So what did you say?"

"I told her to get on her back and make believe her feet hate each other." Chip takes a drag off his Marlboro and blows the smoke straight up.

"Dude, that's it?" asks Stoner.

"Yeah, dude. It's good, isn't it?" Chip looks over at me.

"Weak." I take another hit off the bong. "Do you think Janelle will be there?" I ask Chip.

"Don't know. Don't care," says Chip.

Stoner grabs the bong and takes a hit. "Dude, one time I had this girl who liked to be spanked. I think her name was Becky."

"Yeah, been there," says Chip, grabbing the bong.

"No, dude, I mean she *really* liked to be spanked," says Stoner in a matter of fact sort of way.

"Yeah, dude, been there," says Chip.

"No, dude, I mean, I'd spank her until she cried!"

"Oh dude, never been there," says Chip as he takes a hit.

"J, what do you got?" asks Chip. "Ever fucking spank a girl until she cried?"

"Ahaahaaha," laughs Stoner, grabbing the bong.

"No," is all I say. I could tell them about the time I had two Asian girls in Memphis who liked to fuck each other with a dildo they had nicknamed "Kong" but I'm too high to talk right now and this is getting really boring and we really need to get to the party.

Sometime around five, we change. I put on my black wig, leather skirt, leopard print half-shirt (pointy bra underneath), and realize there's a rip in my black stockings (so I don't wear them). Dressed in drag, we grab the herb, shrooms, and coke, and then we leave.

# 24

"JEREMY FUCKING JENKINS! WELCOME!" says Sharon as she gives me a hug and kiss. She tastes like gin and is wearing a pin that reads: WELCOME TO MY FUCKING PARTY.

Chip and Stoner follow me in to the party and it's impossible to move around with all the people here. Angella is already here. She's wearing a brown pinstriped Calvin Klein suit with her leather Calvin Klein trench coat over the top. She's talking to a guy wearing a blue bra, black spandex shorts, and a white wig that makes him look like a cross-dressing George Washington. I motion over to her and she mouths the word "hi" and I wave and hold up my hand, signaling that I will be over shortly, but I don't think she sees me because she looks like she's interested in cross-dressing George.

A guy wearing no shirt and a yellow skirt is doing coke off the back of a girl wearing army fatigues and a sailor cap. Kyle, Gordon, Face, and the hicks from Omro, they are all here. I say hey to Kyle as I pass him, but he ignores me and takes a drink of his Blatz beer.

He may be pissed at me or just unable to hear me over Kid Rock's "Cowboy", which is playing very loudly. I'm not sure and I'm very high so I move on.

I bump into Chip, who blows smoke in my face and hands me a bag with mushrooms in it. He slaps me on the back, which shifts my bra, and says, "Happy fucking New Year!" then disappears into the crowd with a girl wearing a black silk shirt and a nose ring. I adjust my bra, light a Marlboro, find a beer (Michelob is all I can find in the near vicinity), and walk over to a crowd where Mickey and Mark are talking to their wives and another girl.

Mark is wearing a see-through gown over what I hope is a Speedo and not a bikini.

"Hey guys, what's up?" I take a drink of my beer.

"Not much," says Mark. Everyone else says, "Hi."

"Jeremy, have you met Angel?" asks Janet (a.k.a. Nikki).

"No, nice to meet you."

"You too," says Angel, who's wearing a blue jacket and a big floppy red hat that reads: PIMP DADDY.

"We used to work together," says Janet. "She's very good."

"Oh," I say. A girl named Angel is a stripper? What are the odds? "So do you still, uh, work?"

"No, I stopped a couple months ago, but I'm thinking about starting again. You really can't beat the money."

"Yeah."

"Sure, you have to deal with assholes once in a while and take a beating every now and then, but the money is really good."

"Yeah."

I can tell Clarice is bored so I ask her how the kids are. She says they're okay and that they're with the neighbor, who is an angel for watching them. Then she looks over at Angel and says, "No pun intended," which really isn't the correct use of the phrase, but I let this pass.

"You here with anyone?" asks Mickey.

"Sort of." I look over to where Angella was standing, but she's no longer there.

I tell them I'm sure I'll see them later and continue to mingle, smoke, and drink, not necessarily in that order.

I bump into a guy who's drinking Killian's, smoking a Marlboro Ultra Light, and not wearing a costume. He introduces himself as Dave, says I look ridiculous and that this is a stupid fucking party, and then leaves.

In the living room on the couch I see Angella and George Washington, so I walk over and say hey, and Angella says that this is a fabulous party and introduces me to her friend whom she says is very interesting and tells me his name, but I can't hear her over the Jimmy Eat World song and his back is turned to me. I ask Angella if she needs a beer, and I'm pretty sure she says she's okay, and then George turns around and underneath the wig is a familiar face and I laugh and say, "Hi, Roy. How are you?" Roy gives me a look that simply says please don't tell and I give him a look that simply says Roy, I wouldn't know where to begin. I light another Marlboro, grab a Heineken from a bucket of ice that's sitting on the table in front of the sofa, and tell Angella to have fun. "I definitely will!" she says as I walk away, having trouble unscrewing the cap off my Heineken because I'm laughing so hard.

Despite feeling a little self-conscious over my hairy legs sticking out of my skirt, I feel good, but just to be safe I take two more Advils, washing them down with my Heineken. Kelly from the bar, the strippers from Showgirls, the transsexual from Joe Mamma's (who now ironically is dressed as a man wearing J. Crew), they are all here. Dakota is wearing her pinstriped Armani suit and is working the crowd, carrying around a bottle of tequila, asking in a girly way, "Who wants to do a shot with me?"

Everyone does a shot with her. I do three.

I see Stoner, who sees me and walks over. I ask him how it's going and he says, "Dude, fucking great!" and points over to the waitress from Joe Mamma's, who's drinking Starbucks coffee. I ask what that's about.

"Dude, she has to go to work tonight," says Stoner.

"No shit? That sucks," I say.

"Yeah, I guess it's one of the busiest nights or something," Stoner says. "Bummer, dude."

I notice Fred off in the corner, smoking a Camel.

"Yeah, it is a bummer. See that guy over there?" I ask Stoner.

"Yeah, the guy in the red wig?"

"His name is Fred. Yesterday he bummed me a smoke."

"Herb?"

"No, a cigarette, dumbass."

"Dude, a cigarette? Why are you telling me this?" asks Stoner.

"Because man, it was a good deed."

"What?" asks Stoner.

"Forget about it."

"Dude, I'm out of here. Thanks for the smoke. We'll hook up later," says Stoner.

I tell him okay, wave to the waitress, who waves back, do another shot with Dakota, and walk into a side room that is also filled with people.

My back is turned when I hear, "Jeremy from Jameson, how the fuck are you?" I turn around, see the square head, and stand there a little shocked and still a little repulsed.

"Jack from The Street," I say and offer my hand for some reason. Jack is wearing a tight velvet half-shirt, a fur white mini-skirt, and no wedding ring.

"Good. Good. Lot of hot girls here tonight," says Jack.

"Yeah, I guess."

"Look at her," says Jack as he points to a girl with a panther tattooed on her neck. She is wearing a large brimmed hat that reads: I'M DOWN.

"Yeah, great." I finish my Heineken and wave at Dakota, who gives me the "one minute" sign.

"Three words, Jeremy, three words," says Jack.

Don't say it. Don't fucking say it.

Jack says it and then walks away, heading in the direction of panther girl.

Dakota walks back over. She's now only wearing Armani slacks, has found lemon wedges and salt from somewhere, and wants to know if I'm up for body shots.

"Sure," I say. After two shots, I tell her she's really fucking cool.

She says, "Hey Jeremy, you have to live every day like it's your last." Dakota takes a swig from the bottle and I agree and then I'm distracted by my tumor, but then it passes because I'm so drunk and still a little high and Dakota is standing topless right next to me.

She says she has to go talk to one of her friends and that we should meet up later and I say, "Definitely," and then wonder if G-Dawg's "never fuck a girl named after a city" applies to states as well, and then realize that she's not named North or South Dakota so I shouldn't have an issue.

Jack is talking to the panther girl, sees me, and shoots me a devilish grin that makes me feel sorry for panther girl. Then Troy walks over and says, "Hi." Troy is wearing a T-shirt that reads: ORLANDO that he has cut off at his belly and is wearing a sheet around his waist. I'm just going to assume he's going to another party after this where this is what everyone will be wearing.

"Great party," I say, looking around for a beer. I look over to where the Heinekens were on ice, but only an empty bucket of water is on the table.

"Yeah, it's okay," says Troy. "You been here long?"

"An hour or two. I'm not really sure."

"Yeah, well, it was great seeing you again, Jeremy."

Troy leaves. I'm relieved when I spot a fresh six-pack of Bud Light resting on top of one of the speakers. Nappy Roots is playing on the stereo. I light a Marlboro, grab a Bud Light, and bob my head to the beat while looking around at all the people here.

I'm starting to get into the music when I feel a pair of breasts push up against the back of my leopard print shirt, shifting my bra, and a hand slides around the front, gently going up my skirt.

"Guess who?" says the breasts with what are now semi-hard nipples behind me.

"Uh, Dakota?" I say.

"What?" I turn around and see that it's Jackie. I tell her I'm just joking. Then I comment on how great the Calvin Klein leather trench coat looks on her and all is forgotten.

Her eyes are red and she grabs a Bud Light and asks me for a Marlboro, which I give her, then grab one for myself.

We are talking about nothing, listening to the music and watching everyone when she asks me, "What do you like about me best?"

I take another drink of my beer followed by a drag off my cigarette and ignore the question, hoping it will just pass, and then she asks me again, "What do you like best about me?"

I say, "What do you mean?"

She says, "Physically. What do like best about me physically?"

"Your smile," I say, which draws a disappointed look from her. I watch Dakota walk by. Jackie notices this and looks down at her breasts. Then I say, "I mean, after your breasts, of course. They really did do a good job."

Jackie looks over at Dakota and says, "Not as good as hers. Maybe I should get larger breasts." She thinks about this for a second while drinking her beer. "What do you think?"

"Sure," I say, then I ask her if she wants any mushrooms.

Her red eyes light up and she says, "Hell, yeah," and all is forgotten. I tell her I have to take a piss and that I'll be back. I walk over to the bathroom, which is located right off the living room.

I open the door and find Dr. Robertson and Blanch's cousin, whom I only know from Chip's *Playboy*, or at least I think it was his *Playboy*, nevertheless, it's fucking her, and she's fucking Dr. Robertson while he's sitting on the toilet smoking a Kool. I make eye contact with the Playmate, who says, "Oh, hi. We must have forgotten to lock the door." I look at Dr. Robertson, who is looking at me while I'm holding a beer in one hand and a cigarette in the other.

"Hi, Doc," I say, then feel like I need to make an excuse for the way I'm acting until I see his wedding ring. I smile and say, "Have a good night, Doc," and leave to use the bathroom in the basement. Walking back from the bathroom, I run into G-Dawg, Charlotte, and three other black guys. "My man Jeremy, what's up?" says G-Dawg as he lights up a giant blunt. I say hey, look over at Charlotte and nod, and G-Dawg gives me the look that I know too well, despite barely knowing him. G-Dawg is wearing a leather tank top that stops just below his nipples, exposing the most amazing six-pack I've ever seen. G sees me staring at his abs and says, "Jeremy, the secret is," he leans in close to me, "reverse crunches in between bong hits." I laugh, and G-Dawg looks at me seriously.

"Oh," I say. "I'll remember that."

G-Dawg nods his head and says, "Hell, yeah," then passes me the blunt. I take a hit, pass it back, and then G-Dawg and his crew walk away.

I'm walking around, unable to find Jackie. I bump into Chip, who's coming out of a room with the nose ring girl. He punches me in the arm, smiles, and says, "One hundred."

"Great." I laugh. Angella and Roy walk up to us.

"What's up?" I ask Angella.

"You don't mind that I'm hanging out with George, do you?" asks Angella.

"Not at all," I say. Chip looks over at Roy and makes a small C with his hand.

"Oh, okay," Angella says. Roy looks back at Chip, shrugs his shoulder, and mouths the words "I don't care."

"Well, all right, I'm sure we'll bump into each other later," says Angella as Roy leads her away.

"Yeah, sure." I grab the last two Bud Lights from the six-pack on top of the speaker, handing one off to Chip, who's lighting a Marlboro. Incubus is playing on the stereo.

"Dude, good tune. Rock 'n' roll, man." Chip pulls out a joint that I don't remember him rolling and lights it, passing it to me. I take a small hit because I'm so drunk and so baked that I'm not sure how much more I can take. Chip takes about ten hits and passes it again. I wave him off, and he says, "One more, dude, then it's cashed." I take one last hit and my head begins to hurt.

"Later, dude," says Chip as he spots a girl wearing a tan suit and a smile.

It's eleven o'clock when Mary walks in and the music stops. The music stops because the CD is skipping, so Sharon quickly runs over and puts in Nelly. Mary and I immediately make eye contact and she walks over and says, "Great costume, Jeremy," and then, "It's so smoky in here." Mary is wearing a suit (Yale blue) and her hair is a little shorter and blonder than last year. Mary is also wearing a Calvin Klein leather trench coat. G-Dawg is walking by. He hears Mary's comments and says, "Damn, you're right. It sure is cloudy in here."

"I'm going to find a beer," says Mary.

"I can get one," I slur.

"That's okay, I'll find one and meet you on the porch." Mary smiles and walks away.

Like a forty-ounce of St. Ides getting smashed over my head. This is what I feel when I walk onto the porch. I immediately fall flat on my face. Then I'm out. I'm back on the mountain, seeing the light, and I'm once again taking stock, but this time it's more recent events. The drugs, friends, family, and George Michael are what pass through my head. I'm pretty sure this is it. I have no feeling and everything is slowly fading away. Then I see a figure approach me and I'm pretty sure this isn't going to be good if it's who I think it is. Then I hear someone ask, "Are you okay?"

I open my eyes and realize it's Mary. She's holding two Millers and has a joint hanging out of her mouth. Then I feel okay.

Then my Nokia rings. It's Chip.

All he says is, "DUDE, THE VEGGIES ARE POISONOUS!"

# 25

I rush past Mary back into the house. She says something, but I can't hear her over the music. I scour the room for Chip. It's eleven forty-five. I bump into a guy wearing a skirt (Neiman Marcus, I think) who says I look like someone, but he's not sure who exactly it is I look like. I tell him thanks and continue my search for Jackie. I see Angella, who asks me what's wrong, and I say, "Not now. Have you seen Chip?" She says he was talking to some girl wearing a tan suit, but isn't sure where he is now. I tell Angella thanks anyway, because I'm nice, and I continue to work my way through the crowd looking for Chip.

I see Mickey, who's talking to a real estate agent, and ask him if he's seen Chip. He says, "Yeah, he's right over there on the couch, talking to the girl in the tan suit." I tell him thanks and run over to Chip and ask him what he's talking about and he says that G just got a call from his supplier saying that the mushrooms are poisonous and don't take any.

Chip points over to G, who looks at us and shrugs his shoulders.

"Dude, did you eat any?" asks Chip.

"No man, I didn't," I say.

"Well, then, you've got nothing to worry about."

Chip looks over at the girl in the tan suit. "This is Saman—"

I cut off Chip. "I gave some to Jackie. Have you seen her?"

"Oh dude, no I haven't. Let's find her."

We're walking around the party and can't find Jackie anywhere. Dakota approaches us, only wearing a bikini, and asks us if we want to do flaming shots of Bacardi. I say, "No. Have you seen the girl I was with earlier?"

"Which one?" slurs Dakota.

"The one wearing the Calvin Klein leather trench coat," I slur.

"Which one?" slurs Dakota.

"The one wearing a purple suit," I slur.

"Oh, yeah. I saw her go into the bathroom a while ago," slurs Dakota. "The one right over there." She points to the bathroom just off the living room.

"Okay. Thanks," I slur, and then Chip and I rush over to the bathroom door.

"Sure you don't want to do another shot?" asks Dakota, surprisingly not slurring the question. Then she gets on a table and starts dancing to "Cotton Eye Joe".

The door is locked. "Jackie! Jackie!" I scream. No answer.

"Dude, stand back," says Chip as he puts his shoulder into the door. Nothing. Mark comes over and also tries, but the door doesn't budge. It's eleven fifty-five.

G-Dawg walks over and asks what's going on, and Chip tells him the situation. G-Dawg pulls out his nine and points it at the doorknob.

"What the fuck?" I say, then "NO!" I run in front of the gun, which is really stupid, but it stops G-Dawg. I say that there's a window and I'll get in that way.

It's eleven fifty-eight.

I run around outside, wishing I had worn the stockings because it's really cold. Chip lifts me up to the window, and I see Jackie on the floor, Calvin Klein leather trench coat open, fake breasts exposed, and I can't tell if she's breathing.

I punch the window. Nothing. I punch it again and glass shatters everywhere, mostly inside the bathroom, a lot of it landing on Jackie. Shards of glass are sticking in Jackie when I crawl into the window, blood dripping from my hand, some landing on Jackie. I lean next to her and try to take her pulse, but I'm so drunk, high, and wired that I can't tell if she has one. Outside the door I can hear R.E.M. playing, and everyone is counting down to the New Year.

# 26

THREE, TWO, ONE... HAPPY FUCKING NEW YEAR! We're back to where we started and I'm pretty sure Jackie's dead and it's all my fault. I'm out of cigarettes, which is a bummer because if there was ever a time... I shake Jackie, hoping this will cause her to suddenly awaken, but she's not moving. Chip pokes his head though the broken window and just says, "Dude."

"Wake up, Jackie! Fucking wake up!" I'm screaming and tears are starting to well up in my eyes and Chip still has his head through the window and continues to say, "Dude."

Everyone is screaming and celebrating outside, and they have no idea what has happened. I pick away the glass that's sticking in Jackie, wipe the blood that dripped on her, close her jacket, and scream her name a few more times.

Chip continues to say, "Dude," then lights a Marlboro, sees the look in my eyes, and tosses me one.

I'm picking up the glass that's surrounding Jackie's body and notice a plastic bag hanging from her right pocket.

I pull it out and realize it's the mushrooms I'd given to her earlier in the night. She never took any. It's at this time when Jackie's hand moves. I look at her face and her eyes flutter for about ten seconds, then open.

"What the fuck happened?" Jackie looks up at me.

"Rock 'n' roll!" says Chip, who is trying to get through the window. I motion for him to go back through the house and he says, "All right, dude," and then his head leaves the shattered window.

I tell Jackie what happened, or at least as much as I know, and I still have the tears in my eyes because now I'm just so relieved that she's alive and that I didn't kill her.

"You're fucking crazy," I somehow manage to get out and she laughs, which causes me to laugh with her. I help her up to a sitting position and we sit there laughing for about five minutes.

Jackie looks at me and says, "Fuck, I think I'm going to puke."

This is when I hear the first gunshot.

This is when the screams of celebration turn into screams of terror.

This tends to happen when a man walks into the living room at a party with a sawed off shotgun and starts blowing people away.

# 27

Dakota was dancing on the table to the Doors with an empty bottle of Bacardi in her hand when the bullet hit her square in the chest, between her implants. The impact from the bullet pushed her back off the table. She was dead before she hit the floor.

The second shot was a righteous boom that whistled through the crowd and hit Stoner in the right side of his chest.

“Dude with bad hair... uh... and an eye patch... uh... fucking shot me,” said Stoner while falling to the ground, and then, “Dude,” when he hit the floor.

Some have made it out while others are trapped in the line of fire waiting for the inevitable next shot.

The man with bad hair reloads and fires again, but this time he misses a girl wearing a bright red Gap T-shirt who somehow manages to dive out of the way.

I look over at Jackie, who lifts her head from the toilet and says, “Shit, it’s fucking Greg!” Then she puts her head back in the toilet and continues to vomit.

"I know," I say.

"Where the fuck is he?" screams Greg as he reloads. "Where the fuck is he?"

"Who?" someone screams back.

I unlock the door, crack it open, and I'm about ready to go out there because I don't want any more of my friends to die. This is when Greg fires off another shot. This time it's Jack who wins the unlucky lottery, receiving a bullet right through his forehead. I hear Jack's head hit the floor, and for a second in my head there is a debate about whether this is a good or bad thing. Blood is squirting from the side of Jack's head. He is rolling around on the floor screaming. Some blood squirts all over a girl wearing a blue Banana Republic shirt and she screams.

"He's in the bathroom!" yells Roy.

It's at this moment that I promise if I make it out of here I'm going to stick a fucking rifle up Roy's ass and it will be his last fucking ass story.

Fuck it. I'm sick of all the distractions, all the self-medicating, this uncomfortable fucking bra, all the drugs. It's time.

"Where the fuck is he?" screams Greg again.

"Right here!" I yell, opening the bathroom door. I walk out into the living room, but it's too late because Chip, who was talking to someone who worked for ABC before the gun play, is now storming at Greg, who fires and hits Chip's left arm, sending him to the floor.

I'm standing with my hands up, eyes closed, about fifteen feet in front of Greg. I hear him reload and then hear three shots whiz by my head. I'm still standing. I open my eyes and see G-Dawg standing behind me with his nine extended, blunt in his mouth, gun pointing at Greg, who is now on the floor with three bullet holes in him.

G-Dawg takes a drag off his blunt. He looks down at Greg's body and says, "Damn! That's bad hair!" He looks over at his crew. "Let's get the fuck out of here." G-Dawg disappears.

Red and blue is everywhere. Chip (with one arm) and I carry Stoner out to an ambulance. We pass Dakota's body. She's still clutching the Bacardi bottle. "Dude, am I dying?" asks Stoner in the back of the ambulance. "No, dude," says Chip as he lights a Marlboro.

At the hospital, Chip is reading a *Penthouse* on one side of the bed and I'm on the other side of the bed reading a copy of *The Onion* that I found in the waiting area. Stoner is in and out, occasionally lifting his head, grabbing a bucket next to the bed, and vomiting profusely. It's been two hours.

They removed the bullet and think he has a good chance, but he hasn't said a thing. Chip, who's wearing a large bandage on his left arm, asks me what I think about a girl in the *Penthouse*. I say she's too pale. Chip agrees.

Doctor Robertson stops in and we have an uncomfortable greeting. He asks about Stoner and we say that we don't know and then he asks how I'm feeling and I look over at my friend Stoner then back at him and say, "Okay." We exchange more unneeded pleasantries and then he leaves. Chip and I split a cigarette in the bathroom and continue to sit and wait to see what happens to Stoner.

"Is Dakota dead?" I ask Chip.

"Yeah, dude," says Chip. "So is that Jack guy."

"Wow," is all I say.

"Yeah, dude, fucked up. When did Greg get an eye patch?" asks Chip.

"I don't know." It's just easier this way.

Stoner wakes up again, grabs the bucket, vomits again, and then starts laughing with his head still inside the bucket. “Ahaahaaha.” Stoner lifts his head and looks over at Chip. “Dude, Café Bulimia. Ahaahaaha!”

And this is how we know Stoner is going to be okay.

# 28

Sitting at my parents' house on New Year's Day and my dad is watching football and my mom is asking me about the party and I say it was a long night and she asks something about blood on my clothes and I tell her it's nothing and then I go to the kitchen and mix a screwdriver.

"I thought you were going to quit for the New Year," my mom says.

"Next year," I say.

"Oh." She hands me a tape. "This has our top three favorite *Magnum, P.I.* episodes on it. Enjoy!"

"Okay," I say.

My flight leaves in an hour, so I say goodbye to my parents. My mom starts crying, even though she's going to see me in two days. It's at this point that I realize why people say "Hi Mom!" when they're on TV. As I'm walking out the door she runs after me, holding my iPod, which she charged for me last night.

I stop off at Jackie's to see how she's doing. She says she's okay and that the funeral for Greg is on Wednesday and that I shouldn't feel like I need to attend. To please her, I just say, "Okay," and leave it at that. I want to ask when Dakota's funeral is, but this somehow doesn't seem appropriate. I light a Marlboro and Jackie tells me how she's decided to give up drinking and only do coke and speed. "I can't have another night like that," she says. I agree, say goodbye, tell her she should come to New York sometime, but don't make any definite plans, call a cab, and head to the Sheraton.

As I approach Angella's room, Roy is leaving, but I'm not in the mood for more drama so I nod and don't say anything and walk in. Angella has a blank stare on her face. I ask her how her night was. She says she doesn't want to talk about it.

We talk about the party, Stoner, and the funerals, and I tell her I've got a cab waiting and that I'm going to the airport. I ask if she wants a ride and she says no, that she's got a lot of thinking to do, and I say okay, even though I'm a little curious about what transpired between her and Roy last night. She wishes me good luck on my operation and I wish her good luck with the new collection, and then I leave.

At the airport, I call Chip. He tells me that Dakota's funeral is on Thursday and that he knows I can't make it, but will pass along my condolences.

"Dude, I'm definitely coming out to New York next summer," says Chip. "Later."

I call Sharon, who's still hung over (she spent most of her night talking to the police). She says everything is going to be cool and that she's sorry about Dakota, even though she knows we weren't that close. I ask about Mary, and Sharon says she didn't even know she was at the party and hadn't heard anything, and I say it's probably better that way and she agrees with me for some reason.

"See you next year," says Sharon.

I'm sitting on the runway at General Mitchell Airport, holding my freshly charged iPod. There's a delay and it will be fifteen minutes before liftoff. I call Stoner and he's still in the hospital but doing better and will be able to leave in a day or so. He wishes me well on my operation and then says he can't wait until next year's party.

"Are you crazy?" I ask.

"Ahaahaaha. Maybe a little. Dude, it was a blast, literally. Later, dude," says Stoner.

"Later, man. Yeah, I'll see you next year," I say.

Due to the delay, the flight attendants start their beverage service early and I'm surprised to see that I receive a full can of Coke. "Going home?" the flight attendant asks.

GO HOME.

"Yeah, I guess," I say. She smiles and moves on. I think about the week, and how I guess I'm lucky to have the friends and family I have and be able to GO HOME for the holidays. Maybe I'll start looking at things differently, from a positive perspective. After all, when I think about it, I'm really one lucky guy. I think about the past parties, Angella and Roy, Jackie's blue thong, Mary, Dakota's breasts, and all the others that I've shared my week with. It gives me a good feeling. I put my head back, feeling somewhat content. I notice someone near the front of the plane who looks like Mary. She turns around, but before I can see who it is a lady sitting next to me who's obviously wearing too much makeup spills her hot coffee (maybe Starbucks) on me. I think about the surgery, which *really* has been a constant distraction, realize it's not Mary in the front of the plane, and then a woman in the third row stands up, which is really annoying because she's wearing a shirt that reads...

www.ingramcontent.com/pod-product-compliance
Lightning Source LLC
Chambersburg PA
CBHW021951010726
47494CB00003B/689

* 9 7 8 0 9 8 1 5 1 9 1 0 4 *

# BLACKOUT

Copyright © 2008 by David S. Grant

All rights reserved.

No part of this book may be used or reproduced in any manner whatsoever without written permission, except in the case of brief quotations embodied in critical articles or reviews. For information, address Offense Mechanisms, an imprint of Silverthought Press.

Printed in the United States of America

Published by Offense Mechanisms
www.offensemechanisms.com

ISBN-10: 0-9815191-0-5
ISBN-13: 978-0-9815191-0-4

Designed by Paul Hughes

# BLACKOUT

by DAVID S. GRANT

OFFENSE MECHANISMS
PHILADELPHIA | NEW YORK

## Two Years Later

Welcome back. The surgery was a success. Thanks for asking. Once you've had a brain tumor removed, you see things differently. Insightful words from my doctor once the check cleared.

Run. Close this book and run. This is a story of despair. A tale that makes you weep and then seek counseling. Paragraphs of words, short on lessons, heavy on addictions. My story.

This is a story about drinking. Massive amounts of drinking. This is a story about the worst hangover of your life. The type of hangover you're forced to put on paper for others to see and mock in disgust.

When dealing with a crisis, back story is useless. Here's all you need to know: I had a brain tumor. The surgery was a success. I live in New York and am on vacation in Vegas for my friend Stoner's bachelor party. Chip, another friend, is also here. Chip is in charge of the strippers. My job is prostitute coordination. I'm obsessed with a girl named Mary. It's important to mention that it's New Year's Eve 2006 and I have consumed

narcotics for weeks in preparation for tonight. This is all you need to know.

This is a story about underage sex, and not the good kind.

How would you react if you were standing at a New Year's Eve party and were informed that this would be your last year? What questions would you ask? How would you change? If your answer is to change anything, you've failed the test of life. Live now as if it's your last year here. Drive with the top down and scream from the top of your lungs with a fifth of Jack Daniels in your lap and your handgun of choice in the glove compartment.

Remembering is half the battle. Forgetting is the other half.

In the end I've realized you can get drunk enough to do anything. However, you have to realize that once you're sober these are the things that will lead you to grab a 12 gauge or remain drunk for the rest of your life.

This is story about living.

It's time. My apologies to those who turn this page looking for romance. Maybe next year, if we are both still here. Until then...

Welcome back. That's really all I can say.

# 1

Sometimes the heat in Vegas has nothing to do with the temperature.

There are seven of us in all and Stoner is already baked when we meet at the Bellagio. "Dude, it's my party." Chip doesn't have an excuse, already wobbling as he reaches the bar. It's three in the afternoon.

We drink boilermakers and play poker at Bellagio, then play craps at Caesar's until the complimentary shots of Jim Beam are out, smoke crack behind TI, walk through MGM in two minutes, walk back over to TI and drink frozen mixers while smoking Kool cigarettes and commenting on the length of the waitresses' cocktail dresses, rent two Ferraris and drive to Crazy Horse Too, where we drop two grand on strippers (would have dropped four, but we get thrown out when Stoner's friend Jekyll bites Jasmine's nipple), total one of the Ferraris on the way to Olympic Gardens, leave the Ferrari, go into OG's and drop two more grand, eat sliders with mustard at a restaurant called Lucky Burger, and

then smoke crack next to the lone Ferrari hidden behind the Lucky Burger dumpster.

After sliders, we hop on a helicopter, take a loop around the city, finally landing near the Stratosphere, where we go to the top and drink Bacardi straight up with a slice of chocolate cake. Leave the chopper and walk to Stardust, drink red wine and smoke cigars and sing karaoke songs. Half an hour before midnight, we go to Circus Circus and take the elevator to the roof, where Chip has arranged for a Cambodian stripper to perform for Stoner. I walk over to the open bar, order a shot of dry gin, and then lean over the side of the roof and watch the city lights as midnight, the New Year, approaches. At midnight, the fireworks begin and I look over at Stoner and see that the Cambodian girl is now performing oral sex on him. Chip walks over and explains that she's only a stripper and that this is normal in her country. I turn back to the lights of the Vegas Strip as they shoot to the sky.

"I know a place just off the Strip that has the best Thai." Chip puts his pipe back into his pocket.

"Cool," someone says and we pile into the Ferrari and within minutes pull up to a two-star hotel and walk up to the second floor, where the Thai prostitutes are waiting for us and then after twenty minutes we meet out in the hallway, where we all smoke Kool cigarettes and drink from a warm case of Miller that was left in the hallway by someone. Two guys decide to stay at the hotel with the girls and finish the case of Miller. "Ahaahaa, dude, that was fucking awesome," laughs Stoner as we pile back into the Ferrari and speed back over to the Strip and stop at the Paradise Club, where the strippers are doing a shower scene on stage and Chip works out a deal to get Stoner up on the stage, but he looks too stoned to remember and spends the whole time laugh-

ing hysterically. After the shower, the girls take Stoner backstage, where more laughter is heard, and a bill for one thousand dollars is handed to Chip. When Stoner comes out, he goes over to Chip and whispers something into his ear. Chip gets up and goes backstage, Stoner walks over to me and I'm high and I ask him if his soon-to-be bride knows what's going on tonight and he tells me that it doesn't matter because he's only marrying her for her trust fund and that when she finds out the wedding may be worse than *Kill Bill.* Chip returns with a smile on his face and says, "You're right, it was worth a thousand." At Perfect 10, I get lap dances from girls named Saw and Ginger, but my second dance is cut short when Chip interrupts and says we have to go because they are playing Kanye West music, which is just the same to me because Ginger isn't really into the dance, snorting cocaine while she's grinding on me.

In Bikinis, three rounds of Manhattans are consumed and conversations about both grass skirts and whether or not Mariah Carey is still considered crazy are had. A girl named Anne begins talking with Stoner, but he can't stop laughing so she leaves. The grass skirt conversation carries over when we arrive at Coyote Ugly and begin drinking Old Fashions, even though we ordered gin, and Stoner dances on the bar until we are asked to leave. A joint is smoked inside the House of Blues while waiting for our Sidecars, which we slam in under a minute, and then at Rain, another joint is smoked instead of attempting to get drinks at the overcrowded bar.

Ten minutes later in a club with "Aces" in the name we throw down double shots of dry gin and eat pretzels and then out of our minds all do the funky chicken on the dance floor. In the club we lose two of Stoner's friends and now we're down to three. Chip and I head to

the blackjack tables and lose three hundred each and then drink more dry gin and Chip talks two porn stars into doing a show for Stoner, so we all go up to a room and watch the girls perform oral on each other for twenty minutes or so and then go to the Imperial Palace, where the owner knows Chip and lets us openly smoke hash in his lounge. We meet Nicolas Cage and Chip pitches his new reality show idea to him and Nic sounds interested as he sips a Heineken. They embrace and exchange contact information.

Outside of the casino, Chip falls on his face and while Stoner and I are laughing two squatters help him up and then Chip starts talking to them and it turns out they were actors at one point so Chip gives them his card and asks them where's a good place for breakfast and the squatters both point across the street where we see the sign for Denny's.

At some point after plates of sausage and bacon we hook up with a guy named Earl who is driving the Ferrari with Stoner riding shotgun, a girl named Rose on his lap, and Chip passed out with sunglasses on in the back seat. I ask Earl what time it is and he tells me 4:30 a.m. then pulls out his crack pipe and that's the last thing I remember until I wake up the next morning in Los Angeles with a gun barrel stuck in my mouth.

# 2

At what point in my life am I going to stop fantasizing about removing a police officer's gun from his holster? It's something that has concerned me for quite some time. Right now it doesn't matter as I stare into the barrel of the gun that is connected to the officer standing over me.

Lying flat on my back on a living room floor that reeks of Corona beer and Kool cigarettes, I'm looking out the corners of my eyes trying to figure out where I am. To my right is Chip. The officer has already turned him over and is applying handcuffs. At my left, I see a chair littered with leather whips and beads, and that's how I figure out that I'm at Sharon Winkler's new house in Los Angeles. Also from the Midwest, Sharon started her own escort service, which grew rapidly, forcing the move to a larger market base. Plus, she was really beginning to get into cosmetic surgery, so the move to L.A. was justified in her eyes.

Finance in New York is a bore and not really what anyone sets out to do with their lives. Firefighters, base-

ball players, and astronauts, these are childhood dreams. For even the most conservative upbringing, financial analyst doesn't crack the top ten. A little over a year ago I decided to pursue my dream of writing. I got a job part time as a writer for a satirical newspaper similar to *The Onion*, writing articles on popular culture. Unfortunately, I only got to write two articles before I was moved to the obituary section. Not normal obituaries, but rather strange deaths often caused by random circumstances.

*Sammy O'Henry was golfing when he was struck by lightning, moving approximately 10,000 volts of electricity through his body. He lived. A week later, he was sleepwalking. He went into his garage and mistook a container of antifreeze for apple juice. He never woke up.*

You're probably wondering who would do this in their spare time and thinking how depressing it must be. First, this was (and still is) supposed to be a stepping stone. I'm hoping to get back into the pop culture section of the newspaper. As for the depression, it actually had quite the opposite effect on me. It taught me that at any minute we can be gone. The bus around the corner we don't see, the crazy person who didn't take their medication, or waking up to a police officer with a gun in your face.

*A man only known as Koria travels to Thailand to teach English to underprivileged children. One of his students brings him a fruit called durian. He appreciates the gesture. He eats the fruit, which overheats the body from within. Koria doesn't live to see the end of the day.*

This is a story about living.

The officer slowly lifts me from the floor and then applies handcuffs to me. At some point I attempt to ask what this is about, but my mouth is too dry to talk.

In the background, an Aerosmith video plays, Steven Tyler belting out lyrics of drugs, debauchery, and sex. I can't see the TV at the moment, but I'm guessing he's wearing one of his usual gown-like robe outfits that only he can wear. In my present position, what would Steven Tyler do?

I look over at Chip. It takes two officers to lift him, and he has a grin on his face. Chip has a cigarette in his mouth and is still wearing sunglasses. His glasses are knocked off by the elbow of one of the officers. "My shades!" grunts Chip, cigarette still in mouth.

"Too bad, lost your glasses. You're no longer cool," the officer jokes.

Is Chip cool? Is the situation cool? The LAPD? Definitely not cool.

Sharon walks out. She's wearing a bright pink robe that has a pin with a clover that reads: IRISH GUYS MAKE GOOD LOVERS AND BEER. "What's going on?"

The officer that is holding me by the cuffs, the one with the bushy mustache, tells Sharon that Chip and I are going in for questioning over some fifteen-year-old girl.

"But I know these guys. They couldn't have—"

"We have witnesses," says the cop with the well-trimmed mustache.

Once again I try to say something, but my mouth is not cooperating with me at the moment. Chip looks disoriented as we walk through the door and into the back of the police car. I sit and try to remember the night before. Bits and pieces slowly fill my head: dropping off Stoner at his place, arriving at Sharon's, where her annual New Year's Eve party was winding down, looking for Mary, and finally settling for a conversation with a girl named Patricia that went something like this:

Patricia: Hey, I remember you. You're Jeremy, right?
Me: That's me.
Patricia: What have you been up to?
Me: Nothing, and you?
Patricia: Oh, you know.
Me: {putting a gun to my head}

Other than that, I don't remember much. I know that the sun was up and that Chip wasn't around for most of the morning. I had probably assumed he had crashed in a corner somewhere. He has always preferred hallway corners over beds after a long night.

Outside, cuffed and resting against the squad car, the cops standing in front of us smoking, Chip asks, "So what did we do?"

Silence.

"We have rights. You have to tell us what we did," I barely get out.

"You see this?" One of the cops points to a patch on his sleeve, then blows smoke into my face. "LAPD. We don't have to tell you shit." He laughs. The others laugh as well, staring at our bleached hair. "What are you guys, a couple of surf bums?"

"No, I'm in finance," I say.

"I'm in construction," Chip says.

"Whatever. You guys look like a couple of bums to me."

Inside the car, Chip makes the motion of putting his arms under his legs to move his cuffed hands to the front, but is unable. "Damn, now it's ten inches even. There's no way I can get the cuffs over."

Chip was referencing his penis, which he had recently had lengthened another half-inch to ten inches. (A previous operation put him at nine and a half.)

"Yeah, that's too bad," I say as I move my legs up and swing my arms under, moving my cuffed hands to the front.

Two officers are in the front of the car. The dispatch radio is turned off. A classic rock station is playing. When a song by The Who comes on, the officer with the more trimmed mustache asks bushy mustache what he thinks about when he listens to music. "Do you pretend to be the guitarist, the lead singer, or do you just listen to the music?"

"Mostly just listen," Bushy mustache replies, "but sometimes, like with Van Halen—old Van Halen—I pretend to be Eddie in my head." We approach a red light and he puts on the siren. "Yeah, but that's pretty much it. Only Eddie Van Halen, that's really the only guy. How about you?"

*Eddie Van Halen is (or was, depending on whether it was only the music) cool. In an era where there seemed to be nothing left to do with a guitar, Eddie took it to new levels, and did it with a drink in his hand. Cool.*

"The same. I feel exactly the same way," the trim-mustached cop says.

An awkward silence is had by all until Chip coughs. "Damn cigars. I don't think what Cage gave me was a Cuban. It was pretty harsh."

"Maybe it was only the wrapper," I say.

"The rapper?" Chip adjusts his arms. "Oh, you mean the wrapper was Cuban."

"Yeah, Cuban seed. That's not illegal."

"Cool. That explains it. I don't want to be pissed off at Nic."

Almost to the station, the mood is pretty light since we are pretty sure we will answer a couple questions, explain that we were too hammered to remember anything, and then find someplace to sleep. I overhear them

discussing a fifteen-year-old girl, and it sounds as if she was at the party and then left, so I speak up and ask what happened and the officers tell me to sit back and wait until we get to the precinct for question time. One says, "One of you is going down like the Titanic," which is the last thing I need to hear. Go ahead and reference a movie that took me eight years to finally see and realize that I never really needed to see it.

"Dude, we didn't molest any fifteen-year-old," says Chip. He coughs again.

The trim-mustached cop turns around and looks Chip in the eyes. "The sex is only part of your problem, you asshead. Her death is another."

# 3

***ONE-STAR HANGOVER:***

*Also known as the Monday Night Football disease, the one-star haunts everyone. Even the most conservative social drinkers will experience this. For some, the one-star is a rite of passage to push it to new levels, for others, a public service announcement on the dangers of drinking leading to a career path involving paper products or Snapple distribution. This is social night on the town, a beer with the boys, a glass of wine with the girls. A shot before the big game.*

*It was the late eighties when I experienced my first one-star hangover. Chip and I cut psychology class (taught by a man named Mr. Needles, which was fitting because his hair stood straight up like a porcupine) and headed to a liquor store, where we shoplifted two forty-ounce bottles of Miller High Life and a fifth of J. Bavet brandy. Outside a Burger King, we drank down the forties and discussed who was the strangest person in our psychology class. I voted for Steve, the guy who drooled*

*and was always blowing his nose. Chip voted for Stephanie because she was a whore, but refused to fuck him. After Burger King, we walked down a gravel road, carved obscenities into an abandoned refrigerator, and then threw rocks at a couple kids wearing cowboy hats and shirts with pictures of Disney characters on them.*

*Wandering around, we found an old wise man named Russ who explained to us how women fit into two categories: complex and exotic, and that if you end up with the wrong one you could ruin your life. His theory was that you should only date women with short hair or long hair. Medium length was a sign of indecisiveness. But not too short, he warned—don't want to end up having your vacations at Cape Cod with your girl scoping out the other REALLY short-haired girls. Also, find out if they like James Bond movies. They don't necessarily have to have seen many, just make sure they're not opposed. He seemed really mellow and very open. He taught us about women, surviving, and the early warning signs of syphilis.*

*Unfortunately we never found out which one was the correct choice or how to identify one over the other because Russ had to move on after Chip pointed to his chain of keys and asked if one of the keys was to unlock his dreams. "This grocery cart isn't going to push itself" was how he put it as he moved on. For the next two hours we swayed around town, only stopping to buy chicken wings and cigarettes, wishing we were old enough to drive. Eventually we bought two forties from a homeless guy because drinking brandy straight is always a little harsh.*

*The brandy was gone before the forties. We passed out early and awoke the next day feeling weak with dry mouths.*

*No pain and no signs of illness, with full memory of the afternoon before and the fun we had. With all bodily functions intact, I knew this would become a recurring event. We learned three lessons: water is your friend, cheeseburgers always taste best when you have a hangover, and Gatorade isn't just for athletes.*

*Let's face it, working is bullshit. Everyone needs a way to unwind. Watching sitcoms, working out, collecting stamps. Drinking a tall boy.*

*When you go into the office tomorrow, look around. One out of every three are experiencing a one-star hangover (they are the ones enjoying their coffee slightly more than the rest) and feeling pretty damn good about it.*

To my left is a man wearing a blue flannel shirt with black Doc Martins. His breath smells of bacon. I look down and realize I'm wearing extremely faded jeans. At my right is a guy wearing a Harley Davidson leather jacket who continues shifting from one foot to the other, never able to just stand still, occasionally looking down at my faded jeans. I look over and see Chip, three people down. The speaker informs us to look forward. Number five is told to stand still. Number five is wearing the leather coat. I catch another whiff of bacon and come to the realization that it's not even real bacon but some type of low-fat brand, or maybe SizzleLean. Two down, a man wearing a Dodgers hat backwards is chewing tobacco and spitting on the floor in front of us.

The voice from the speaker tells us to turn right. As we turn, the man in the Dodgers hat begins choking. We pause. Chip goes over and performs the Heimlich maneuver and knocks him on the back, jarring the tobacco from the back of his throat. The voice over the speaker tells us to go back to our places.

"That's number four," says Chip as he passes me on his way back to his spot in the line. I know what this is about. Chip is referencing his number of saves as he glances down at my jeans.

Five years ago, Chip was working at a construction site just north of Chicago when a car veered off the road and burst into flames. Chip was the first to make it over to the car, pulling out a man before he burst into flames himself. This was his first save. Since then, he has rescued a girl from a shark, talked a Starbucks cashier out of suicide (to be fair, she had drunk six cappuccinos that day), and now this, saving a fellow lineup associate from choking on his own tobacco.

I've never had a save. It's not that I haven't had the opportunities. Usually, I freeze. Sometimes it just doesn't seem important. I've never been mistaken for Batman. That's not to say I've never tried. There was one time when a car lost control and flipped over, ending up in a steep ditch. I rushed over and could see a mother and daughter moving around. With all of my might I tried to open the door, but was unable to do so. Luckily, another person showed up. She was able to lift and open the door.

Zero. My number of saves at this point.

*Betty and Guy Carlson were owners of the Carlson Vineyards. It was their life dream to own a vineyard. One day when checking on the wine fermentation tanks, Betty slipped. She tried to steady herself by grabbing Guy. Both died in the tanks. An estimated thirty cases of wine were destroyed.*

The speaker says number four and number eight must stay; the rest are free to go. I look down. I'm holding number four. I've got a bad feeling who has number eight. The nightmare continues.

Chip and I are placed into a holding cell, awaiting questions. We just stare at each other and say, "What the fuck?" We take turns saying this to each other. The guy who almost died choking on his tobacco hugs Chip on his way out. Despite my current predicament, I can't help but be a little jealous of Chip and his saves.

Five minutes pass and then I'm pulled out of the cell by a Detective Jackson. "It's best if you come clean. We know it was Chip and not you, so if you come clean we won't press charges." Jackson leads me into a dimly lit room with only a metal table and two chairs, very NYPD-like. One glaring difference of course is that Jackson doesn't reek of alcohol. That would be me.

"Come clean about what?" I ask. "Charges?"

The detective slams his fist down on the table (very Sipowicz-like) and then moves in closer. "A fifteen-year-old was raped and murdered last night and you don't give a shit! You know what? Fuck it. I want to see you go down, too. I know you're holding back on me."

"I don't know what you're talking about. I—we—didn't do anything. We were in Vegas." Then I think about this for a second. "Fifteen?" I clear my throat. "You think we did this?"

"Ah yes, Vegas. You were with Earl Santana, correct?"

Who?

"Ye—uh, shouldn't I have a lawyer?"

"That's up to you, if you want to look guilty and show involvement in all of this."

"Involvement?" I look at the mirror, wondering who is on the other side. Maybe they have Chip over there, waiting for me to flip. I look back over at Detective Jackson. "Fifteen?"

There's a knock at the door. Sharon Winkler is standing with a half-smile on her face. She's wearing a

pin that reads: WAR! SOMETIMES THAT'S THE ONLY WAY. Behind her is a man with a dark complexion and carefully parted hair.

"I'm Michael Stone. I'm representing Jeremy," he says to the detective. "We've posted bail, so if there are any more questions..."

The detective stares at me for a second, then throws his arms up in the air. "Take him. I've got nothing for the asshead, but we will." The detective points at me. "This isn't over."

Bail is also posted for Chip. We walk out of the jailhouse. "Who posted bail?" I ask.

"Stoner," says Michael Stone. "Well, not Stoner, but his friend."

Chip lights a Marlboro. "Who's the friend?"

"His name is Earl," Stone says. "I'm his lawyer, and now I'm your lawyer."

Chip takes a deep drag and looks at Mr. Stone. "Okay, so some guy named Earl bailed us out, and your name is..."

"Michael Stone."

"Sounds made up." I'm thinking this, but Chip says it out loud. Chip looks over at me.

"Chip, easy, he's helping us—"

"No, actually," Michael Stone pulls out a pack of Kools, "he's right. My name isn't Michael Stone. The name is fake, but believe me, this situation you are in is very real."

I look back at the police station. In the window two stories up, Detective Jackson is looking down at us. I look over at Chip. "We have to go see Stoner."

"Definitely," says Chip. He looks over at Sharon and adds, "You have a joint we can share first?"

# 4

Michael Stone is driving with me and Sharon in the back seat. Chip is riding shotgun, smoking hash out of a brass pipe and explaining our side of the story. Billy Joel's "Captain Jack" is playing on the radio.

"Wow, what a story!" says Sharon. "You should send it in to *Reader's Digest*!"

"Really?" Chip hands the pipe back to Sharon.

"No," laughs Sharon, grabbing the pipe from Chip.

Stone speaks up. "Seriously, though, you need to be careful who you talk to, Chip, or you'll be sleeping with the pirates."

Looking straight ahead at the road, Chip asks, "Pirates?"

"Yeah, pirates. If this is a setup, then someone did a hell of a job, and they want you to either rot in jail or sleep with the pirates." Michael looks over at Chip, who is still confused. "Bottom of the ocean. That's where the pirates sleep."

The rest of the ride is quiet as we ponder our destinies. I think about whether or not I will ever get a save. Maybe on my flight back there will be a terrorist and I will have to step in, or possibly a man clutching his chest, requiring CPR. Rescuing a child from a kid snatcher in the airport as everyone watches me, the ultimate save. My mind drifts to a dark place where the future looks bleak, a little New Jersey mixed with the rain of the Pacific Northwest. I realize my first save must be to save myself. I feel the need to drink. A lot.

We pull off onto a side street, somewhere in West Hollywood. Out the window I see two homeless people heckling someone who looks like Bob Saget and an old woman who looks a little like Mrs. Garrett from *The Facts of Life* carrying a sack of potatoes.

"Dudes, what happened?" asks Stoner, meeting us outside the duplex he's living in. "I can't believe you got arrested. That's fucked up, dude."

"Man, it's all fucked up. They think I fucked some child and then killed her." Chip lights a Marlboro.

There's a pause because it hasn't quite been put like this, out in the open and all. Maybe this was a setup. Maybe we had better be careful, or else we'll end up like pirates.

"No way, dude. You were with me. Shit, Earl drove us home last night. Let me give him a call."

Michael Stone moves closer. "Call Earl. Let's see what that motherfucker is up to."

Stoner looks at me, then over at Chip. He lowers his voice. "Do I know him?"

"He's cool," I say. "He's Michael Stone, Chip's—I mean *our*—lawyer."

"Oh cool." Stoner offers his hand and slaps Michael Stone's before he has a chance to offer a proper handshake. "Earl is my dealer," says Stoner, still looking at

Michael Stone. “Let’s go. You’re driving, Stone?” Stoner throws the keys. They land short of Michael Stone, who is forced to bend over and pick them up. “Ahaahaaa,” Stoner laughs.

We meet Earl at a strip club near Santa Monica named Bottoms. Plaques cover the walls as we enter through the doors next to the stage. A woman wearing a yellow bikini dances on the stage while a cover band plays next to the pole. The band is playing a KISS song. For some reason I comment on how the cover band sounds good, even though they don’t. I always feel the need to comment on cover bands. Even if they are just okay, I’ll say they’re great. If a cover band sucks, I’ll say they’re okay and then start talking about cover bands I’ve seen that are better, only I never remember their names, only places I’ve seen them. I eventually just start sounding like an alcoholic because of all the bars I list. I really have a cover band problem.

Earl, Stoner, and Chip are looking at the plaques while Michael Stone and Sharon go to find a table.

I join them. Earl sees me, looks over at Chip and points to the plaques. “Never been a plaque man, myself,” says Earl. “Medals are where it’s at.”

“Medals?” I ask.

“Yeah, you know, gold, silver, and bronze. It really means something. That’s why the Olympics uses medals. It would be a damn shame if they used certificates. Can you imagine?”

“Ribbons for me,” says Chip. “Nothing beats the good ol’ red, white, and blue.”

“Ahaaaahaaa,” Stoner laughs, “but the plaques are great for, you know, cutting lines and shit. Dual purposes.”

“Good point,” says Earl.

Michael Stone calls to let us know we have a table. "It's away from the door," he says in a matter of fact sort of way.

On our way to the table, we come to the agreement that we are anti-certificate people, especially the certificate of attendance bullshit given out to students of private schools and tax attorneys that attend conferences.

We order drinks. Chip and Stoner order Bloody Marys while the rest of us order drinks with rum. My drink comes with a slice of orange. Ordinarily I would not have a problem with this except that I have been seeing this a lot more lately: overuse of fruit in drinks. As far as I'm concerned, we should just stop all of this right now. Moving forward, there shouldn't be any fruit allowed unless it's a Bloody Mary (where the groceries are always welcome). I had someone tell me I was crazy and that things haven't changed. I hope they are right, because I would hate to someday order a Jack and Coke and find a slice of mango in it when my drink is delivered.

"It was definitely morning. I'll testify to that," says Earl to Michael Stone, looking over at Stoner.

Stoner leans in. "Earl doesn't really like cops, so let's keep the questioning to a minimum if possible."

"No problem," says Stone. "We'll probably just need a statement to support your alibi." Michael points at Chip. "Then we'll talk with the D.A. and see if we can get the counts dropped. No need to waste everyone's time."

"Come to think of it, I may have an outstanding warrant or two." Earl looks over at Stone. "Is that going to be a problem?"

"For me, no." Michael Stone scans the table, stopping at Earl. "For you, yes, a huge fucking deal." Stone laughs. "We'll figure out something. You probably won't have to testify anyway."

Everyone eats club sandwiches except for Earl, who eats a cheeseburger with only mustard. Sharon and Michael go up to the bar and order shots of pineapple juice with vodka. Back at the table, Earl looks over at Chip and starts laughing.

"What?" Chip looks around the table. "What is it?"

"Man." Earl continues laughing. "Man, you ever smoke weed soaked in gasoline?"

"Yes I have," Stoner says and then laughs. "Ahaaahaaa, that's my smoke of choice!"

We only stay at Bottoms for a couple hours. Stone gets Earl's statement and then we're heading back to the precinct to talk to the district attorney. Michael Stone is driving back with Chip riding next to him while I'm sprawled out in the back seat. Chip is calling Michael Stone stiff because there's really no movement when he drives, like a board.

*I stare out the window and close my eyes. In a few minutes I see a long field in front of me, about a quarter mile long with a light at the end. Looking back, I see a field of sunflowers. A storm is kicking up. Something is pulling me to go back, but I know I need to keep moving forward. The sunflowers bob violently as the winds of the storm pick up behind. From within the darkening field behind there's a faint voice that urges me to move on. I look back again, forward, out to the open field and hear a phone ring. I walk toward the ringing even though I can't see the phone and then I'm standing in an empty conference room with a laptop and projector set up. Someone walks in and dims the lights. I don't get a good look of who it is, but he looks vaguely familiar...*

Waking up from the dream, I feel groggy. The dream shakes me, and I'm unsure what it means. Chip's phone rings and he debates answering it because he doesn't recognize the number. Eventually he does and it's Nico-

las Cage. I got woken up by a Nic Cage phone call. Despite being on our way to the police station, Chip, as promised, pitches his movie idea to Nic.

"It's like a Tarantino movie, Nic. The ending is in the beginning and the ending is in the middle. I guess the only difference is there won't be a cameo by Quentin in this movie."

Cage must have enjoyed Chip's joke because Chip is doing his laugh-along laugh. He continues to explain some very nondescript details of the nonexistent movie and they set a meeting to discuss.

"Dude, don't you need a script or screenplay or something?" I ask.

Chip points to his head. "It's all here, man. No problems."

"Cool." What the hell, have you seen the movies Cage has picked over the past couple of years? Maybe it will work out.

*Sam Underwood, a famous snake magician who was slated to have his own national special leading to a possible talk show, dies six hours after a cobra strikes his neck during the warm up for his big special.*

Back in L.A. we pull off at a 7-11 because Chip needs smokes. I'm looking over the burrito selection and am somewhat appalled by the selection because there is chicken, fish, and vegetable, but no beef. Michael Stone is standing in line with a box of cheap cigars, eyeing up the CDs that line the counter. He picks up a Clint Black CD and I quickly jump over and say, "No, you don't want to do that, do you?" Stone puts the CD away and we leave. On the way out of the store I wonder whether or not this could technically count as a save. After all, it was Clint Black. In the end I decide no since this would only cause mental issues and there was no actual risk of physical injury. I really feel like I'd be a different man

if I could just get that one save. The first one is always the harshest. Oh wait... That's herb, not saves.

Chip lights up a Marlboro and blows about ten percent of the smoke out the half-inch crack in his window, the rest ricocheting back at everyone in the car. "Man, if I did have to do time, I don't know how I could possibly do it without these." Chip holds up his cigarette. "Most prisons are smoke free now. Can you believe that shit?" Chip takes a big drag. "Thank God I don't have to deal with that fucking shit, but I'll tell you what," Chip leans back and points at me with his cigarette, "if I was famous, I'd have a carton of these sitting in my dressing room. Hell yeah. Marlboro cigarettes, a bottle of Wild Turkey, and a machine gun." Chip looks back at me. "What three items would you have?"

What would Steven Tyler have? Probably prostitutes, condoms, and sex toys.

"Uh, not sure. Probably something like, um, a bowl of M&Ms, an acoustic guitar, and the DVD of *Point Break*."

Chip stares back at me. "You must be fucking joking. Tell me you're fucking joking, right?"

I laugh. Chip laughs.

Truth is, I was only joking about the guitar.

# 5

***TWO-STAR HANGOVER:***

*You make it in to work, although no actual work will be completed. Water is always around, and Vitamin Water has never tasted so good. Two-star hangovers are common for those who order a shot with every third beer. Binge drinkers.*

*At twenty-one years of age, Chip and I attended a party somewhere in the middle of nowhere that promised two half-barrels of beer. Six beer bongs, two shot-gunned cans, and a fifth of brandy later, we were driving around looking for a liquor store that we never found. Instead, we pulled into a bar. We knew it was a bar because it had an orange neon sign with big letters that read BAR.*

*The night involved the following: six pitchers of Miller Lite, one pitcher of Newcastle, two glasses of Scotch, six shots of Jägermeister, two shots of vodka (on a dare), four packs of cigarettes, twenty-five games of pool, four bottles of Budweiser, and finally, two glasses of cognac.*

*There is a woman at the bar. Okay, it was the bartender, who was a single mom by day, who was flirting with me. It was strange because as the night went on she seemed to be getting really fucking fresh with me. While she was pouring a pitcher of beer I made my move and asked if when she got off she wanted to go have a drink. She said maybe, and then I got defensive to the point where she stopped serving me. I left screaming, calling her a "fucking dirty whore." It was not my brightest moment, yet I've had many two-star nights, so it's possible this has happened many times, hence the reason I can tell you this story, vividly etched in my mind.*

*Sometime around 2:10 a.m. an unsuspecting person got vomited on when I didn't see them sitting on the toilet. I felt like I was going to die and was sure no one was feeling worse than me. Well, maybe one other person was.*

*The next morning, there's the feeling that if you were to get pulled over, you may be charged with a DUI. You risk it anyway because you can't miss work. Before work you stop at an ATM (because, of course, all you have left from the night before is ATM receipts) and try to put your card into the receipt slot.*

*Truth is that your job isn't that important (to you or the company), so you end up leaving at ten o'clock in the morning after you've officially crashed and catch your head bobbing as your eyes close at your desk. On the way home you find something greasy (usually involves McDonald's) and then eat more than you've eaten the previous three days combined. A nap is always just a short period of time away. This is some of the best sleep a man can have.*

In the precinct we're on a different floor than before. I think we're on the third, but it's hard to tell because the

staircases are spiral and somewhat disorienting. We sit down and the District Attorney walks in, introduces himself, points at me, and says, "He can go. We are not charging him."

"Jeremy," I say. "My name is Jeremy."

"Jeremy, you can go." The D.A. points at me again to make sure we know he's talking to me and not just staring at me.

Chip looks at me and then over at the D.A. "He can stay if he wants to." He then attempts to light a cigarette, which the D.A. quickly grabs from his mouth.

"No smoking."

"Shit." Chip looks over at me. "I fucking knew it. I told you."

Michael Stone jumps in and explains that he has two witnesses. First, there's Johnny (Chip looks over at me, I softly say, "Stoner," and Chip smiles and shakes his head), and then there's his friend Earl. Both were with Chip when the alleged incident happened.

"Earl, ah yes, the drug dealer. I wouldn't bring him near this place if I were you, Michael Stone." The D.A. looks over at me. "And him..."

"Well, he doesn't remember, so..." Stone trails off.

"That's convenient," says the D.A. I give him a half-smile. He continues, "Well, here's the thing, Mr. Stone. My suggestion is that you get your witnesses here fast because not only are we moving forward with charges on Chip, we have been told a conviction is the only acceptable outcome."

"What the hell is this?" Stone stands up.

The D.A. laughs. "Well, it turns out the girl is Louie Lorde's daughter." Michael Stone groans. "From your groan I assume you know that he is a State Representative. A Congressman, if you'd rather."

Michael Stone looks over at Chip and shakes his head. “This is not good, man.”

Michael Stone’s dressing room would contain a palm tree, a fake passport, and a telescope to spy on people outside of his window.

“What?” Chip begins to look worried. “Dude, she was fifteen. There’s no way I would fuck that!”

The D.A. opens the door. Two police officers come in, cuff Chip, and remove him from the room.

“Don’t worry, Chip. You’re innocent. I’ll take care of this.” Michael Stone glares at the D.A.

The D.A. laughs. “Oh, one other thing, due to the circumstances and the high profile for this case, the court date is being fast tracked. See you in court,” more laughter, “next week.”

“Fuck,” Stone says under his breath, then looks over at me. “Get Stoner and Earl the fuck over here by tomorrow. We need to start on Chip’s case.

*Vince Buckley, a famous Greek playwright, died when an eagle dropped a tortoise on his head. Mr. Buckley was found clutching a new script named* Tales from the Sky.

To be honest, I don’t believe in Michael Stone, so I decide to meet up with Stoner and Sharon at a bar called Happy Ending in Manhattan Beach. I’m there early, so I grab a seat at the bar and order a Rolling Rock only because I haven’t had one for a long time and am feeling a little crazy tonight. With my green bottle in front of me, I look across the bar and see a guy who looks a lot like Oliver Stone. I squint to get a clearer look, but it turns out to be no one, just someone who looks a little bit like John Lithgow with a tad more hair.

“See the upright chairs and the glass tables?” Sharon asks as I look around.

“Sure.” I look out even though I’m feeling a little bit stupid because I’m looking at tables and chairs.

"This is totally a coke bar. I bet the residue alone off the tops of the tables could keep us up for an entire week. The chairs are so you can sit at the end and lean over."

I look around, but it doesn't really seem like anything remotely close to cocaine use is happening. Just a modern bar with people wearing hip hats and yes, glass tables. Not exactly the seventies in here with crazy disco music, flared collars, and anal sex coming of age.

As I come to the conclusion that this is not a coke bar, a couple next to us pulls out a bag, carves up two lines, and snorts them within seconds. It is important to note that the man is wearing a turtleneck and the woman a conservative blouse. Welcome to 2007. It's not quite the seventies, but it's 2007!

Sharon shakes her head. "Told you. Enough to keep us up all week. That's how much shit is on those tables."

This seems like an odd thing to say, but then again, this is Sharon, the party girl, so you come to expect odd things. Yes, odd things and free sex. Party girls are great.

"Ahaaahaaa," Stoner laughs as he watches the couple carve up a couple more lines. "Crazy shit. What do you think of my new do?"

Stoner has shaved his head.

Stoner's dressing room would contain a pipe, video tapes of *All in the Family*, and a five-gallon bucket of herb.

"It's cool," I say. "Dude, you are really tan. You almost look like—"

"Ahaaahaaaha, I know. I went to a tanning salon after I got it shaved this morning. Someone told me I look like Damon Wayans."

Michael Stone approaches. "There's my star witness." He pats Stoner on the shoulder. "What's with the shaved head? You look like—"

"Yeah," we all say.

A bartender comes over and Michael Stone orders a Captain Morgan and Coke. The waiter explains that they are all out of Captain, but they will substitute with their house rum. "It's simply the best," the bartender assures Michael Stone. Stone stares down the bartender for a minute, then looks back at us and tells us we're going to another bar around the corner named the Bitter End.

Walking out of the bar, Sharon asks me to smell her neck. I shrug, thinking I misunderstood her. "Smell me. It's a new cologne. Chip and I are going to start marketing it."

I take a whiff, but the odor of the bar and smokers out front paralyze my senses for a moment.

"I can't tell. Right now you smell like a bar."

"That's it!" Sharon continues. "It's called SMOKE, the scent of adventure! What do you think?"

I smell her neck again, shrug my shoulders, and walk over to the Bitter End.

Inside, there are no glass tables. There are wooden chairs placed around a few picnic tables. A couple guys with leather jackets with stained white T-shirts underneath stand by the jukebox looking for songs, but never actually playing anything. Sharon looks around and then proclaims, "Now this—this is a heroin bar."

She points out the leather straps hanging over the bar and how those are used by patrons to shoot up when they want, although according to Sharon they never do this at the bar but behind a partition near the pool tables. I look over and see at least three sets of Converse All Stars underneath. "Looks pretty busy right now," I say. Sharon just looks at me and nods.

I think I'm starting to understand.

Sharon's dressing room would contain the latest *National Enquirer*, a pair of tall leather boots, and a five-gallon bucket of KY Jelly.

While Michael Stone explains the next steps to Stoner and what the process of the trial will entail, Sharon informs me that Mary is still interested in seeing me. "At least she'll go out on a date, maybe a dinner thing with you."

I find this hard to believe, given the fact that each time Mary and I have gotten close, something bad like a person busting through the door of a party and people being murdered in front of us happens. Bad things. Other than that, we appear to be perfect for each other. She is a ten! Anyway, I get Mary's number from Sharon and tell her I'll call her tonight. I have no plans to call her. It will just be easier this way. The more I think about it, the more I'm convinced it would be a bad idea to call Mary. No one wants to hear that lately you've been spending your time in a police station because you may or may not be an accomplice to raping and murdering a fifteen-year-old girl, and oh yeah, it's a Congressman's daughter. Now where would you like to have dinner?

# 6

*The conference room is dark. I bump myself on three chairs as I move to my seat. Somehow I know this is my seat, even though no one else is here, just empty chairs neatly placed around the table. The projector towards the back is showing a PowerPoint presentation, which provides the only light. The first slide shows a badge from the LAPD, only a badge. The host of this meeting is holding a laser pointer and points to the center of the badge. No words are spoken. The slide stays on the badge for several minutes. I want to look back and see who is conducting the meeting, but a strong feeling, a presence in the room, is strongly suggesting I do not. The next slide is a picture of my boss. Again, no words are spoken, and the red dot from the laser pointer rests on my boss's forehead. My boss appears to have just said something incredibly witty in his mind because his right eyebrow is pointed up. This is a very common expression for him, one that can usually be seen six to seven hundred times a day. The projector is moved slightly to focus better. While it is being moved, I get a glimpse of the host. It is*

*God. Only God and I are in this meeting. The next slide says the word DREAMS, followed by a slide that is blank. The presentation is reversed, to DREAMS and then back to a blank page. I really want to look back and see God, but the other presence in the room is not allowing this. It's possible that the presentation has another slide with the word REVENGE, but I'm not sure because all I hear is laughter and then the projector is shut off. This is when I wake up in a cold sweat.*

It's midnight and I'm unable to get back to sleep. I've never been one for dream interpretation, but it was pretty clear to me that my dream had something to do with either not reaching my potential, reaching the goals I REALLY wanted, the fact that I see God only in a dim light within my world, or possibly that I've been spending way too much time in meetings with mindless PowerPoint presentations and laser pointers.

*Don Capiano was cooking for his wife, who was supposed to be home within the hour. He was tossing a garden salad with a light dressing. There was fresh bread from the Italian market (Gino's) down the street, fruit from the stand around the corner, lamb chops in the oven, and a light pasta cooking on the range. The oven exploded, sending a lamb chop into the air, hitting Don square in the temple. An instant death.*

This is a story about living.

I call Mary and we reminisce about the last time we saw each other, talk about where the best pot is coming from these days (we both agree Houston seems to have the best distribution at the moment), and then arrange to meet for dinner the next day (actually the same day, but she doesn't correct me). Since I'm staying at a motel tonight (nowhere else to go), I decide to order food, but realize my phone isn't working so I go across the street to a full service deli hidden behind a gas station. I can

hear laughter and the sound of poker chips hitting a table from the back room. I buy a Butterfinger, a turkey sandwich, and a bottle of vodka.

Back in the room I watch *Law and Order: Criminal Intent* followed by *Law and Order: Special Victims Unit.* I switch channels and watch Ben Affleck, who is on David Letterman, but I can't watch for very long because I just don't find Ben Affleck very amusing. On HBO is a movie about a distrustful female police officer with a drinking problem tracking down a serial killer, but the TV goes out. I'm still staring at the television (even though it's blank) when I take the last gulp of vodka. After this, I fall into a deep sleep.

I wake up to the sound of an ambulance because the guy in the room next to me apparently killed himself last night by stabbing himself over and over with a steak knife that he bought from Sears. I open my door and see a lot of people standing around and then an officer asks me if I heard the screaming last night. He pokes his head into my room, sees the empty vodka bottle next to the bed, and shakes his head in disgust. A guy wearing a nondescript red button-down shirt tucked into jeans and white sneakers (the nineties Jerry Seinfeld look) approaches me and tells me that he doesn't think it was suicide, but that he was murdered by a random person who preys on motels like the one we're at. "He was one of those heavy sleepers," he says, emphasizing the word "heavy." I consider packing up my shit and checking out, but then I remember what this guy is wearing and just assume he is full of shit. If anything, he probably killed the guy. I make a mental note to not drink a full bottle of vodka before falling asleep.

I'm supposed to meet Chip at an amusement park called Tony and Tina's Go-Kart World, but he cancels because he has to meet with Michael Stone and review

his case. I mention I should be there since I will probably have to take the stand, but he tells me that Stone only wants to talk to him. Bored, with nothing to do, I take a couple laps around the go-kart tracks, knocking a few tykes off the side, then eat two hotdogs with a guy named Andrew who really likes sauerkraut. We talk about the difference between Republicans and Democrats and come to the conclusion that there really isn't much so we look for beers, but alcohol is not allowed at the park so we say our goodbyes and leave.

I call Stoner, who invites me out to get a tattoo. This doesn't sound appealing to me at the moment, so I lie and tell him I'll be there shortly because it's just easier that way. Back at the motel I can hear someone named Red getting fucked by a prostitute in the room above me. I watch the ceiling because there's one area that the bed is pushing down and it looks like the whole room may collapse. This would be a very bad way to go.

*Man checked into motel, sitting on his bed after a full day of go-karts and hotdogs, is crushed by a prostitute and a man named Red who likes to call his women whores while having sex.*

The rest of the afternoon is spent staring across the street at the deli with a poker game in the back and looking up at the ceiling, all while listening to some guy get his rocks off in a motel on a Wednesday afternoon.

Outside of the restaurant it's a little chilly and I'm only wearing a light sweater because I overheard the weather on a television in the motel lobby and it is supposed to be a cool, yet mild night. Weathermen are as useful as black highlighters. I light a Marlboro Light and begin humming the tune to Bugs Bunny for some reason and a guy wearing a warm looking Raiders jacket approaches me and mumbles something about "God's snow."

"Snow?" I say. "No, it's not quite that cold out."

"No, man, not that kind of snow. What the fuck, man?" He looks around. "Do you want to buy some of God's snow, you know, angel dust?"

I now understand that I'm either being asked to buy drugs from a dealer or a cop, so I just shrug him away. He won't leave.

"Fucking PCP man, how much do you want?"

I have to put my hand on his shoulder and push him away. It's now obvious to me that this is not even a drug dealer, but a homeless man with a pocket full of flour trying to make a quick buck. We begin to tangle when I see Mary about a hundred feet away. I quickly whip out a twenty-dollar bill and tell him to take it. He proceeds to give me a small bag of flour, but I tell him to just leave and push him away. He leaves, just as Mary approaches. About five feet away, he asks someone else if they want to buy "God's snow."

Mary is wearing a red dress with white stars. She reeks of good herb when she walks up to Harry's Steakhouse. I decided it would be best to meet outside and go in. Mary has a fear of finding people in crowded places and I have a problem with drinking too much before dates begin.

I order a pint of Stella, Mary a glass of Chardonnay. My Stella arrives approximately two minutes before the wine, so I've already got half of my beer consumed when the waiter returns. Mary is distracted by the menu so I order another beer.

We both order chicken but then I decide on the steak and then I get Mary caught up on the trial and inform her of our ironclad alibi. I can see the concern around our star witness being referred to as "Stoner" by me, but she seems content with the explanation when I tell her it's my longtime pal Johnny.

I go to the restroom and there's an attendant so after I take a piss I dig for a dollar but I only have twenties so I just walk by him without washing my hands. I get a couple of strange looks but I figure there would have been more strange looks had I used the restaurant's precious towel and water supply.

Mary is on the phone when I get back to the table. When finished, she tells me that was her aunt and that she went skydiving today. I mention that I did that once, but then the acid wore off. She shakes her head and laughs because she thinks I'm joking.

"Some people just have so much more energy, it seems," Mary says. "Do you know what I mean?"

"I guess." Even though I don't.

"I've got a younger brother. You wouldn't believe what he's doing." Mary sees our food coming from the kitchen and feels it's necessary to point (it's important to note that the kitchen is over two hundred feet away). "I mean, he's studying to be a pyrotechnician."

"Oh, you mean those guys who do the explosions on stages at rock concerts? That's cool."

"No, that's so eighties." Mary laughs. "It's all about game show productions now."

"Really?"

"Oh yeah, have you seen these prime time shows today? They are in gigantic theatres, with state of the art acoustics. Next will be explosions for the viewers' pleasure."

"Crazy," I say.

"They are the new rock stars."

"Regis and Howie Mandel are the new rock stars?"

"Yes they are. Are you ready?"

"I don't think I'll ever be ready for that."

Dinner arrives (I finally decided on a New York strip, Mary, the roasted chicken) and Mary asks, “So where are you staying?”

“I’ve been staying at Stoner’s for most of the week, and of course New Year’s was spent at Sharon’s, uh, place.”

“Yeah, what’s going on at Sharon’s place, anyway?”

“I’ve stopped asking her questions. Anyway, Stoner is preparing for the trial. I believe he’s having dinner with Michael Stone tonight, so I’m staying at a motel.”

Sensing an uncomfortable moment, I quickly order another beer. “Tonight I’m going to stay in a motel.” There, I said it.

“Creepy,” she says.

Mary’s dressing room would contain a freezer of steaks, a hemp sweater, and a picture of Tom Petty.

“A little bit, yeah, it can be. I really don’t care for when cars pull in around 3 a.m. Always with their bright lights on, lighting up the motel room.”

“God, that would be the least of my concerns. What about the conversations? I mean, usually the parking is right out front of the rooms and you can hear whatever anyone is saying in the early morning. I hate that.”

“I guess.” I finish my beer and wave the glass at the waiter. Mary still has half her original glass of wine left. This is never going to work.

Mary quickly drinks the rest of her wine and then waves her glass as well.

Is this love?

“Ugh, the whole motel scene is like a serial killer buffet.” Mary giggles.

“Oh well, I’ll be fine.” Our drinks arrive and we both take big drinks and then Mary asks if I want to go dancing, which of course I don’t, but of course I tell her that

is a great idea and we agree that Agave, a new club close by, will be our destination.

On our way to Agave Mary has to use the restroom so we stop at a bar called Texas Heroes. When Mary is gone I duck out and smoke a Marlboro Light and then come back in and order two gin and tonics. Mary returns and smiles when she sips her drink. A country song by I think Clint Black starts playing.

"Soundtrack for cutters," I say.

"Cutters?"

I spill some of my drink because I take too large of a sip. "You know, cutters. People who cut themselves out of depression, a need for attention."

"Oh."

"There's really two types. First you have your normal cutters that carve things like initials and such onto their arms. Sometimes other body parts, but they really do like arms."

"Jeremy, I really don't—"

I ignore Mary, take a drink, and continue. "Then you have your body choppers. These are ones who start off as cutters, usually when they are young, but then eventually graduate into body choppers as adults. Oftentimes they find their victims—"

"Enough." Mary puts her hand over my mouth. "I don't want to hear about any more of this. Why do you even know all of this?"

I don't answer. Instead I take a drink and it's at this time I remember that GIN + ANYTHING = FIGHT. I grab Mary's drink from her (saying I think the gin is bad) and quickly order a Stella and a glass of Chardonnay. We sip our drinks and everything returns back to normal. After a couple of minutes I finish my beer and Mary motions to the bartender to get me another, even though she has barely touched her wine. This is love.

At Agave, we dance to the latest Usher song. Mary is unbelievable. After Usher, a Black Eyed Peas song plays, and then after this we go to a back room where everyone is openly smoking herb and talking about the morning's issue of *Variety*, which had an article about Eddie Murphy and how he is planning a big comeback.

Back on the dance floor the DJ begins playing reggae music and both Mary and I agree that this type of music is useless unless on a beach or scoring a bag of herb. On our way out we stop at the bar and have shots of Kamikazes, then Mary asks me if I want to spend the night at her place.

I'm a little shocked when we get to Mary's and I see all of the statues of dead presidents and how she has put fake mustaches on all of them.

She disappears for a minute to return only wearing a black towel. For a moment she looks like Batwoman, which is strange though because it's just a black towel wrapped around her. Considering my zero saves, no one has ever mistaken me for Batman.

Mary removes the towel and then slowly undresses me, starting with my shirt, then working down to my pants and boxers. She asks if I've ever had sex in a kitchen and I tell her no but this is probably a lie. I'm sure I have but was too drunk or high to remember.

On the kitchen counter, Mary is on top of me when we both climax. She screams, "Hallelujah!" I immediately make a mental note that I need to talk to a psychiatrist when I get back to New York.

# 7

It's noon the next day when I meet Chip at the Hard Rock Café. We both have severe hangover issues, so we order cheeseburgers and Bloody Marys. "Time to kick into overdrive," he says.

I have no idea what that means, but I'm assuming I'm going to be drunk before noon again.

"I just wish I could remember more." Chip is fidgeting with the pickle in his drink. "I mean, what the hell did we do? I don't remember shit."

"I know, I don't either. Thank God Stoner and Earl can place us between Vegas and L.A., otherwise we'd be fucked."

"Totally fucked." Chip takes a bite of his pickle. "Look over there. I'm totally getting eye fucked by that cougar." Our waitress behind us hears Chip.

"She was asking about you. Do you want me to give her your number?"

"No thanks. Got enough problems at the moment. She is a hot cougar, though."

Cougars are women in the 35-45 range who go to bars looking to hook up with men. They are typically jaded, overdone from a makeup perspective, and a cheap drunk. Vodka is their drink of choice. Panthers are women 25-35, out of college and not only looking to get laid, but also looking for the eventual Mr. Right. Cougars eventually graduate to Wolverines, which are women older than 45, more pathetic, and will drink anything you put in front of them.

"Probably smart." I motion over toward the cougar. "Staying away from her and all."

"No fuck, I really have enough on my plate right now."

"When is Stoner coming?"

"Soon." I order another round of Bloody Marys.

I call my office voicemail. Four messages from Jim in Sales asking about an accounts receivable report he needs to show customers so that they can see that our customers are paying us. I couldn't make this up if I tried. I call Jim, but he's on the phone so I get to hear one of the top three on-hold songs. Today I get "Hello Dolly". If I hang on long enough, I'll be lucky enough to hear "Hit the Road, Jack" and "Smooth Operator". Eventually Jim answers (two-thirds of the way through Louis Armstrong) and tells me that he already got it from Brad. It doesn't sound like they miss me much back at the office.

Chip is staring back at the cougar. "I hope Stoner shows up soon, because I'm starting to get a little uncomfortable. I've never picked up a girl at a Hard Rock Café before." Chip takes a drink of his Bloody. "He'd better not be getting another fucking tattoo."

"That would be strange. I guess you'd have rock music in common, you know, the cougar and you." I disgust myself with this comment but for whatever reason

continue to try to make a joke out of it. "Hey, you could always take her to the Rock and Roll Hall of Fame."

"Never," says Chip. "That hall of fame is just like a Hard Rock, but without the cheeseburgers. Not to mention it's in Cleveland." Chip slams his drink and looks at me. "Never."

The new Justin Timberlake song comes on; Chip and I look at each other in disgust. We both may throw up in our mouths at the same time. It's hard to say and a little uncomfortable to ask.

*There really isn't any cool music today. Miles Davis was cool, Coltrane, very cool, and then I guess there's The Strokes. That's pretty much all there is for cool music.*

Still no word from Stoner, so we go to a record store and make fun of the guy behind the counter with a choppy goatee and sunglasses because he doesn't have any Bob Dylan records. He tells us he does have the new CD for The Fray, but no Dylan. The guy explains to us the growth of Bob Dylan and how he went through an electric phase, but no one really accepted it so he went back to acoustic. We both laugh at him and tell him he should really just close his store. He agrees. We leave.

Inside a hotel bar named Ambitions we drink three rounds of Captain and Cokes, play two games of Cricket, and then go outside to smoke a cigarette. Outside, a guy with battered Air Jordan shoes is picking a fight with a guy wearing what appear to be incredibly expensive moccasins. They are mostly yelling and threatening each other even though it looks like neither one of them is going to throw a punch. In fact, it looks as though neither one has ever thrown a punch.

"Shit is different here, way different." Chip takes a long drag. "These motherfuckers all grew up with pools."

I smoke and nod.

"No one who grew up with a pool ever wants to fight."

We go back inside and order one more round of drinks. I suspect my drink isn't correct, so I have the bartender taste it. I was right; it wasn't a Captain and Coke but rather a Jack and Coke. Chip and I are unable to comprehend this and the bartender clearly doesn't understand the magnitude of the mistake he just made. We decide we will never go to Ambitions ever again.

Hungry again, we go to a deli with cafeteria-style seating. We each get a slice of pizza and grab a seat at a table where a man wearing a Philadelphia Eagles jacket is sitting and eating what appears to be a turkey club (possibly without mayonnaise). He nods at us and then tells us that he's in California for vacation. "Two weeks in the sun, having fun," he tells us for some reason then heads to the restroom.

A woman with giant red sunglasses, holding a large pizza, walks by and trips on my chair, falling forward, the pizza in the air, her head going to land on the floor. I'm paralyzed, watching. It's Chip who amazingly reaches out and catches her head before the impact. With the other hand he catches the pizza as if his last name is Torentini.

Another save for Chip. Another failed opportunity for me.

A couple minutes later the man in the green jacket returns and stands next to the table we are sitting at. Chip looks up at him.

"Can I help you?"

"Where's my tray?"

"Your what?" Chip looks over at me, confused.

"My tray. My sandwich." Pause. "My motherfucking sandwich. Where did it go?"

"Oh, that guy must have taken it." I point to a man in white who is collecting trays from the tables.

The tourist doesn't look. His eyes stay locked on mine. "Why didn't you tell him I wasn't finished?"

"Uh... I didn't know."

"How could you not know? There was a square of my sandwich left. A fucking quarter of my turkey club sandwich was still there."

"Sorry, I didn't know."

Chip stands up next to the man. "We didn't know. It wasn't our fault." Chip looks over at me. "We're sorry about your sandwich."

"Great. Sorry really helps." And then the man leaves.

Chip's phone is buzzing. "I don't recognize the number. Maybe it's Stoner."

I look across the tables and see an Asian family of four all eating pasta. The mother and two daughters leave to go to the restroom.

"Fuck! Fuck!" Chip screams to his phone, then slams it down on the table. He puts his head in his hands.

As the Asian man (the father) continues to eat, the man in white comes over and grabs the half-eaten plates of pasta and takes them away. The Asian man is too involved in his own meal to notice. I look over at Chip.

"What?"

"Stoner, fucking Stoner."

"Where is he?"

"No, it's not that."

"What, then?"

"He's dead."

# 8

***THREE-STAR HANGOVER:***

*In the morning you are a snooze button addict. The sole purpose of hitting the button has nothing to do with waking up every nine minutes, but rather to rise out of bed and throw up. Your day begins with four cups of coffee, two sausage rolls, and a liter of Coke. You then go back to bed. Work before noon is out of the question. Eventually you wake up, still a little buzzed, but not enough to matter. Coherent enough to feel the three packs of cigarettes still resonating in your lungs as you try to breathe.*

*Work is considered then blown off as soon as you reach the couch. Your day is now court dramas and talk shows. It's times like this when food delivery is the most important service in the world. Chinese, Mexican, or Italian, it doesn't matter because it all sounds amazing. As long as it comes with another liter of Coke.*

*Drinking a flight of wine sounds harmless: three or four glasses, about two ounces in each. Drinking ten flights is potentially painful. I meet a girl named Dana*

*who sets up a double date with one of her friends from work and a guy she's seeing (Kenny and Samantha). Innocent enough. We meet at the Grapevine, a place known for its expensive wine, and, of course, their flights. I start off with the flight of California Reds and before I know it we have sixteen glasses and seven bottles (most empty) in front of us. Kenny is the type of person who likes to put his hand on my arm when he talks, which keeps me on edge regardless of the amount of wine, and Samantha is very secretive, only talking so that one person can hear her. This couple is a social nightmare. Later in the evening after a flight called "Good Times" I stumble, walking from the bathroom. Instead of taking this as a sign that I've had enough to drink (I have friends who at that moment would go straight home; I've never understood this) I immediately order another flight of "Good Times". Kenny and Samantha are giggling and then Samantha whispers something into Dana's ear that makes her blush. Kenny slides over and asks me if Dana and I would like to go over to his place for a nightcap. "We can all have a nice glass of red and then turn in." Kenny says this with his hand on my arm.*

*Plush black carpeting, a fireplace, and a Jacuzzi greet us as we walk into Kenny's apartment. Kenny would be a true player if this was 1975. Instead, now he's just sad. The smell of incense is in the air. Kenny and Samantha disappear. When they come back, she is wearing a bikini and he is wearing a Speedo. "We've got other suits, if you're interested," says Kenny as he grabs and opens a bottle of red wine. Dana looks over at me and I shrug my shoulders, then spot a bottle of Jack Daniels on the kitchen counter. I grab the bottle and take three consecutive swigs and then hand the bottle to Dana, who holds it, looks at Kenny in his Speedo, then looks back at me with a look of disgust. She leaves me standing there, bot-*

*tle of Jack in hand, Kenny and Samantha eyeballing me. Let's just say I finished the Jack and leave it at that. It was at that moment I decided to never date anyone named Dana.*

*Back on the couch, the court dramas are over and you fall asleep around 5 p.m. because there's nothing more to watch on television, wake up around 9, stay up for a couple hours then go back to sleep. The reality is that the three star hangover is the most depressing. A good night had, but it costs you an extra night. As you try to doze off around midnight, you consider having a beer to help you go to sleep. On the plus side, if you're ever having one of those weeks where it feels like a Thursday but is actually Wednesday, have yourself a three-star night and the next time you'll be coherent is Friday. Sure beats having to work an extra day, even if it's only in your head.*

Chip's trial starts tomorrow and we have no idea what happened to Stoner so we go see Earl, who is now Chip's only alibi, at a lounge he frequents called the Cave.

The Cave is not your typical lounge. It's more of a dive bar located right outside Compton. In front of the establishment old men sit in lawn chairs and complain about the Dodgers, global warming, and the LAPD, not necessarily in that order. They throw pennies at white people as they walk by. These men have never had a dream.

Inside, Earl is waiting at a table with a lamp on it. Next to him is another black man, and next to him is Michael Stone. Chip and I pull up chairs.

"Let me introduce you fellas to Detroit," says Earl, looking over at the man next to him.

I extend my hand. "Are you from Detroit?"

"No man, I'm from Long Beach. They call me Detroit because I lean to the side when I drive.

"He's cool like that," says Earl. "Now what the fuck happened to Stoner? I just fucking talked to him yesterday morning."

"I don't know," Chip mumbles. He looks over at Michael Stone. "Do you know anything?"

Stone calls a waiter over and then makes her wait once she gets to the table. He looks long at Chip. "He was your main witness. Now..." He looks over at Earl. "Now we may need to put—"

"No fucking way. I've got warrants out for my black ass."

"He was our friend," says Chip.

We order drinks. Chip looks unsure, so Earl orders a drink called the Turkey Special. It consists of Wild Turkey whiskey. The ice cubes are made from Heineken.

Earl looks over at Chip and lights a Newport. "Don't worry, man. I'll testify if I have to. No big deal." Earl looks around. "It's cool, you can smoke in here. No one is going to say anything."

Chip and I immediately grab our cigarettes. Detroit lights a Backwoods cigar.

"Damn, that stinks," says Earl as our drinks arrive.

Chip can barely lift the drink to his mouth, he is shaking so much. He takes a big drink. "I didn't do it. They have to know I didn't do it."

"I know," Michael Stone says calmly. "Let's just see how the trial goes. It's possible they don't even have any hard evidence."

"Really?" I ask.

"No, but you never know." Michael Stone takes a drink of his Bass, then pulls out a pack of Merit 100s and lights one up. "Usually the D.A. has a solid case in these matters, but you never know." Stone takes a puff

from his Merit. "And she was fifteen and a Congressman's daughter."

A song by Elton John begins playing in the background. Detroit grunts and says, "Now here's a white boy who could sing. You whites never recognize good music. Like The Fray. Everyone thinks they're cool if they listen to The Fray." Detroit takes a drag off of his cigar. "The Fray can kiss my black ass."

Earl nods and points at me. "Music and hats. Your people have no clue."

"Hats?"

"Yeah, visors. What the fuck? White people always wearing them visors, look like you always coming from a tennis match."

Chip drinks down the Turkey Special and says, "I've seen lots of black guys wear visors, except they usually wear it tilted, off to the side."

"True. That shit's true." Earl lights another Newport. "But we stopped doing that shit back in 2002." Earl looks over at Detroit. "2002?"

"Yeah," says Detroit. "2002... That was a bad motherfucking year."

Michael Stone clears his throat. "Enough. Now Jeremy, do you remember anything from that night?"

I look over at Chip, then back over at Michael Stone. "I don't remember a thing."

"Well, let's just see how it goes. I'm not crazy about putting Earl or your friend Sharon on the stand." Michael Stone takes a deep breath. "No offense, but they don't really scream 'credible witnesses'."

"I can't testify," says Earl. "I'll be in the courtroom, but no motherfucker's gonna know my name."

Chip puts his hand through his hair. "Well, then what's the plan?"

Michael Stone leans forward. “We'll see, but you're probably going to have to take the stand.”

Chip orders another Turkey Special.

# 9

Inside the courtroom, there's a heavy feeling (not heavy as in smoking pot, or heavy like SMOKE, the scent of adventure, but more of a heavy something amazing is going to happen type mood). Courtrooms attract strange people. The normal people are here: lawyers, witnesses, family of the victim, and court personnel. There's also another group here: the family wearing straw hats, Earl, and Mark-Paul Gosselaar, who to the average American means nothing, but being a scholar of reality television I know he is the actor who played Zack Morris on *Saved by the Bell.* The bailiff stands tall, but is acting like he has Tourette's because he keeps yelling out, "Hot damn!" Strange feelings throughout the courtroom today. Heavy.

I sit near the back behind Earl and look over at Chip at the defense table. He looks back my way with a grin that is either stress or the aftereffects of the joint we smoked thirty minutes ago. Probably the herb; it was that good. It was really sticky in the bag. Even now, sit-

ting here in the courtroom, my fingers are still a little sticky from the herb.

The D.A. announces himself (all I know is his name is Italian, maybe Tony) and begins his opening statement, beginning with the dead Congressman's daughter and how she was only fifteen and oh yeah, she had sex prior to her murder. There is a pause as he explains that there is no such thing as consensual sex with a fifteen-year-old and that this is considered rape. The D.A. traces back through the incidents of the night leading up to the end. I'm reminded of Chip's movie pitch to Nic Cage: "It's like a Tarantino movie. The ending's in the beginning, the beginning is in the middle, and Quentin makes a cameo." Today it appears Zack is filling in for Quentin. Mark-Paul catches me staring and looks over. I grimace, wondering what in the hell he's doing here. The D.A. ends his opening argument, saying, "Rape! Embarrassment! Murder!" three times as he stands in front of the jurors.

The jurors are also an interesting group. Three of them are middle aged women, all with glasses and second chins. Two of the men look like police officers because of their mustaches. Six women with stripper-like smiles, all checking each other out. It's hard to say whether it's out of jealousy or if they are turned on by each other. I bet they are turned on. The last juror looks a lot like Dustin Diamond, the guy who played Screech on *Saved by the Bell.*

Michael Stone gives his statement, which consists mostly of "what if" questions to the jury that I find hard to follow. His statement ends with, "Who knows, maybe it was me. Do we really know?" It's at this point I realize Chip is in big trouble.

Chip looks back at me and yells, "What the fuck!"

The judge scolds Chip and the courtroom erupts in laughter. The start of the trial has a very sitcom feel to it. *Law and Order* (judge, lawyers, and law enforcement) meets *Hee Haw* (family with straw hats) meets *In Living Color* (Earl and Detroit). There is also an unnatural number of people wearing "Property of..." T-shirts in the courtroom. Seems suspicious, but I guess that's the point of the justice system, to be suspicious of all. I realize that Detroit doesn't only lean when he drives, he also leans in the court of law. Right now Detroit is leaning a little to the right.

The morning consists of the District Attorney questioning the detectives responsible for the case. They have an eye witness that pulled Chip out of a lineup and fingerprints in the room where the murder occurred. The words "molested", "raped", and "murdered" continue to be said. Each time one of these words is uttered, the D.A. looks over at the jury and nods. Despite the D.A.'s case depending on a lot of hearsay, Michael Stone isn't objecting. Only at the end when the police officer is asked if Chip should be given the death penalty for what crimes he is accused of does Stone jump up and object, although I'm pretty sure he was only objecting because he thought the police officer was pointing at him, not Chip. When asked whether he wants to cross-examine the officer, Stone declines, leading Chip to shout, "What the fuck!" again, which again leads to a courtroom of laughter. Even the judge appears to be chuckling. Chip follows this up with a request for a recess so he can go smoke. The judge frowns but grants the court a ten-minute recess. Outside, Michael Stone tells Chip not to worry, he's got a plan. When Chip asks him what the plan is, Stone laughs and tells him he wouldn't understand.

I meet Mary for lunch and we have buffalo chicken wraps and I explain how awful things are going and tell her that I'm going to have Michael Stone put me on the stand. "It can't hurt, can it?"

Mary agrees and then adds, "Well, maybe it can hurt. It's not like you remember anything—or do you?"

"Maybe I do remember, just maybe I do."

I'm not sure if this is Michael Stone's great plan, but he puts Sharon Winkler on the stand. She swears that she's "pretty sure" we did not show up until after the murder happened. It's when Michael Stone emphasizes that Sharon is "pretty sure" to the jury that I really know Chip is in big trouble.

The transcript from the prosecutor's cross-examination of Sharon Winkler:

D.A.: How many people live at your house?

Sharon: It depends. Anywhere from five to twelve. I have a lot of friends.

D.A.: Friends? Hmmm. That's an interesting way to put it.

Sharon: Yeah, well—

D.A.: Never mind that. Miss Winkler, I have one more question. When you answer, please remember that you swore to tell the truth and can be imprisoned for up to twenty years for perjury.

Sharon: Uh, yes.

D.A.: Do you run a brothel?

Sharon: Excuse me?

D.A.: A whorehouse, a dude ranch, a place, Miss Winkler, where men come and spend money to sleep with women?

Pause.

Sharon: Yes.

Chip looks back at me and we both nod. This explains a lot. This also may very well mean Chip is going to prison for a very long time.

## 10

*The PowerPoint presentation tonight begins with a picture of Stoner with the caption NOT LIVING, followed by a picture of someone I don't recognize with the caption LIVING (It may or may not be me; I tend not to look at myself very closely. It could have been Screech, for all I know). The next slide says the word REVENGE. I look over at God, who is laughing as if someone behind him is cracking a joke, but when I look back I don't see anyone behind him. He clicks on his keyboard and the next slide is projected. It's Mary, a picture of her in the red dress. The room is filled with the Whitesnake song "Is This Love" and God laughs while pointing at Mary with his laser pointer. I can hear footsteps behind me as if someone is dancing and there's a faint smell of SMOKE (the scent of adventure), and then finally a tap on my back. I turn around, but again, no one is there. This is followed by another slide with the caption REVENGE.*

Once you've had a brain tumor, everything else is supposed to be easier. This is not the case today. We're

at a cemetery outside of Anaheim watching Stoner be laid to rest. In my head I can still hear him laughing.

Funerals are a time to look back, but also look forward. So they say, "they" being mostly psychiatrists, I think. Unfortunately there's too much going on with Chip for me to allow myself to grieve. During the memorial the night before, the casket was closed, but there was a basket placed next to the casket, allowing family and friends to drop in pictures and other items to be buried with Stoner. As the casket is lowered, I see the basket. It is filled with pipes and bags of herb. I think the priest is allergic to herb because every time he gets close to the basket he begins sneezing. A tear rushes down Chip's cheek. Stoner's family is in shambles, barely able to keep it together. Chip leans over to me. "Why him? It's just not fair. Everyone liked Johnny. He was *Stoner*, man."

I look over and see Stoner's fiancée. She looks—I don't know the expression—I guess broken. Lost. Out of all of the people, the crooked, the ill, the wicked, Stoner is gone. I think back to the night before. Revenge.

"We need to find out who did this," Chip says out loud, even though I think he meant to keep it inside.

We don't even need to know why. At this point it really doesn't matter. This just isn't right. It wasn't supposed to go down like this, not with Stoner. Not Stoner.

"No one enjoyed life more," says Chip.

"Yeah," is all I can say. I'm now having difficulty keeping it together.

*Sanjay Cooper was driving his sporty new boat on the Hudson River when a duck flew at him and hit him in the head, knocking him unconscious, sending the boat exploding into an oil tanker.*

Some of Stoner's family are going to the bar. They invite us along, so we go with them to a place called the

Dragon, a place owned by an Asian woman I've heard is known to deal heroin as long as you're Asian.

Chip and I order Alabama Slammers, Stoner's favorite drink. We don't allow the glasses to touch the bar before we're ordering another round.

Stoner's sister Sheri orders two sides of French fries and sticks them into her mouth one after another.

"Look at her," Chip says. "It's just disgusting how some people give in to despair."

We both guzzle down our drinks and order another round.

"I want to take the stand," I say.

"Dude, I can't let you do that. Who knows?"

"Who knows what?" I ask.

"Maybe they'll end up trying to pin some of this shit on you. It's not like you know what happened."

"Maybe." I call the bartender over and get another round. "Maybe I do know what happened."

Chip motions with his head across the bar. "See that girl over there? She's a stripper from Legs, down the street. She's the main act."

"No shit?"

"Yeah, I can tell because of the mole right below her neck. When she was giving me a lap dance, it was pressed against my eye. Look, I think she notices me."

"I don't know, man. I can't tell if she's smiling or sulking."

"No shit. Strippers only know how to smile or look sultry, almost depressed. At least the good ones are like that." Chip looks outside because he wants to have a cigarette. "Let's go smoke."

Outside, Chip lights a Marlboro.

"Dude, you can't take the stand and lie. You'll get nailed for perjury. We gave statements, and you're not that good of a liar."

I light a Marlboro Light. "It's not up to you anymore, Chip. I'm going to do whatever the fuck I want to do. It's my choice."

"Remember that time I had you call in sick to work for me?" Chip laughs. "You're just not a good liar, man."

"Just let me do whatever I want."

"Fuck it, dude. Whatever."

"That's right, whatever. It's my fucking life."

This is a story about living.

I decide to go see Earl and see what I can do to get him to testify for Chip. He explains that most of his warrants are for skipping assault trials, so if he comes forward he's going away for at least a few years. "I still think I'll do it, you know, take the motherfucking stand and all, but I've just got to wait and see." Earl scratches his head. "If I do this, it's for Stoner. I wouldn't go away for people I don't know very well, but Stoner, that was one cool cat."

"Yeah, he was..."

"Hey man, you want to take a ride with me? Got to go pick up my laundry."

Knowing there is a very good chance he isn't picking up his laundry, I go anyway to try to convince him that he really doesn't have a choice and must take the stand. Whether he does it for Chip or for Stoner, I really don't care. All that I know at this moment is that I'm riding shotgun in Earl's Cadillac, going to pick up his laundry.

We drive to someplace near Long Beach where, as I suspected, Earl is picking up herb. I'm not sure exactly how much he is planning to pick up, but the empty duffle bag he carries into the ranch-style house is one of the largest bags I've ever seen.

Inside, there are four men, two with unkempt afros and the other two wearing dark glasses and chains like Easy E used to wear before he died from AIDS. They are all drinking cans of Budweiser. One of the guys wearing sunglasses is playing with a yo-yo, doing tricks and calling them out.

"WALK THE DOG!"

Earl taps me on the shoulder and tells me to hang tight. He leaves with one of the afro men to a room in the back. The second afro man nods at me and asks, "How you know Earl?"

"Friend of a friend," I say.

"Which friend?"

"Stoner."

"Ah man, I heard." Afro man pulls out a miniature cigar and lights it with a Zippo lighter that has the Playboy emblem on it. "He was over here once with Earl, very cool. Sorry to hear of his demise."

"AROUND THE WORLD!"

"You want to smoke some?" the guy in sunglasses and gold chain not playing with a yo-yo asks.

"Sure."

He goes to a closet behind the couch and pulls out a four-foot-high bong, and then grabs a bag from a trap door located in front of the TV.

"Killer shit," I'm assured as the mega-bong is loaded.

I take the first hit and almost fall on my ass. "This is killer shit." I smile.

"JUMPING ROPE!"

"It's from Houston," the guy with the afro tells me. "All of the good shit is coming from Houston these days."

"Why is that?" I ask.

"Don't ask that question. Never question where the killer shit is coming from."

Earl comes back. His duffle bag is full. We hang out for a few more minutes. When we leave, the guy who went back with Earl comes up to me and says, "Sorry about your friend Stoner. God bless." Then he proceeds to pull out a nine-millimeter gun and point it at my face and say, "I'm gonna shoot you." Everyone laughs.

"ROCKET TO THE MOON!"

The ride back is very enjoyable because the Cadillac is filled with the sweet scent of good herb.

"Fucking Houston," says Earl. "Damn, they know what they're doing."

At Earl's request, I test out some of the new herb and assure him it's the killer shit he's expecting. Back in L.A., Earl mentions that he's glad I came along today and that he will take the stand if Michael Stone needs him to.

Mary and I meet for dinner at a seafood place that was her pick after I found that my favorite Italian place, Stulleto's, was no longer open. Really not a big fan of seafood, but fuck it, I figure I can always order the blackened swordfish, which tastes pretty much like a steak anyway. We meet at a place called Craig's Crab Shack. Jay Z is playing when we sit down. The tables are candlelit, yet there's a very Chili's atmosphere to Craig's.

Mary orders the crab and I order the fish and chips, since they do not have swordfish on the menu. She tells me about a new bar called the Mermaid where there's a pool and the guests are encouraged to swim while drinking.

"The only rule is that you don't pee in the pool. Isn't it funny that regardless how old we get we still have to remind people of that?" I tell her that it sounds like fun,

even though it doesn't. Once our food arrives I mention how good the fish is, even though it isn't.

After dinner, we try to get tickets for *The Producers*, which on the west coast is starring for a limited time Tom Hanks and James Caan, but the show is sold out and scalpers want over five hundred dollars for shitty seats so out of options we go to the Mermaid. Fucking Tom Hanks.

The Mermaid is a disaster because right when we walk in someone jumps into the pool, splashing Mary. I don't feel good, probably from the fish I was forced to consume. Despite all of this we order a bottle of Pinot grigio and quickly drink our first glasses and then pour out second glasses, emptying the bottle. As I lift my glass, my elbow hits the bottle, causing it to fall off the table and crash to the ground and shatter. Tiny shards of glass spray all the way to the side of the pool. We leave about five minutes after the incident, not because we are told to, but because I'm pretty sure I'm going to be getting sick soon and with all that has happened at the Mermaid I would rather that not happen here.

# 11

***FOUR-STAR HANGOVER:***

*You first notice it on your pillow case. Eventually when you look in the mirror you realize where the blood came from. You almost fall in the shower. When you're out of the shower, your skin smells of tequila. You brush your teeth but it's no use because each tooth has an individual sweater wrapped around it. It doesn't matter because you are able to function normally, or so you think. You've had seven hours of sleep yet are still completely wasted. Ever drive to work in the morning and see four squad cars with one guy in a suit pulled over, walking the line? That's right, even the cops call their friends when this happens. Everyone enjoys a four-star drunk.*

*Matt was his name, I think. He worked in the finance department and was given tickets to a private party being thrown at a new club named All Night Long. When we walked in we were greeted with champagne and a bag of cocaine, both of which were gone in an hour. This was followed by a whiskey tasting and then another bag of*

*cocaine. We attempted to talk to a group of girls who claimed they were cheerleaders for the Chicago Bulls, but I doubt that was the case, not that it mattered because after All Night Long we ran down the street with our shirts off singing the theme to* The Jetsons. *A random guy yelled at me and told me to put my shirt back on so I went over and punched him in the face and then we continued running until we came across a Guinness party so we stopped in and had a couple pints and found a girl with a Russian accent who had some cocaine to share in exchange for some attention. After an hour of conversation and eight lines we left and went to a disco named Strutter where Matt got asked to join an orgy but declined because the women were too short. Two shots of Skyy vodka later and we were out in the parking lot fighting over who could hold their drugs better. We both either simultaneously knocked each other out (like* Rocky*) or both passed out from exhaustion because we woke up an hour later on the asphalt outside the bar and remembered the bartender had promised us one more round of shots. I was out for the next five hours but have no recollection and have no idea how I got home. The next day I recall sitting next to a guy who referred to AA as "The Double A" and kept telling me he wasn't in AA because he was too drunk to take thirteen steps, and I was so drunk I agreed. After all, at that point, twelve, thirteen, it doesn't really matter because we aren't making it past the first one.*

*The best part of the four-star is that you can always continue right where you left off. An eye-opener (usually a Bloody Mary) has never tasted so good. Unless you operate heavy machinery, I highly suggest a Bloody on your way to work when working on a four-star. Keep the buzz alive. Continue drinking. Life is good. Don't feel bad walking into a bar when the sun is bright and the chil-*

*dren are playing outside. It's okay. You're living in the land of the free, home of the corner bar. Cheers!*

*Once you make it in to work it's a breeze because you have no idea how drunk you still are. You are now one of the tens of thousands of functioning alcoholics. Welcome home.*

Day two of Chip's trial begins worse than day one.

The judge is acting as if he's had a few eye-openers this morning. He starts off by pointing at two gorgeous women sitting in the back, behind Mark-Paul, who is also once again present at the trial. "Star fuckers," the judge says to the bailiff, then, "Don't put that down. That's off the record," to the court reporter. The judge shakes his head and then continues ranting. "There are more star fuckers in this city than there are bums. It's unbelievable, everywhere you turn." He looks for his gavel. "Okay, let's get started. Michael Stone, what do you got for me today?"

"Hot damn!" yells the bailiff.

How about a mistrial? I wonder to myself, then realize that there is no way there could possibly be more star fuckers in Los Angeles than bums.

Michael Stone stands and looks around the courtroom, then looks over at the jury, then down at Chip, then back to the jury, finally resting his eyes on the judge, who is shaking his head. "Yes, Mr. Stone?"

Stone looks back at the women in the back then says, "I call Chip Dorsey to the stand."

Collectively around the courtroom you hear everyone ask, "His last name is Dorsey?"

Chip is shaking like a dog shitting razor blades. Clearly he was not expecting Stone to put him up on the stand yet. He looks back at me. I give a reassuring nod

that probably comes across more like a confused shrug. He walks up to the stand, puts his hand on the Bible and swears to tell the truth, then sits down and makes a face as if something smells, and says, "What the fuck?" This causes the courtroom to erupt in laughter and the judge to bang his gavel a couple times and demand order while he stares at the women in the back.

One of the women turns to the other and mumbles, "What a dweeb," which I wasn't sure was even a word anymore. I'm not even sure if I knew what the word dweeb meant when I was calling people it. I do know that the word went out with VHS, glow in the dark condoms, and the band Candlebox.

Michael Stone pulls on his yellow tie as he approaches Chip. "Where were you the night of the incident?"

"Vegas." Chip clears his throat. "At Stoner's—I mean my friend Johnny's—bachelor party." Michael Stone looks over at the strippers in the jury box.

Michael Stone giggles. "And did you boys have fun in Vegas?" He looks back over at the jury box.

"Uh, yeah, sure. It's Vegas."

"And what time were you back at Sharon Winkler's house?"

The D.A. jumps up. "Objection! That is not Sharon Winkler's house, but rather a house of sin!"

The judge grins. "Maybe, but I'm going to allow it." He looks over at the jury. "I think we all want to see where this is going."

Stone looks back at the D.A. "I will repeat my question: what time were you at Sharon Winkler's house?"

Confused, Chip says, "I don't know for sure, but I know it was in the morning, later than when the police say, but again, it's hard to say, because..."

"You were drunk?" asks Michael Stone.

"Well, yes, it was a—"

"A bachelor party, of course." Michael Stone looks back over at the jury box and smiles. "How did you get home?"

"OBJECTION!" the D.A. screams.

Both are called up to speak to the judge. "We can't allow you to speak of the recently departed, Mr. Stone."

"But this is my whole case. This is my client's alibi."

The judge takes a deep breath. "If you don't like my ruling, fuck it, that's what the appeals court is for. However, this is my court, my rules. No talk of Johnny."

Both Stone and the D.A. back away. Stone paces in front of Chip, his hand on his chin as if he had a goatee to stroke, pondering his next move. He stops for a moment, then shakes his head and continues pacing. This continues for a couple minutes until the judge insists that Michael Stone continue. Stone nods and pauses, then looks over at the jury. While still looking at the jury, Stone asks Chip, "How many women have you slept with?"

Chip, who was beginning to slouch, sits up. "You mean, had sex with?"

Everyone begins laughing.

"Lots of sex!" the bailiff screams.

"Yes, had sex with. How many?" Michael Stone reiterates.

"I believe it's now at 139." Chip winks at one of the girls sitting in the back of the room.

Michael Stone is still looking at the jury. "So it's obvious getting girls isn't a problem for you?"

Chip giggles. "Well, I should say not." Laughter continues.

"139!" the bailiff says.

Stone turns to Chip. "So, hypothetically, getting shot down is no big deal. You wouldn't snap, nor have you ever abused a girl."

"No way, man. That's not my style. I'm no Ike. I can always just go and bang some other skank."

"Right, you are no Ike Turner and there really ARE many skanks in the sea." Michael Stone turns back to the jury. "There is no way my client would turn on a girl, regardless of her age, because of rejection. It just doesn't make sense."

Sitting back in the courtroom, I'm not sure if Stone put any doubt in the jury's head, but at least for five minutes he didn't seem to make things worse.

Stone turns to the D.A. "Your witness."

The D.A. slowly rises from the table and places his hands on his hips. "139 women, that's a lot. Are you sure you're not exaggerating?"

Chip looks at the judge. "I swear, 139 is my number."

The judge laughs. "Continue."

"Chip, do you recognize that girl over there?" The D.A. points to a girl in the third row.

"No, why? Is she one of my 139 and I don't remember?" asks Chip.

Michael Stone laughs into his hands.

The D.A. smirks. "Uh, no, that's the girl who walked in on you and the girl you allegedly murdered." He pauses. "Recognize her now?"

Chip shrugs his shoulders and mumbles, "I don't know who she is."

"SHE," the D.A. pauses, "has signed a sworn affidavit that she saw you on top of the Congressman's daughter!"

The D.A. pauses for dramatic effect, but this is broken when the bailiff jumps and yells, "Touchdown!"

"Order, order," from the judge. "Continue."

The D.A. continues, "SHE saw you on top of the Congressman's daughter, RAPING her!"

The jury gasps in unison.

"In fact, not only that, but she says you have a small penis, the smallest one she has ever seen."

The jury gasps again.

"Like an acorn."

Chip looks confused.

The D.A. repeats three words: "rape", "embarrassment", and "murder".

The D.A. walks up to Chip until he's only a couple of feet from him. "Maybe she mentioned to you how small your penis was, you snapped, and murdered her!" The D.A. is now about a foot away from Chip. He looks back at me and I can see in his eyes what he is thinking: What would Steven Tyler do?

"Embarrassed of your small penis, maybe she made fun of you, but you had had enough. Isn't that right, Chip Dorsey!" The D.A. is face to face with Chip.

Chip stands up and before Michael Stone can scream "NO!" Chip pulls out his ten inches, actually brushing against the D.A.'s head as he whips it out.

The jury gasps.

The judge stares at Chip, then at the D.A.

The D.A. stares back at his star witness, who can only shrug her shoulders.

The strippers in the jury box smile.

Detroit leans to the left.

Chip stares at the girls in the back.

I stare at Mark-Paul Gosselaar, still wondering what he is doing here.

The judge looks down at Chip's penis, then stands as he looks at the D.A. and pounds his gavel.

"Case dismissed!"

Despite Stoner's death, Chip's innocence is a reason to celebrate in Sharon Winkler's eyes, so she throws a DIDN'T DO A FIFTEEN-YEAR-OLD AND NOT GOING TO HAVE TO DO FIFTEEN pool party.

Chip and I show up and there's already well over a hundred people around the pool, mostly hot women who may or may not be prostitutes. A girl named Lucy offers me a hit off her bowl, I accept, and then spend the next fifteen minutes discussing the show *House* and whether either of us like it or despise it (neither of us reach a conclusion on the subject). I try to call Mary, but she's not answering and then I remember that she mentioned something about yoga. I take another hit from Lucy's bowl and am then introduced to her friend Tosha, who has bleached blond hair, bright red lipstick, and tender looking legs. All of us take another hit and begin to get very high. I walk around and try to find Chip, but at this point there are well over three hundred people at the party so instead I find a Heineken and then go back to Lucy and Tosha. They are placing ice cubes on their shoulders, watching the water trickle down their bodies as they debate whether or not to remove their bikini tops. Together they decide that as long as they are smoking herb they really shouldn't be running around the pool topless. I drink my Heineken quickly and then take another hit of herb that clearly must be from Houston because I can barely open my mouth when Lucy and Tosha ask me if I want to go inside with them.

We walk up a spiral staircase to the third floor and enter a room that has been painted light pink. When Lucy removes her top I mention that I'm sort of seeing someone, but this doesn't seem to bother her. Watching Lucy, I don't even notice Tosha, who behind me is com-

pletely nude and is already playing with a vibrator that looks like a turtle at the base, but with a really long neck.

I don't bother fighting off their advances. Lucy jumps on top of me while Tosha rips off my pants. Tosha jerks me off while Lucy rubs her crotch on my chest and then they both yell, "SWITCH!" and then they both run out of the room. In walks a tall black woman named Bianca and an Asian girl named Wu. Wu grabs my penis and starts blowing me and then guides me into Bianca, who is bent over the end of the bed. After my third thrust into Bianca, Tosha returns to the room with a bowl and I take a hit and continue to have sex with Bianca until they all yell, "SWITCH!" In walks another blonde named Joyce and a muscular brunette with short hair named Michelle. Joyce slowly approaches and then turns around and rubs her ass on my penis while reaching around and pinching my nipples. Then she moves to my back and reaches around, stroking my penis. Michelle comes up and I reach around to find out that Michelle is actually Michael and that he has a penis. Lucy comes in with the bowl so I take another hit, but even this herb isn't strong enough for this to happen so I yell, "SWITCH!" and everyone leaves.

# 12

I'm still staying at the motel because there's just too much drama everywhere else. Chip is staying with one of the star fuckers from his trial, and Sharon's place is just too weird now that I know it's a brothel. I mean, I suspected such, but KNOWING is another game I'm really not in the mood for right now.

*Robby Williams owned a bar. The day after paying off the establishment he slipped on the floor behind his bar and fell on a bottle of Absolut Citron. The bottle broke and slashed his main artery.*

My room has a bed, a television, and a mirror that looks very out of place to the right of the television. I watch both *The Simpsons* and my shoes as I lie on my back. I also have a sink that's not in the bathroom, but right outside. I have to say, I like this. It makes me want to be a cleaner person. Maybe this motel has changed me, or maybe I just need to smoke some herb. I reach into my pocket and pull out a small bag that Earl gave me and grab some Top rolling papers and make a huge joint that I smoke only halfway because it's not even

dark outside yet, but it is enough to make me jump when the phone rings. I wonder if this herb has been soaked in gasoline.

It's Mary. She asks me how long I'm going to be staying and I tell her probably only two more days, but that Chip is thinking about staying. "He's got some possible movie thing he's working on," I tell her. She asks me if I want to catch dinner and of course I agree. While I'm clipping my fingernails she asks me if I want Mexican and I agree this sounds good so we decide to meet in two hours at a place called Pedro's.

I finish my nails then wash my face again (the sink is right there), then try to decide whether to wear my white with black stripes shirt or my plain blue shirt and my phone rings again. It's Chip. He tells me to meet him at a bar named Sam's Place and then hangs up. Sam's is three miles away so I call a taxi and finish the rest of my joint while I wait for the cab to pick me up.

Chip is sitting at a table in the corner and stands when I approach him and gives me a strange half-way hug, the kind where a man grabs hold of another man's elbow and shoulders touch. Not necessarily uncomfortable, but, because this is Chip, definitely unsettling. We order pints of Magners cider. Chip orders chicken wings, and I go to the bathroom. On the walls I see "BUSH DOES BONGS", "The Jews have ruined Hollyweird", and "I love L.A." I laugh at the last one, which was written with a thick black Sharpie. Fucking tourists.

Back at the table, Chip has finished his Magners and has another one on the way. He is very fidgety and finally I just assume he wanted to have a couple beers to unwind, but then he tells me, "I got his name."

"Whose name?"

"The guy who killed Stoner. I got his name."

Chip's Magners arrives. I drink my first one down, pouring some down the side of my face. I order another. "From who?"

"Earl. He called me and gave me the name. His name is Louis Recker, some actor or something like that."

"How did Earl get his name?"

"Don't know, but he says it's definitely him, and he's going to set up a meeting with him."

You can never have too much information.

"He's going to let us know when the meeting is." Chip finishes his second beer. "So, if, you know..."

Our eyes lock. We both slowly nod at each other.

I have always believed that Mexican restaurants should smell like a mix of tequila and burritos, and Pedro's definitely passes the test. Mary is waiting at the bar drinking a margarita on the rocks when I show up.

Apparently I'm still processing everything Chip has told me because Mary asks me what's wrong.

"Let's sit first," I tell her.

"Oh my God, you guys know who did it!"

Mary is too smart for me. No way can this be love.

I change the subject and talk about how much I miss New York, and then Mary tells me that although she likes New York it's a little too close to Connecticut for her. "I would rather be raped than have to live in Connecticut." She goes to the bathroom.

When Mary returns I'm on my phone, listening to my messages. "Just people, mostly just my neighbor, who's watching my apartment back home. He's one of those classic big body, small head guys. Makes me laugh every time I see him."

"Oh yeah," Mary agrees. "I love small head, big body, especially when they wear oversized hats to try to hide

their small heads." Mary orders enchiladas and another margarita. I do the same. "Still, it's nice to have someone watch your place while you're gone."

"That's true, but he's only doing it so he can use my shower."

"That's strange. Why does he shower at your place?"

"Because he grows drugs in his bathtub."

Mary laughs at first, thinking I'm joking, then realizes I'm not and says, "Gnarly." Then, with a serious look, she says, "You're not going to do anything, are you?"

Unfortunately I realize the conversation has come full circle and that we are discussing Louis Recker. "No, of course not," I assure her.

Despite the fact that I will miss my motel sink, I go over to Mary's. At her place we drink red wine and talk for over an hour about our love of caves and how we both could see ourselves someday living in a cave for about a month, although we both agree that after a month we would definitely have had enough. Another bottle of wine and Mary falls asleep on the couch. For over an hour I look around her apartment, trying to understand the sculptures and mustaches then decide it's really not worth it because I probably don't want to know. I'm tired, but can't fall asleep. Instead I think about the past few days and all that has happened and how I'm still okay, but feel there's unfinished business to attend to. I do eventually close my eyes, but only after I fantasize about breaking Louis Recker's neck.

# 13

***FOUR-AND-A-HALF-STAR HANGOVER:***

*The 4½-star hangover (a.k.a. the 4.5, a.k.a. the crazy as fuck hangover) usually has you waking up wondering first how many people are pissed off and second (more importantly) whether anyone is actively looking for you. The crazy as fuck drunk can also be translated as the "good gag" drunk.*

*After a college barrel party my friend Chip and I decided to get a case of beer and just relax at home, maybe watch a movie or play some video games.* Pulp Fiction *is not that long of a movie yet the case of beer is gone so we set out and got another case of beer and also some herb from a guy known as Nemo who at the time was our friend and is now doing five years for selling a police officer a machine gun. Nemo hooked us up with some amazing herb (called The Chronic at the time) and we smoked and drank while making prank phone calls. The calls started off with people we knew. Teachers. Classmates. Then it escalated to the elderly. Call up Betty and let her*

*know it's Johnny, from many years ago. Nine times out of ten they take the bait. "Oh yeah, Johnny, what's wrong?" They ask what's wrong because it's 2 a.m. You reminisce with Betty, Gladice, Adrian. Make them trust you and believe that at one point you did have a relationship, a bond, something sexual. They are too old to remember. Then tell them you have AIDS and that they had better go get checked out.*

*When all of the herb is smoked and the beer is gone, we go to the grocery store and get a couple of roasted chicken breasts. Wait for innocent bystanders to walk by. A woman in her twenties works best. Run up from behind her and quickly rub the chicken in her face. We do this and then proclaim YOU HAVE FIVE MINUTES TO LIVE! Watch her expression. Once you've felt a roasted chicken breast rubbed all over your face, you will believe anything. Most of the time, we wouldn't even wait and tell them we were joking, just leave the victims wondering if they really did just get poisoned... Nope, it was just "the roaster".*

*As bad as your head feels the next day, it's your hands that look the worst. Holding roasted chicken for hours and then being too drunk to wash your hands isn't good for your skin. Don't even think about the smell. Let's just say your neighbors will complain. The most important thing to remember is that everyone had fun.*

The next morning I'm in front of my sink at the motel shaving with one arm behind my back because I often wonder what it's like to be in prison. From the alarm clock the radio is playing. It's the new drug song by Velvet Revolver and it's playing so loud that I don't even hear my phone ring. I notice I have voicemail once I've finished shaving. It's Chip. He tells me to come over to

the star fucker's house for a good morning Bloody Mary. Now I may have cleaned up a bit recently, but who am I to turn down an eye-opener from a good friend?

*Jessica Chen joined the Peace Corps to see the world and help others. Two weeks into her mission, she was trampled by elephants.*

The star fucker's name is Rachel and her friend (another star fucker) is named Cherri, although I suspect that may not be her real name. Also, at this point I can't even put a face to the name because when I walk into the house Cherri is bent down blowing some guy who looks like Jon Stewart. Chip is sitting on the couch next to Rachel, watching SportsCenter. I whisper, "Is that Jon Stewart?" and Chip says no, he just looks similar, but don't feel bad because he thinks Cherri has made the same mistake.

Two minutes pass and Cherri finishes (so does the Jon Stewart look-alike), and they along with Rachel leave the room. Chip enjoys a Marlboro and I a Marlboro Light. I ask him how he knows the star fuckers and he tells me it doesn't really matter and I agree so we smoke in silence.

Putting out his butt, Chip asks me, "How much time do you think you could do?" Chip blows his final puff of smoke into the air. "I've been thinking about this a lot, with the trial and all. For a while there, even though I know I didn't do anything, I was a little worried I was going to be doing some time."

"I always thought a month would be interesting, but as far as how many years?"

Rachel comes in with two Bloody Marys, puts them down in front of us, and then leaves.

Chip smiles. "You really do have to love star fuckers."

"Yeah, I guess." I take a drink of the Bloody—spicy, very good. "I guess it would depend who I was doing the time for, you know, like what crime would be worth trading prison time for."

"Exactly," says Chip. "So you know where I'm going with this..."

I take a long drink, light another cigarette. "Of course I do."

Chip's phone rings. He answers. "Oh, hey, Nic. I was hoping you would call back. Sure, I've got a minute, and a new idea." Chip covers the phone and whispers to me, "It's Nic Cage."

Chip explains to Nic his idea for a movie that involves a man convicted of a crime he didn't commit and then absolves himself by the size of his penis. "Dude, this is a guaranteed box office smash!" Chip says three times. Apparently on the other end Nic Cage is interested because Chip sounds excited and is drinking fast while explaining to Nic Cage that he wouldn't have to be totally nude, just his back side for effect.

While Chip is on the phone, Cherri enters the room and sits next to me. Cherri tells me about why she likes independent films (they always have a driving scene that lasts over five minutes long, usually a camera looking at the landscape of America), that she likes "mini" travel games because they're not as embarrassing, and that her last real boyfriend was some guy who only tried to get roles in reality shows. This was the reason she only went after Hollywood stars now. "Do you want Jon Stewart's autograph? I can get it if you'd like." She says something about my resemblance to Tom Selleck or Tom Green and then puts her hand on my knee, but I push her away and I don't know if this is because I love Mary or because I'm repulsed by Cherri. She looks back at me

and tells me that we're a lot alike. "We each put our pants on one leg at a time."

How this became the great equalizer, I don't know. That's like saying if you have two legs, we're all the same. Tell that to a homeless person while he's pissing on himself. "Hey, I'm just like you. I put my pants on one leg at a time... Of course, I don't piss on my pants."

"Nic is very interested. He's presenting it to his agent tomorrow." Chip shuts his phone. "Rachel, going to need a couple more Bloodys out here.

"So what do you think?" Chip asks. "How many years do you think you could do?"

"I don't know. If it was family, I'm not sure there would be a limit, but with friends, it all depends on whether it's worth it, you know, is that really what's best for the situation?"

"True," Chip ponders this for a moment, "but I'll be honest, Stoner gone makes me feel like I lost family."

"Me too." Rachel is topless when she brings us our drinks. "Plus, you have this whole Nic Cage thing going..."

Chip watches Rachel walk away. "You're right," then adds while still looking at Rachel, "Do you think those are fake? Uh, fuck it. It really doesn't matter."

We both have a cigarette and sit in silence. The only sound is the ice cubes in the Bloody Marys when we take a drink. Inside, I'm finally able to start to grieve for Stoner. I remember how cool it was to hang out with him and how much fun he always seemed to have. My last sip of my Bloody Mary is all vodka. I take the last drag of my cigarette. "I'll do eight to ten for Stoner."

Chip looks over at me. "Fuck it. So will I."

This is a story about revenge.

# 14

The next morning Chip calls me at 7 a.m. and tells me that we need to be at the bar we met Earl at last time, the Cave, because this is where Louis Recker is going to show up around two o'clock. I don't ask how Earl knows this or what he did to set this up, but at this point it really doesn't matter. I go back to sleep and wake up two hours later. I spend five minutes showering and an hour at the sink doing what, I don't know, but it makes me feel good.

*George Sanchez bought his wife roses and edible panties for Valentines Day. Later that night, Mr. Sanchez choked to death.*

I turn on the television. The movie *Gone in 60 Seconds* starring Nic Cage is on. I find it interesting how little effort Nic Cage gives in the movie. The defining moment is when he has his "crew" stand around and listen to the song "Low Rider". After they hum along to this song they are able to go steal cars. Makes perfect sense.

After the movie I feel like watching videos, but MTV has *Road Rules* on and William Shatner is hosting some countdown on VH1 so I shut off the television and go meet Chip. On my way I stop off at an ATM and take out two hundred dollars. While retrieving my money and waiting for my receipt to print I feel the barrel of a gun press into my back. "Put your card back into the machine and take out all of your money," a muffled voice tells me. I explain that I can't. I can only take out two hundred a day. This must not be his first ATM heist because he tells me that all I have to do is give him the two hundred dollars I just took out. I place my hand holding my money over my left shoulder and tell him to take it. I feel the man's breath on my neck and he whispers, "Next time, it would be a lot easier if you would just pay for 'God's snow'." I turn around, but the fake drug dealer has left. I turn back and take another two hundred dollars out from the ATM.

It's around noon when I arrive at the Cave. Chip and I both order the Turkey Special and cheeseburgers. I order mine medium-well. Chip orders his rare, drawing a look of concern from the waiter, prompting Chip to say, "Fuck it, just make it rare."

A family of four enters. Two kids, both about nine years old, give or take. The kids are full of energy, running around the table, knocking into each other, and overall making a lot of noise. Most of the restaurant's patrons are incredibly annoyed, but Chip and I don't really care about a bunch of nine-year-olds at this point. We are more concerned about our Turkey Specials and if the guest of honor is going to show.

We don't speak until our food arrives. We both stare at the nine-year-olds. Our cheeseburgers are half-gone before Chip speaks.

"How many nine-year-olds do you think you could take on?"

"I think you've had too many Turkey Specials. Haven't you learned your lesson with minors?"

"Not sex with nine-year-olds. How many do you think you could take on, you know, man, as in fight?"

We both remember at the same time that we can smoke, so we both light up. No one else in the establishment is smoking, but then again no one seems to mind either.

"I don't know. All at once, maybe four or five," I say. "Kids can be quite exhausting."

Mary calls and wants to talk about the latest Tom Hanks movie, which she is being told by everyone to go see, but she doesn't really want to go see it, because it is Tom Hanks and if anyone is overrated it's definitely him. "Tom Hanks just isn't that cool of a guy to me," Mary says. She hangs up.

*Samuel L. Jackson, now he's always been cool (especially if you refer to him as Sam Jackson). Then there's Robert De Niro (extra cool when it's Bobby De Niro), and Tom Selleck's mustache.*

I go to the bathroom and notice that right above the urinal where I'm standing someone has written the words GO HOME.

"What if they're lined up? I think I could take about fifteen of them out. You figure that if you kick them in the head, most are going to go down." Chip thinks about this for second. "Yeah, I would say fifteen would be about right. A nice pile of nine-year-olds."

"Well, if they're lined up, I would have to say—"

Chip cuts me off. "There he is. Earl told me the guy looked like what would happen if Carrot Top and Lewis Black had a son."

I look over to where Chip is staring. "Yeah, well, that's definitely him then." We sit and stare for a minute. "What are we going to do?"

Chip motions for me to look under the table. I look under and he's got a gun in his hands. "Man, I don't know."

Chip looks back up. "You think? Just want to beat his ass?"

"Then crack his skull against the floor," I look at Chip, "repeatedly."

"Cool. You see the rail about a foot off the bottom of the bar?"

"Yes." I lean my body so that I can see the bar.

"Let's wedge that motherfucker's head and stomp it down."

"Cool. For Stoner."

"For Stoner."

We get up and walk up to Louis Recker. As we approach, he turns around. Louis looks over my shoulder and his eyes widen, and then we hear the gunshot.

I hit the ground, as does Chip.

Louis Recker also hits the ground, but because he has been shot in the face.

Earl walks up and plants another bullet in his skull.

A splash of blood hits the side of my face.

"What the fuck, Earl!" Chip yells.

The lights dim in the Cave. The doors are locked. "It's cool. This place is cool. It's my place." Earl orders a couple of busboys to clean up Louis Recker. "This is my place. Where else can I go and have a smoke and relax in California?"

As the busboys begin cleaning up the blood, Earl kicks at Louis. "Can't have people take out my customers. That's just not good business."

Chip looks confused, and so am I. "So, Louis was a dealer?"

"No, Louis Recker was a struggling actor who lost too many jobs to Damon Wayans. He shot Stoner because he thought he was Wayans. Damn, though, still doesn't change the fact that Stoner was my customer. Man has to protect his business."

*Johnny Kingston, a.k.a. "Stoner", born in Wisconsin, lived in L.A. Stoner enjoyed life to the fullest through adventure and experimentation. His only crime? Being too tan.*

# 15

***FIVE-STAR HANGOVER:***

*Your head has a second heartbeat. When you wake up, you are never in your bed, and people are usually standing around you. Sometimes you don't sleep, but rather slip into a coma. Always and I repeat you are always fully dressed when you wake up. More times than not, you will open your eyes and find yourself in a hospital room, an IV in your arm.*

*At Jewish weddings, a glass is broken to signify the bond between a man and woman becoming husband and wife. At an Irish wedding, glass is broken everywhere, usually the aftermath of several fights ending in mugs of half-drunk beer being smashed over the heads of family members and friends.*

*A friend of a friend named O'Callahan was getting married and invited me to the reception. The bar was before the hall where the seating and dancing was happening. I never made it past the bar. At 9 p.m. I was having a discussion about World War II (a subject I could not know*

*less about) with a man who if you gave me a screwdriver and three hours I wouldn't have been able to remove the bottle from his hands. At 9:30 p.m. I was asked whether or not I had ever mainlined whiskey and since I asked what kind of whiskey everyone assumed I was in so they stuck a needle in my arm and shot alcohol straight into my veins. Even as the needle was left dangling in my arm and I could feel my brain shutting down it seemed like a great idea.*

*The rest of the night has been pieced together by three guys (or "accomplices" as the police would refer to them), things that later trigger my memory, and police reports. To summarize: I stole a cop car and drove it two miles while honking the horn and screaming obscenities out the window, then puked in a cop car, then crashed a cop car. From here I'm told I stole a gun from an officer, shot up a Burger King when they wouldn't allow me to have my Whopper my way, and then ended up at my boss's doorstep, where I threatened to blow my head off if he didn't give me a raise. Keep in mind, this wasn't part of my entrance essay to Harvard. Also keep in mind I was only seventeen, otherwise I would still be serving time.*

*Including the court dates, mandatory treatment, and embarrassment, the hangover lasts about six months. The second heartbeat, about three days.*

Chip is on the phone with Nic Cage. His movie idea has been given a green light and Cage is going to play Chip in the movie of his life. He explains that there will be a man charged with a crime involving a fifteen-year-old girl, a murder of a key witness, and then a very cliché ending where a black drug dealer shoots someone.

Apparently Cage loves this. Then again, his last few choices...

While Chip explains the details, Mary calls me and tells me that she heard about what happened to Louis Recker and was glad nothing happened to either Chip or myself (the detail that we were there really isn't that important at this point). Apparently it was leaked to the papers that Louis Recker killed Stoner, although the details weren't very clear how Louis Recker was murdered. Earl.

"He really did look like Damon Wayans," says Mary.

We talk for a while longer and Mary tells me how much she is going to miss me, and this strikes a nerve and a silent minute passes, and then I ask her to move to New York and stay with me. I tell her that even if it's just for a while it will be fun and she's at a place right now in her life where she can just pick up and go if she wants to.

"Well, Jeremy, I can't believe you're asking me this. I—" is all I hear, then my cell phone cuts out. I'm staring at my phone in disgust when Chip shuts off his phone and tells me that he's going to meet Nic Cage for breakfast and that I should come because he knows of a place that has the best sausages in the world, not to mention the world's best Bloody Marys.

Nic Cage is running late, so we order. Chip orders scrambled eggs and sausages and I get a western omelet. "No sausages? What the fuck?" says Chip and then I tell him I'm allergic because it's just easier to say this.

Behind us two women are in a frenzy because Fred Durst just walked in and is sitting alone. He orders a plate of sausages. Chip looks over at me and nods as if to say if it's good enough for Fred it should be good enough for me.

Our Bloody Marys arrive and we each take a sip and then step outside to get some air and smoke. I tell Chip I just asked Mary to come with me to New York and he's

blown away by that and is really blown away because I still don't know her answer.

"Why don't you just call her back?"

"I don't know. Let's go back inside. I don't like it when the ice melts and my Bloody has that watered down taste."

Walking back inside, I notice a vending machine that has a Nut Roll candy bar and I mention how that has to be the worst candy bar ever made. As our waitress approaches, Chip says he thinks that the Crispy M&Ms are absolutely the worse, and I tend to agree. Our waitress says licorice is by far the most awful and Chip and I just stare at each because there could not be a more wrong answer to our question than licorice.

Our food is gone and we are on our third round of Bloody Marys and I can't help but overhear the two girls behind us and how one of them is "totally absolutely" going to go over and try to hook up with Fred Durst and how neither one of them have ever done anyone famous. Finally, having had enough, I turn around and initially am mildly surprised by how attractive they are, but then explain that the last thing either one of them wants to do is hook up with Fred Durst and convince them that if they are looking for a Hollywood star to fuck they really need to put the bar a little higher.

I turn around and Chip is smiling. "That's number one," says Chip. "I'm officially giving you a save for that one."

I think about this for second. I even feel proud for a few seconds.

"No, I didn't save anyone's life."

"Even more so." Chip waves to Nic Cage as he walks in. The girls behind me are now going crazy as he sits down next to us. "What you did there is even better, be-

cause if you fuck Fred Durst you will still be alive but feel bad every day."

Nic Cage stares at me. "You want to fuck Fred Durst?"

"No," I motion back with my head, "those girls were going to."

"Bad idea," says Cage. "I know what that's like." Nic looks over at Chip. "Is that you? That smell, what is that?"

"It's called SMOKE, the scent of adventure." Chip smiles.

"I like it. Reminds me of a woman I met at a biker rally in North Dakota," says Nic. "Betty. Her name was Betty." Cage nods. "Scent of adventure... I like that."

Chip and Nic Cage begin discussing the movie, but then I interrupt them because I need to pack and start heading east. Chip and I say our goodbyes (Dr. Dre-style handshake) and then agree to meet up in a couple months.

Back at the motel, I pack my things, wash my face one final time in the sink, check to see if Mary called, and then sit on the end of the bed and close my eyes. It's been pulling at me for a couple days, but with the cops, the trial, the murders, and watching Detroit lean, I never had a chance to stop and let it pull me in. With my feet on the floor, I lean back on the bed, accidentally turning on the TV. Oprah is on. I quickly throw the remote at the TV. It turns off as if it's a sign for something.

Again, I lean back and close my eyes, taking deep breaths.

I can still hear it.

Probably always will.

"Ahaahaaahaa."

You can die at any moment.

My phone rings. I look over. It's Mary.
This is a story about living.

## ABOUT THE PUBLISHER

Offense Mechanisms is an imprint of Silverthought Press, an independent publisher of speculative, transgressive, and experimental fiction. Since 2005, Silverthought has released nine novels and three anthologies of short fiction. In addition to critical praise, Silverthought publications have received honors from the Independent Publisher Book Awards, the DIY Book Festival, and the New York Book Festival. For more information about Silverthought and its Offense Mechanisms and Megan's Closet imprints, visit:

http://www.silverthought.com

## ABOUT THE AUTHOR

David S. Grant, the author of *Bleach and Blackout,* was born in West Allis, WI. David's first novel, *Corporate Porn,* was published in 2005 by Silverthought Press. Major writing influences include Bret Easton Ellis, F. Scott Fitzgerald, Chuck Palahniuk, and Hunter S. Thompson. David has also published several short fiction pieces with various literary journals and websites including *The Writing Journal, The Reader's Retreat, The Falling Star Magazine, The Sink,* and *Lifted Magazine.* Grant has three corporate degrees and now lives and works in New York City. He is currently working on a prequel to *Bleach* titled *Bliss.* For more information, please visit David's website at:

http://www.davidsgrant.com